# Arrow

Also by
Samantha M. Clark

*The Boy, the Boat, and the Beast*

# Arrow

### SAMANTHA M. CLARK

A Paula Wiseman Book
Simon & Schuster Books for Young Readers
New York   London   Toronto   Sydney   New Delhi

SIMON & SCHUSTER BOOKS FOR YOUNG READERS
An imprint of Simon & Schuster Children's Publishing Division
1230 Avenue of the Americas, New York, New York 10020

SIMON & SCHUSTER BOOKS FOR YOUNG READERS
and related marks are trademarks of Simon & Schuster, Inc.
For information about special discounts for bulk purchases, please contact
Simon & Schuster Special Sales at 1-866-506-1949 or business@simonandschuster.com.
The Simon & Schuster Speakers Bureau can bring authors to your live event.
For more information or to book an event, contact the Simon & Schuster Speakers
Bureau at 1-866-248-3049 or visit our website at www.simonspeakers.com.
The text for this book was set in Adobe Caslon Pro.
The illustrations for this book were rendered digitally.
Manufactured in the United States of America
0521 FFG
First Edition
10 9 8 7 6 5 4 3 2 1
Library of Congress Cataloging-in-Publication Data
Names: Clark, Samantha M., author.
Title: Arrow / Samantha M. Clark.
Description: First edition. | New York : Simon & Schuster Books for Young Readers, [2021] |
Audience: Ages 8-12. | Audience: Grades 4-6. | Summary: Twelve-year-old Arrow was
raised by the Guardian Tree in a rainforest protected by a magical veil, but now the
veil is deteriorating and humans have entered, changing his life forever.
Identifiers: LCCN 2020045574 (print) | LCCN 2020045575 (ebook) |
ISBN 9781534465978 (hardcover) | ISBN 9781534465992 (ebook)
Subjects: CYAC: Magic—Fiction. | Rainforests—Fiction. | Trees—Fiction. |
Environmental protection—Fiction. | Foundlings—Fiction. | Fantasy.
Classification: LCC PZ7.1.C579 Arr 2021 (print) |
LCC PZ7.1.C579 (ebook) | DDC [Fic]—dc23
LC record available at https://lccn.loc.gov/2020045574
LC ebook record available at https://lccn.loc.gov/2020045575

*For my de Freitas and Gomes family*
*who made Guyana their home*

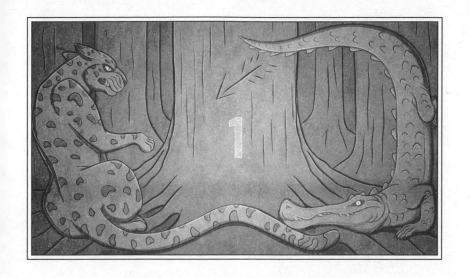

MY END BEGAN THE DAY THE SKY TURNED RED.

WE SHOOK. WE TREMBLED. WE STARTED TO BLEED. BUT THIS
WOULD BE ONLY THE START, A SMALL TASTE OF THE BATTLE TO
COME. OUR QUIET WORLD HAD BEEN CHANGING, AND I
COULD ONLY HOPE SOME WOULD SURVIVE.

Arrow was high above the ground when the boom sounded. Stretched out along a branch, he peered at the gecko perched on his wrist. He had been watching, narrow-eyed, as the gecko's neck billowed then shrunk, billowed, then shrunk, its mouth wide open, waiting for its next meal to fly by. Arrow had been about to shift—a small, almost imperceptible movement—to coax the gecko's webbed feet to scurry across his skin, over his shoulders, and down his other arm to his waiting hand. He had played the game many times before; he was good at it.

But the gecko wouldn't be captured that day.

First came a scream that tore open the sky. Closer. Closer it came. Louder. Louder it wailed.

It silenced the forest. Focused attention. Arrow snapped taut, and the gecko jumped away, but Arrow didn't follow. His eyes were on the glimmer of blue between the treetops and the line of black fracturing its calm.

*Screech.*

*Crunch.*

*BOOM!*

The forest shook. Arrow lost his footing. His hand caught a branch, his elbow hooked a tree limb. His breath shallowed.

"What was that?"

"Sit down," I told him, as he leaned forward, peering into the brush.

"But what can make those noises?"

"Nothing for you."

His weight shifted; his feet scrambled to the next branch down.

"Don't go!" I told him. "It's too dangerous."

Lives had already flickered out. The losses had been etched in the soil. It had been quick for some; others had passed on what little they knew before their voices had disappeared.

Another boom, and great clouds of gray and red belched into the sky.

Arrow faltered. The clamor of his heart hammered through the soles of his feet.

"Stay here," I said, sensing his itch to follow the roar, to find the source.

He listened for the intrusion, craning his neck to pluck more information out of the air. Then he lifted his heels. "I won't be long."

"Arrow!"

But his soles pounded across the earth, up the tree trunk, through the branches, along the lianas. Down. Up. Down. Cautious but driven forward. Until he stopped short.

The vision had already been laid out for me. South, near the mouth of the river, where the water plunged over the cliff, a flaming metal bird had crashed, punching a crater into the ground. Red-and-orange tongues twisted into the sky, trying to escape cloaks of black. The broken bird crackled and spit as the fire devoured it.

Arrow stayed back, the heat like a wall, but his eyes were wide. He had never seen fire this tall, or a metal bird up close. And he had never seen one in flames.

I wished he would return. That was not a place for a boy of only twelve rings. And I knew he wasn't alone.

Another thud had followed the first—a smaller one, a man. He had landed hard on the scorched ground farther back from the river's edge, a windcatcher dragging behind him. He wasn't far from the blaze, though, and hadn't stood since his body had crumpled onto the dirt. Most likely he'd been unconscious as he had descended. He should've been thankful he hadn't gone over the edge, down with the water, onto the froth at the rocky base of the mountain. Instead he lay still, his slowed heartbeat pulsating into the soil.

The man's arm moved, shoulder twitching against the ground.

Arrow's toes dug beneath the forest's carpet of leaves as he leaned forward for a closer look. He took in the burning bird, the sleeping man, and the ribbon of thick, rainbow-tinged liquid between them. Arrow had never seen the colorful liquid before, but he could see how the flames sought it out, lapped it up, hungered for its taste.

A gust blew in, and the giant red windcatcher lying near the bird bloated with air. Its bottom edge grazed the ground, soaking up the liquid, as the wind raced across the cliff. Flames picked up the scent, lunged, and caught the end of the windcatcher. The fire bit at the red fabric, swallowed inch after inch, spit out black ash as the windcatcher drifted closer to the man.

Arrow's feet lifted, and I wanted to plead for him to stay, but I knew my words would be lost to him this far away.

*Thud, thud, thud,* and Arrow was next to the man. His hand grabbed the back of the man's shirt; his arm hooked under the man's armpit. He pulled, pulled, heels digging into the dirt. The man was heavy, his body a sloth. A tug, and the man moved—but the flaming windcatcher followed. It was still tethered to his back.

Arrow's pulse quickened. He tugged on the ropes, and one came loose. A metal claw at its end had opened and set it free. Arrow found a lever that opened the other claw, then threw the ropes to the side. He heaved harder, all his weight pushing down on the earth until he gained traction. Finally he pulled the man away. The windcatcher writhed and twisted in the air as the flames devoured it, until all that was left was black dust.

With the man out of danger, Arrow laid him on the ground. The man stirred, a groan rising up from his throat.

Arrow raced back, back, back to the safety of the trees as I whispered a thank-you.

The man started to wake, pushing himself up. But his shoulders slumped, and he collapsed again.

I wished for Arrow to leave, to come home, but he waited, heart drumming onto the silt. He peered from around a trunk, watching the man, willing him to stand, to walk away from the waves of heat radiating off the still-burning metal bird.

Until the fire jumped.

Arrow saw flames inch closer across the thin line of rainbow-tinged liquid. Saw them reach for the man. Saw them leap.

He called out, but it was too late.

The man's scream echoed into the blackened clouds above. He jumped up, swatting at the flames tearing at his boot. His eyes caught the river and he ran for the bank, swung his legs into the fast-rushing water. The fire was doused in the fray, but the man had to pull himself out of the river before he was swept away.

Cradling his burnt foot, the man squinted at his metal bird as the bones sighed into the crater. His eyes narrowed at the ropes unclasped from his back and lying scorched on the ground.

He glanced around quickly, and Arrow slunk out of sight, finally retreating back, back, back to me.

Night had begun to descend by the time he got home. Heart wild, Arrow breathed deeply as he climbed to his nest of palm leaves tied between my branches. "He's like me," he whispered. "But bigger. Much bigger."

"Older," I told him. "He's a man."

"A man," Arrow repeated. "Where did he come from?"

"I felt his machine from the north," I said. "The outside world."

"What's he doing here?" Arrow's breath was quick as he settled on the branches but not from his climb.

"You should sleep, Arrow."

"Sleep? How can I sleep now?" His voice was exasperated. "There's another one like me in the forest."

Cradling his chin in his right hand and the tip of his arrow arm, where it ended at his wrist, he gazed at the star starting to blink above and smiled.

As night fell, so did the flames. Soon only embers glowed on the carcass of the metal bird, as the man sat on the ground and watched. Finally he slumped over, his body heavy with exhaustion.

The rainforest relaxed. A little.

But with the sun rose the fear. In all except the boy.

"Stay, Arrow," I told him as he hurried down my branches.

The boy's excitement had grown with the sun's light. He was filled with curiosity.

But I knew the danger of that.

"I've got an idea," he said, jumping to the leafy floor. "Maybe the man is here for a reason. Maybe he's here to help."

"That's not why he's here, Arrow."

"You don't know."

"His metal bird fell from the sky. The curtain is failing, and he came through a hole in it. There was no purpose behind it. It was a mistake."

Arrow's eyes twitched from me to the direction of the man and back. "But he might know something. Maybe I can learn from him."

"You won't—"

But he was off, threading through the trunks.

"Arrow," I called, but the boy didn't turn back. "Don't let him see you!"

My warnings wouldn't keep Arrow away from the circle of blackened ground and the man who lay asleep in its middle. At least Arrow held caution close to his heart. He perched high in the branches, nestled with the monkeys, all eyes peering down at the strange man in the colorful clothes below.

Even charred and dirty, the man showed off the colors of the birds. His legs were as blue as parrot wings, his torso as yellow as a kiskadee's belly, and on his chest was a marking of some kind, a spray of lines fanning upward like the crown of the stinkbird.

He slept most of the day, his body as still as a waiting caiman, until the sun was directly overhead—then the man sat straight up and screamed. His "AAAAHHHH" echoed through the treetops, scavenged by the mimicking birds. But the man didn't notice. He cradled his burnt foot, rocking back and forth as his bottom dug into the ground.

Arrow tensed with each of the man's shivers, as though the pain were his own. His toes gripped the branch beneath him, and he leaned as close as he could without falling or being noticed.

After a while, the man's shudders ceased. The soil shifted as he rose up on his one good foot. Hobbling, he made it to a rivulet where the water escaped the drag of the cliff. The man pulled at his clothes, crying out again as the crusty material exposed red and yellow welts on his skin. Then, taking deep breaths, he dipped his foot into the cool water and quickly drew it out again.

The palm of Arrow's right hand pressed into the bark, but he heeded my words. He didn't leave his hiding place; instead he quieted the chittering monkeys around him. Arrow watched as the man ripped a strip from the bottom of his shirt and wrapped it around his injured foot. He watched as the man struggled to stand, prodded at the charred bones of his dead bird with a stick, then shook his head in disgust. And he watched as the man peered at the green around him, holding his belly to stifle its growls.

9

Arrow stayed until dusk, and I waited for his footsteps to head my way. Instead they thumped quickly to the east and west, stopping then starting, getting heavier with each pause.

Finally they journeyed back toward the man.

"Don't let him see you," I whispered again, wishing he could hear from that distance. Hoping he'd remember.

Arrow stopped short of approaching. He crouched behind the shrubs inland from the river's edge. His wild heartbeat pulsed from his soles as he leaned forward for a better look. This close, Arrow could see the new hair growing on the man's jawline, the muscles flexed under his kiskadee shirt, and the glint of metal that peered out from his belt. It all made Arrow pause longer, and that quick ticking of his heart let me know his curiosity was growing.

The man was seated now, his injured leg stretched out against the ground, the other heel digging a ditch of worry in the ash. His eyes shifted between his dead bird, the green trees, and the water that rushed past him to the edge of the cliff. Shift, shift, shift.

Arrow couldn't feel the man's consternation. He only saw the need.

Sliding from his hiding place, Arrow scurried from trunk to trunk until he was gazing at the man's back.

His heart skipped in anticipation. He sucked in a breath, then stepped out into the sun.

A loud chitter came from the trees as the monkeys

protested, their concern mirroring my own. But when the man turned in their direction, he faced away from Arrow. My smart boy.

Arrow's footsteps were light, but slow—too slow for my liking—and got dangerously close. I waited—wondering, hoping—as his padding stopped. He laid down the bounty he had collected, then ran silently back to the safety of the trees. His right hand grabbed branches and his left elbow hooked around tree limbs as Arrow pulled himself up to a high spot where he could spy while hidden. He exhaled and steadied himself, his left arm hugging his body tight to the trunk. Then he quieted the others, took a deep breath, and whistled, bright and melodic, like a bird.

The sound tugged at the man's attention, but he didn't turn around. Arrow whistled again, longer this time. Then I felt the ash under the man stir. His fingertips dug into the burnt dirt as he glanced around, curious, cautious, fearful. Until he saw what Arrow had left.

Slowly, the man stood on his good foot, limped to the gift, and dragged it back to where he felt safe. As he bit into the fruit, his eyes searched the branches.

Arrow stayed hidden, watching, watching, watching. I wished he'd come back to me.

Finally the man collapsed back onto the ground. Arrow stood, worry spilling from him. But the man wasn't dead, only asleep. Arrow must've seen this too; warmth seeped into the bark around him as his worry lessened and happiness grew. As the sun dropped lower, he started back home, the young monkeys hanging off him with excitement.

"Hurry," I whispered. I knew what was coming, had felt the vibrations in the air.

Too quickly a noise reverberated in the sky, a loud *tum, tum, tum* twisted over a whine. Arrow tensed as his eyes turned up.

"Don't go!" I screamed uselessly to the boy. "Come back!"

Arrow took off south again. The farther he got, the louder the *Tum Tum Tum* became. He was still far from where the metal bird had crashed, but he knew the noise was coming from there. He raced toward it, not bothering to hide. As he ran forward, the birds and monkeys fled back, but Arrow continued on, his feet barely touching the ground.

Finally he neared the Burnt Circle, and Arrow fell to his knees.

The sky was filled with a metal creature that looked different from the first. This one was bulbous, like a giant tree frog, held aloft by spinning arms over its head. It hovered above the ground, about half the height of the nearest tree. And below its insect-like legs was the man, curled up with his arm protecting his face.

"NO!" Arrow shouted. He didn't know what kind of monster loomed like that in the sky. It was so big and so close to the man, it looked like it would crush him. Arrow tried to stand so he could help, but wind from the spinning arms shoved him back onto the dead leaves.

The man must have heard Arrow's cry, because he twisted, his elbow piercing the dirt. His tense body told me he had seen the boy this time.

The metal frog rose into the air, and with it went the man. Ropes were tied around his chest and connected to the inside of the airborne beast. Another man peered out of a gaping hole in the creature's side. He hoisted up the rope until the kiskadee-clothed man was swallowed up.

Higher and higher the beast rose, leaving behind a cloud of leaves, dust, and ash picked up by the swirling wind. Then its nose tilted down and the metal frog sped away.

Arrow stood, his feet unsteady as the dust settled around and on top of him. He watched the whirling giant roar across the sky until it disappeared, sadness seeping from his soles. For the loss of this new human, I understood, this new possibility.

"This isn't the end," I whispered, wishing I could pull him close. "They'll be back."

IT STARTED IN THE SOIL. EARTHWORMS SLOWED,
LOST THEIR APPETITE, STOPPED EATING. THEY WERE DYING.
SO TOO THE BACTERIA AND MITES. DEAD. DISSOLVED. GONE.

"You should not have helped him." I didn't like how stern my words to Arrow were, but he needed to understand the dangers. "You cannot trust humans."

It was late, dark, but Arrow was not friendly with sleep. He was perched in his nest, mouth open as he moved back and forth trying to catch the few raindrops that dripped from the sky.

"I'm human, and you trust me."

Curly swung into Arrow's nest, chattering, and the boy welcomed the small monkey onto his lap.

"You are different," I said. "You grew up here, like the Forest Dwellers from rings ago. That man is not one of us. He's not from here. We cannot trust him to protect us."

"But I'm not from here either. Not really."

"The forest has been your home for as long as you can remember. You are not one of those humans now. You are part of us, Arrow."

Arrow wiped the water from his brow, and his consternation soaked into my branches. He wasn't convinced of my words. The pull of a long-forgotten past still had a grip on him.

"I'm just saying that we don't know anything about the man," Arrow said. "He could be like me. He might be nice. He's bigger and . . ." Arrow looked at the ends of his arms, his right with a hand that stroked Curly's black fur, his left pointed at the wrist like an arrow. "The man might know how to mend the Anima because—"

"He won't."

"He might. He had that machine. He knows things we don't."

"Arrow, machines don't bring up the magic. Only those from the earth can do that. The humans from outside don't even know what the Anima is. The Forest Dwellers tried to teach about it. The Imposters were the ones who called it 'magic,' but they sneered the word as though it weren't real. No, we must mend the Anima, our magic, on our own. We have to dig deep." I hoped he could hear the urgency in my words as much as I felt it in my roots.

Arrow shook his head, dropping his hand from Curly's back. "You keep saying that, but I've tried, and it hasn't worked. There has to be more to it."

I wished I had better answers for him. "That is all I know. The humans who lived with the forest said they would 'dig deep' to get the Anima. That is what I do. It must be what the humans do too. I trust that you will find it. You have to keep trying."

Arrow sighed and gazed at the carving he had placed on my bark many rings ago. Reaching out, he traced the small arrow, the line of its base, the angle of its tip, and the feathers at its back end.

"Tell me again about the humans who used to live here," he said. "And don't leave out any details. There must be something I'm missing."

Curly patted Arrow's hand so he would continue stroking her fur. Arrow obeyed.

"I believe I've told you every detail, but it was so long ago. It has been twelve ring cycles since you came to the forest; multiply that by five or more, and that's how long it's been since the previous humans lived here. Still, it cannot hurt to go through the story again."

I paused, gathered all the images of the old Forest Dwellers, their faces, their dreams, their actions. "They were good people," I told the boy. "Caring. Loving. Responsible. Their families had lived in the forest for generations. Since before I had rooted. Long before I became the Guardian Tree. And there were so many of them. The abandoned village to the north was only one of their homesteads. They lived nestled within the trees all over the forest."

"They slept in a nest like me?"

"No. They slept in huts, in hammocks low to the ground. But I think they would've been very jealous of your nest."

Arrow smiled.

"There were mothers and fathers and children," I continued. "I got to know many generations of the same family. And each generation would pass down their knowledge. The mothers and fathers would teach their children everything they needed to know to survive in the forest. How to find and grow food, how to protect themselves from hunter animals, how to heal themselves from injuries and sickness."

"Get to the best part," Arrow said. He shifted, disturbing Curly, who complained in loud chatters.

"Yes, the best part. Just as the Forest Dwellers had their own human families, they also welcomed us, everything within the forest, to be their family. They taught me what they discovered, and I taught them what we needed. They never took too much, and always gave back more. Together, we kept each other healthy."

"Like families do."

"Yes, like families."

"And the magic thrived," Arrow said, want written across his face.

"Oh yes. You think the forest is beautiful now. Then, it was many, many, many times as big. Far more animals roamed the soil and branches. Lots more Curlys were running around. And the flowers. Deep in the forest, where we are now, the night would be almost as bright as the day with the glow from their petals. Orchids would shine from hundreds of tree trunks. Fungi would rise out of the soil and burst into light all around the roots. Fireflies and butterflies and spiders and worms would compete to be the brightest and most beautiful. Everything was alive and growing as far as all the roots in the entire forest could spread. And the Forest Dwellers would dance and sing and play in the magical glow."

Arrow smiled, but he cast his eyes to the orchid next to his nest, the one that had glowed every night for most of his life but was now lit only by the moonlight that filtered through the forest canopy.

"And when they drew on the magic, on the Anima of the forest," I continued, "they would sit on the soil, close their eyes, and . . ."

Arrow sat up. "And what?"

"They would dig deep. That's what they told their younger generations."

18

Arrow slumped again. "There must be something more. They would just sit there and dig?"

"They wouldn't always dig. And they wouldn't always sit. Sometimes they would stand. Sometimes they would dream. Sometimes they would dance." I paused, wondering what other details I could tell him. Wondering what would help. "I—"

"I haven't tried dancing," Arrow said, hope in his words. "Maybe that will bring the Anima back."

Curly chittered in annoyance as Arrow moved her off his lap, but the little black monkey scampered onto the branch above. She could tell when something important was about to happen.

Arrow hopped from branch to branch until his soles hit the soil. He glanced back up at me, uncertainty in his eyes.

"How did they dance?"

"There would be music, drumming, and they would sing . . ."

"Like the birds?" Arrow glanced at my branches as though expecting the birds to wake and perform.

"Yes." I reached out to the night owls, and they began to hoot. Curly banged her palms on my branches and slapped my leaves in time to the music of the owls. "Then the humans would . . ." How to describe this? "Move. Wriggle. Stomp around in time with the beat."

Arrow moved. He wriggled. He stomped around my

roots, the pounding of his feet matching the slapping of Curly's palms. And all the time he kept his eyes squeezed closed, trying to dig deep with every stamp of his heels, every slap of his toes, to dig down to the magic.

Finally he paused. He opened one eye. "Am I doing it? Can you feel more Anima?"

I flexed my roots, but the bitterness that had invaded the soil since the magic had begun to die was still there. How I wished I could tell him something different. "I'm sorry, Arrow. That's not working either."

His shoulders drooped, and he climbed back up to his nest. Curly patted his arm and grinned, reassuring Arrow that he would mend the Anima one day. But I could feel in the energy that flowed from him into my bark, he was not so sure.

"There were so many more humans when the Forest Dwellers were here," Arrow said. "You said the older ones knew about the Anima and would tell the children. But you've only got me, and I'm just a child. What if we need more humans? Or I have to be older to mend it? If we wait for me to get older, it might be all gone before we get it back."

Cold sadness leached into the leaves as he lay down and Curly tucked herself into his chest again. He was getting tired now, the day's activity finally sapping his stamina.

"I don't think it is your number of rings," I told him.

"But you don't know. The human who fell from the sky is older. He'll know more than I do," he said, his eyes fluttering closed. "Maybe he left something that can help. Tomorrow I'll search the Burnt Circle. I'll try to find something."

"No," I said. "You must stay away from there, Arrow. It could be dangerous. We must mend the Anima ourselves. Do you understand?"

But I could not be sure Arrow had heard. Sleep had found him, and he was already breathing heavily, perhaps dreaming of finding magic inside the burnt metal bird.

He was stubborn, so stubborn, but he was also determined. And perhaps he had to learn his own lessons. After all, I had trusted all humans once, and I had learned not to.

I had taken a chance with Arrow. It was a risk, but he was so young. I hoped he could grow to be like the old humans, the Forest Dwellers, if I could teach him their ways. And he had, so far.

But with the magic fading fast and the curtain around the forest shredding quicker than I could control, I didn't know how much longer we'd survive if we couldn't find more Anima.

Arrow was my only hope.

True to his word, the boy ignored my repeated warnings and went to the Burnt Circle early the next morning, and the next, and the next. He spent his days exploring every inch of the charred ground. The rest of the forest stayed back, watching him from the trees, sending me images laced with worry. But this boy of twelve rings was stuffed full of curiosity, and he wouldn't be stopped.

21

His feet grew black with ash as he searched the ground. Eyes blazing, arms and feet rummaging. The frogs kept an eye on him, showing me Arrow's image as he touched the great bird itself, the broken bones jutting out at strange angles. He peered inside, and the monkeys watching from the branches screeched, but the boy waved their cautions away. He strode around the carcass, the body so much bigger than him. It lay on its side, its long tail twisted and snapped. One wing was crumpled beneath it, the other stubby with a jagged edge. And at the top, a hole was cut into its body, like a door, enticing Arrow to look for answers.

He jumped, trying to see inside, and the monkeys screamed louder. Arrow reached up but couldn't grab hold. He stepped onto a ledge, but the carcass rocked, and he scampered away. At the back, under the tail, he spied another opening, not large enough for his whole body, but at least his head. With the monkeys crying after him, Arrow peered inside.

The bowels of the carcass were hollow. Sunlight streamed through tiny holes in its skin, lighting a confused nest of colorful threads, metal shards, and what looked like curved hands, lying on their side, where humans could've been comfortable. The Kiskadee Man must've sat there.

Arrow pulled his head back out, squinting against the brighter sun.

He had not found anything that looked like it would mend the Anima, but the boy would not be deterred. He examined other areas of the Burnt Circle, where the Kiskadee Man had lain, where he had eaten the fruit Arrow had brought him and been hoisted into the flying bullfrog, then swept away.

Arrow kicked the leftover mango skins, which were already starting to rot and feed the charred earth. He outlined the indents in the ash, made by the man's body. He placed his small foot in the large print left by the man's shoe.

And he frowned at a glint coming from under the burnt dirt.

Arrow wiped away the earth and pulled out a small golden circle. He rubbed his thumb over the protruding image, the same picture as the stinkbird that had been on the man's shirt. The circle had a hole at the top, and Arrow held the piece high to watch the sun poke through it. With the disc clasped in his hand, Arrow ran to the line of trees, pulled a palm strand, separated a fiber thread, then hung the circle on it. After pulling the end knot tight with his teeth, he slung the thread over his neck so the disc shined next to his heart.

Fingering the gold circle with his right hand, Arrow gazed at the sky, in the direction the bullfrog had flown. He was no doubt playing the images of the Kiskadee Man in his head, wondering where he was, where he had come from.

And if he would return.

But while Arrow searched the scorched ground to the south, more of the curtain shredded in the north.

We would not be alone for long.

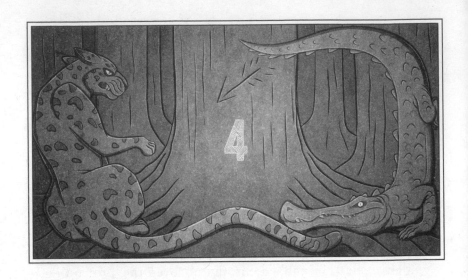

THE SMALLEST COFFEE TREE IN THE NORTH WAS BURSTING WITH SEEDS,
UNTIL IT FELT SOMETHING STRANGE, SOMETHING WRONG, SOMETHING
UNWELCOME IN ITS ROOTS. AND ALL THE SEEDS ON THAT SIDE
SUDDENLY LET GO OF THEIR BRANCHES AND FELL TO THE GROUND.

Four moons trailed a path over the forest, and the birds and other animals began to join Arrow in the Burnt Circle, cautious, sniffing, curious. With each moon that passed, their bravery grew. Arrow had hidden the disc within the folds of his nest and searched for other trinkets he could collect, anything he believed would give him the secret to these humans, to how they lived, and if they could fix the Anima.

My fear of the humans didn't lessen, despite Arrow's hope. I pulled enough magic to patch the wound in the curtain where the Kiskadee Man had fallen through, but I couldn't close it completely. I knew it would crack open again.

Meanwhile, in the north, rips like large open sores appeared in the curtain faster than I could mend them. It wasn't long before I felt footsteps draw closer, closer, closer. I hoped their owner would retreat, wouldn't see, but the tears were too big to be missed by searching eyes.

The footsteps came with another pair, light, cautious, hopeful. A fly showed the humans to me, sending their image and sound. It was a girl around Arrow's age, and a boy who was older. As they crept nearer, apprehension swarmed around them, but it didn't keep the children away.

"Look at this," the girl said, reaching out tentative hands. "There's a hole in the rock. I don't remember seeing it here before."

"Me neither," the boy replied. "Don't get too close."

"There are trees on the other side. Real trees! Maybe there's something we can use." The girl stepped toward the opening. "Come on."

The boy didn't move. "I don't think this is a good idea. Who knows what's in there."

I wished, wished, wished they would stay away. We needed more time for Arrow to mend the forest's Anima. Then I could repair the curtain and we'd be hidden once again.

"What do you think is in there? A treasure trove guarded

by a bloodthirsty dragon?" The girl thrust an elbow in the boy's direction.

He scowled at her, and the girl laughed. He didn't join in, though. His attention was squarely on the passage before them. "Something's not right. We've scavenged here plenty of times. Why haven't we seen this before?"

"I don't know." The girl shrugged. "It's not like we've been looking at the rocks much. We just missed it."

"Maybe," the boy said, but he didn't sound convinced.

Their words hung in the air, and I sent a silent plea for them to leave. But the girl broke the quiet. "Come on, Val. Trees!"

But the boy, Val, narrowed his eyes.

"Fine, stay. But I'm going in," the girl said.

"No. We'll tell the others, then send a scout party."

"We can be the scout party," the girl said. "Come on."

"No! That's not our job."

"You never want me to do anything," the girl mumbled.

"Of course not! You're my sister. I'm trying to keep you safe. Let's go." Val turned and strode away.

*Go. Go. Go*, I silently told the girl. *Listen to your brother.* But her toes stayed firmly pointed in the direction of the hole.

Finally a foot lifted out of the dry sand and came down closer to the curtain, then another, then another.

The boy shouted, "Petari! No."

"Just a peek," his sister said. She was as stubborn as Arrow. And as brave.

I wished she weren't.

Then Petari stepped through the hole in our curtain.

Her energy felt weaker than Arrow's, filtered through the hard bottoms of her shoes, but I could still feel her heartbeat lift, hear her breath falter. Inside the curtain must've seemed like a dream to her. Green, lush, alive. So unlike the world she knew.

"This is amazing," she said.

"Come back," Val called. But he followed the words with, "What's it like?"

"See for yourself." She grinned. "Come on. Stop being a baby."

His feet tapped, tapped, tapped the ground; then he scurried through the passage too. "I'm not a baby. We're supposed to be scavenging. This could be dangerous."

"I don't care. I don't want to just scavenge the same spots again and again. I want to scout." Petari soaked in the greens of the leaves, the browns of the sky-tall trunks, the pinks of the flowers of the trumpet tree. The sunlight was dimmer here, trickling through the forest canopy, but sharp rays bounced light from bloom to bloom.

"It smells so good," she said. "What is that?"

"It smells like the hydro farm Luco and I raided, but this is much better." The boy's energy perked up with every glance around.

"What's it from?" Petari asked.

"It's humidity. Water in the air."

"Water in the air!" Petari's eyes grew wide, and that pushed a smile onto the boy's face.

"Yeah, it's brill, isn't it?" he said.

Petari spun around, breathing in deeply, filling her lungs with the water in the air. "How can it be so different just on the other side of the rock?"

Her brother gazed up at the wall of rock they'd walked through, and I wondered if the tears in the curtain looked suspicious. If they did, the boy didn't seem to notice.

"I don't know," he said. "The rock goes up pretty high, but I don't see why that would make a difference. It's weird. It's like this is a completely different place, but it's only separated by a few feet of rock."

"However it works, I'm not complaining," Petari said. "Let's see what else is in here." She took off running, leaving behind Val's calls to "Slow down! Don't run! We need to go back." His words flitted into the trees, as Petari skipped over roots, and I braced for the worst.

I wished she would heed the boy's warning. I wished they would both run back through the hole in the rock and never come looking for it again.

But they were entranced by this world of green. Val was soon walking too, feet trailing the girl, eyes looking all around.

Each was quiet, breaths held so as not to wake from what must have seemed like a dream. But with every timid step in, their noses swelled with the smells of the forest. Damp leaves on the ground. Fungi on the trees. Animals breathing and sweating and pooping. Life all around them, crisp and clean.

The opposite of their dry and dusty realm outside.

Their smiles grew bigger as they trod on, rubbing fingers on bark and tracing veins on leaves.

The girl led them inward, her bravery building, hope buoying her feet. Over high roots, under low branches, around thick trunks. Stopping only when she heard the chatter.

"There!" She pointed to near the treetops. "Come on."

"Wait," Val said, "are those monkeys?"

"They look just like the pictures in the books." The thrill rode over Petari's breath.

"Don't get close," Val said. "You don't know what they're like."

"They're small."

"But still. In the books, they can be vicious."

Petari pushed ahead. "Only the big ones."

Their feet followed the monkeys, who were swinging from branch to branch, leading the boy and girl farther into the forest until, breathing heavily, the children stopped.

"Val, look!" the girl said, jumping as she pointed. "Is that real fruit? It looks like the picture on the fruit cocktail cans."

Eyes like bright suns, they stared in wonder at the trees. Tall trees with smooth green coconuts, shorter trees with rows of yellow bananas, bushy trees with green almonds. The boy ran to a trunk, then jumped and jumped until his hand caught the end of a bunch of bananas and pulled it down.

"It looks ripe," he said, turning the fruit over in his hand.

"How can you tell?"

"Dad showed me pictures in one of his books. Watch." Val gripped the top and pulled the yellow skin down in strips. The fruit inside sparkled in the sun. Petari quickly snapped off the top, brought it to her mouth, and—

Val ripped it away. "Wait! What if this is a trap?"

"Are you serious? What kind of trap?"

"I don't know." Val glanced around. "This place is suspicious. What if people put that hole in the rock to lure kids in here then poison them with this fruit?"

Petari snatched the banana back. "Poisonous fruit? Growing from a tree? Really?"

"Poisonous stuff does grow on trees. And people could make a tree grow poisonous fruit, you know."

Val tried to grab the banana back, but Petari quickly bit down on the textured goodness. She smiled, her eyes lit up, tongue licking every morsel from her lips.

"If this is poisonous, I— Oh no. No!" She grabbed her stomach, bent over, then collapsed onto her knees.

The boy grabbed her elbow to keep her upright.

"Petari!" Fear hung from Val's voice. "I knew this was a bad idea. I—"

"Ha ha ha ha." Petari threw her head back, laughing. Her brother stood quickly, his mouth pressed into a thin line.

"Not funny," he said, crossing his arms. I had to admit I agreed with him. The bananas in this forest are loved by all.

"Very funny." Petari grinned and pulled another banana from the bunch. "Go on. Try it. They're so good."

Val gave her a side-eye look, sniffed his banana, then nibbled the end. His mouth ticked up into a broad smile. He stuffed the rest into his mouth, then pulled down another and another, until their bellies were full.

"We have to show the others," Petari said. "We should take some with us, so they can see we're not lying."

"When they don't hear our stomachs rumbling, they'll know we're not lying," Val said. "But yeah, let's take some. Only what we can hide, though. We don't want questions if we get caught by the goons."

"Good idea." Petari grabbed two bananas and pressed them against her belly, concealing them carefully under her shirt. She grinned at the boy. "*This* is the best discovery since you found that stash of toilet paper."

Val nodded. "Hey, maybe the fruit will make Ruthie better."

Petari plucked another banana from the bunch and peeled it. "Told you it was a good idea to come in here."

My hope dwindled. If we could not close the curtain soon, these two would no doubt return, maybe with others.

And what if they went only a few steps farther? What if their gaze twisted between the trees? What if they found—

"Val, look!" Petari froze.

I knew then that the forest was doomed.

The girl's arm stretched out, one finger pointing to a thin gap in the growth. The air around Val vibrated when he spied what she had. Beams that were horizontal instead of reaching for the sky. Colors and shapes that were not of nature.

Petari hurried forward, but her brother whipped out a protective arm. "Wait!" He threw her a frown. "I'll go first." And he stepped closer.

As the forest opened to the savanna, their eyes widened.

The old structure had no walls, just poles and a roof. Grass and small trees had begun to reclaim the spot, but the structure was still intact and enjoyed by the chittering monkeys hanging in the shade it offered.

Beyond, the humans saw the village that had been left so many years before. The huts, the fences, the open field where the young Forest Dwellers would kick a ball and cheer when it was corralled within lines.

"Do you see anyone?" Petari asked, stretching her neck as though a few inches could reveal the world.

Val shook his head. "I don't think anyone's been here for a long time. And look!" He ran, Petari close on his heels. "A river. A proper river, with water still in it."

Petari gazed at the glistening water so close to her toes. She reached down but stopped when the boy said, "It'll be polluted."

"Even in here?"

"The water's polluted everywhere. You think here will be different?"

Petari pouted. "Mercou will know how to filter it. And look over there." She pointed at the thick forest on the other side of the river. "How many tasty foods do you think are over there?"

Val stared at the girl. "Don't get any ideas. Who knows how many dangerous creatures live in this water. Remember the story Dad told us about that giant shark that attacked people at a beach?"

"That was just a movie. Wasn't it?"

But Val didn't answer.

"Besides," Petari continued, "wasn't that in the ocean?"

"Oceans connect to rivers."

"They do?" Petari's eyes widened, her heart ticking up at this news. I had never heard stories of giant sharks attacking people at a beach, but it had spooked the girl. Good.

She turned away from the river and gazed back at the village. "Still, we were wrong before. *This* is the best discovery ever."

As they retraced their steps back through the trees to the hole that had brought them through the curtain to their great discovery, excitement spun in the air around them. Petari lifted one palm, and Val slapped it with his own. Smiles beamed bright on their faces.

I felt their footsteps retreat toward where stone ruled the land, where the soil was dusty and the air was dry. But I knew they'd be back. I knew they'd be back *soon*.

Any hope I had held of the forest staying hidden drained away.

I reached into the soil, connected with the root network, and alerted the rest of the forest.

THE BLIGHT CREPT INTO MORE TREES. IN THE NORTH, ONE
LEAF ON A YOUNG RUBBER TREE SPECKLED. THEN ANOTHER.
AND ANOTHER. UNTIL THEY WERE ALL COVERED IN DOTS.

"Arrow!" I called, but he was too far to hear my words. He was still taking in every inch of the Burnt Circle.

The images from the dragonflies showed me he had enticed Curly to join him. Curly's brothers and sisters had followed, peering into the carcass of the metal bird as though they'd discovered lost treasure. None were listening for me.

I tried to dig deeper, to summon more Anima. But there wasn't enough to stitch the hole in the curtain back together again.

I had always known this day would come, when our secret would be secret no more and we would be exposed to the humans again. But I had hoped it would be many, many rings from now. If we'd had more time, we could've discovered why the magic was diminishing. We could've fixed it, thickened the curtain, stayed hidden forever.

But focusing on problems would do no good. I needed solutions. And I needed them fast.

That's when I felt the cold fear that had seeped into the charred soil. Arrow was in trouble.

I asked frogs for help, and they showed me the boy.

He was gazing at his palm, a frown clouding his face. I quickly understood why. I felt a small tap on the surface of the soil, then a slickness. Rainbow liquid had dropped from the carcass of the metal bird. This machine sap had been brought into the forest by the Imposters too, and it had ignited just as quickly.

The images of the fire devouring the liquid when the bird had crashed out of the sky flooded back to me.

There was no fire for it to feed now, but what if it created one? Uncontrolled fire was dangerous in the forest.

I did not like Arrow being so close to that liquid.

I did not like it being so close to our trees.

Arrow must've recognized it too. He retreated quickly, worry creeping onto the ground around him. He rushed to the river's edge, tearing at his hand where it had touched the rainbow liquid. Smart. I didn't want it to hurt him the way it had hurt the Kiskadee Man.

While Arrow scrubbed, the footsteps returned in the north. The Petari girl and her brother, Val. They came back even quicker than I had expected, and I was not prepared.

Arrow was too far to hear me call, and he had his own troubles.

Even worse, the children weren't alone. This time, they were joined by a small herd. None of the footsteps were as heavy as the Kiskadee Man's, and none of their energy was as old. All of these humans were still children, some around Arrow's age, like Petari, some younger, and some older.

But they were still dangerous.

Many were laden down, walking on their heels to balance what they held in their arms, or walking on their toes to stabilize what they carried on their backs.

They came through the hole one by one, each stopping when they were inside. I didn't need the dragonflies to know the children were gazing around in awe at the lush growth, just like Petari and Val had. Their words confirmed it.

"Wow!"

"It's incredible."

"How is this here?"

"Why didn't we find this sooner?"

The herd chatted happily, slapped hands, patted shoulders, as fear spread through my roots.

"You sure you didn't see anyone in here?" asked an older female with short hair as red as a scarlet macaw's belly.

"No one." Petari shook her head decisively.

"Doesn't mean there aren't any people," said an older male. He was as tall as a grown caiman is long and as skinny as a spider's legs.

"We'll find out," the Macaw Girl said with a smirk.

Petari's toes pointed purposefully toward the village, ready to lead the others. "Come on."

"*I'll* show the way," Val said, pushing Petari back. "We saw some monkeys that might be trouble, so stay close."

I did not know why *he* was so quick to lead. Anxiety swirled around his every step, as he glanced behind and ahead. He did not like being in front.

Petari pouted but didn't argue.

The herd's footsteps trod, trod, trod along the path, crushing vines, stomping worms. The humans hooted and hollered as they walked, until the older ones quieted them with loud shushes. But they could still be heard across the river. Their heavy feet pounding the ground, heels snapping twigs, and squeaks ringing out from metal carts with small wheels, which the herd pushed across the dried leaves and soil.

The terrain was hard for them, and when they reached the downed branch, I hoped they would give up and go home.

"Hold up, Storma." The Caiman Boy raised his hand to

the Macaw Girl near the back of the herd, then turned to Petari and Val. "How much longer?"

"Not too much more," Petari said. She hopped on her toes, excitement squelching under her feet.

The Macaw Girl, Storma, ran up to the front. "All right. Come on, people. Lift!"

The herd was not to be stopped. The children gathered around the carts, lifted them across the branch, and continued on their journey.

"Arrow!" I cried as soon as I felt his footsteps were close enough that he could hear me.

"The metal bird was bleeding that rainbow liquid. Did you feel it on the soil?" He was lively after his adventure, swinging Curly as they journeyed back. Elated that he had been of use. I didn't know how long that feeling would last.

"Yes, but—"

"I fixed it, though. I put sapodilla sap over the hole, and it's not coming out anymore." The soil beneath him warmed with pride.

"Good thinking, Arrow. I knew that bird was dangerous. But we have other dangers inside the curtain now. More humans have entered, in the north."

"What?" He stopped walking, and Curly jumped onto his arm. "What do you mean? They're in the forest?"

"Yes, in the forest. A herd of them came through a rip in the curtain. They're headed for the abandoned village."

Arrow's feet picked up speed, a mixture of nerves and excitement in his wake. "Is it the Kiskadee Man?"

"No, not the Kiskadee Man. These are other humans. They walked in from the north."

Arrow stopped still.

"Walked?"

"Yes. The curtain is shredding there. I couldn't fix it with the magic."

"Are they . . . ?" Consternation flooded from the boy. He swallowed. "Are they the same ones who abandoned me?"

"These humans are too young to be the one who left you. But they could be from the same community. There's no way of knowing. Whoever they are, they will be bad for us."

Arrow slouched as anxiety swept into the air around him. Curly clutched his neck tight as if to comfort.

"What do we do now?" the boy asked.

"We watch. We learn. We do whatever we can to make sure they don't destroy the forest. And if we find a way to make them leave, we use it."

He nodded. "Okay. And when we get the magic fixed, we'll block them out for good." My boy. He understood. He knew the dangers.

"Yes," I told him. "Watch them, but make sure they don't see you. We must keep them north of the river. At least then we'll have some protection."

"I will." Arrow grabbed hold of a thick, woody liana

vine and quickly climbed up the kapok tree, his feet pushing against bark, right hand pulling on branches, and left elbow levering him around tree limbs. High up, he untied the strong hemp rope he kept around his waist, then stuck his foot into the end with the small lassoed hoop. The other end held a bigger lasso, and he threw it over the vine, and then pushed it down around his shoulders with his right hand and the end of his arrow arm until it was under his armpits. Secure, he pushed off and slid through the air toward the abandoned village.

The humans plowed their way slowly on the uneven ground of dirt, rocks, and leaves. The youngest were slower and held up the group, and more than a few times comments like, "How much longer?" and "Are you sure you know where you're going?" were tossed at Petari and Val. The boy shied from the words, but Petari batted them back with, "Soon. You'll see. It's perfect!"

When the herd sighted their first banana trees, hearts rapped faster and eyes widened. Bellies that had previously been silent screamed to be filled.

"See, Luco?" Val pulled down a banana. "It's brill, huh?"

"You weren't kidding," said the Caiman Boy, Luco. He seemed to be the oldest, with maybe fifteen or sixteen rings on his slender frame. "This place is stacked with food. We could eat here forever."

Hands grabbed bananas. Teeth bit through skins, until

41

Val showed the others how to peel. The herd almost missed Petari's chants of, "Come on. There's more. This way!"

Luco laughed. "I'm not sure we need anything more than this. I've only had that banana-flavored pudding. This is so much better."

"I know." Petari grinned. "But this is just the beginning of the good stuff."

"I'm ready for more," Storma said, stepping closer.

"You always want more," Luco said with a grin.

"Nothing wrong with that." She smirked and turned to Val and Petari. "Show us."

Val straightened at attention like a lemur. "It's just through there."

"Eyes out!" Luco called to the group. And their shouts and hollers over the bananas quieted as they began to move again.

"Lead the way, Val," Storma said.

Val did, Petari close behind, and the other humans trailing like ants through the tree trunks until they saw the opening.

Arrow and Curly were already perched on a branch on the south side of the village when the human herd stepped into the sunlight from the north. Arrow gasped, and Curly slapped a small paw against the boy's lips.

Like rainwater spilling from between two rocks, the herd spread out around the abandoned village. Carried items were dropped on the ground, forgotten, carts left in their pathway. Eyes widened, mouths hung open, steps were cautious.

"Stay here," Storma shouted. She ran into the center of the village. Luco did the same, while the others obeyed the girl's command. The two darted from hut to hut like hummingbirds looking for nectar. They peered under, around, and inside, until they heard a loud squeak from their group. Storma looked back under a deep scowl, one finger slammed against her lips. One of the smaller children had clamped her palms over her mouth, but she jumped up and down in place like she was holding back a stream of words that couldn't wait to get out. After Luco gave Storma an approving nod, they returned to the rest of the herd and the girl finally released her mouth.

"Water!" she shouted, pointing at the river. "Real water!"

The whole herd followed her fingertip ... then they were running, skipping, cheering to the river's edge.

"Told you," Petari said. "Isn't it beautiful?"

"I've never seen this much water in my life," Storma said.

"Mercou, can you filter it?" Luco asked a boy with a halo of black hair.

"I can try," the boy said, grinning.

"What's over there?" Storma pointed at the forest on the other side of the river. Pointed in my direction. My roots stiffened.

Val shrugged. "Probably more of the same."

"Maybe people." Storma flashed Luco a frown.

"The river's too wide for anyone to get over here," Luco said. "But we'll be cautious."

Hidden high in the ficus tree, Arrow and Curly were frozen, just like I had taught them to do when they saw Claw or one of her pups. Stay small. Stay silent. Stay still.

But the boy's eyes took in all their movements, and his heartbeat, pulsing into the bark through the soles of his feet, gave away his fear and anticipation.

The abandoned village now held more humans than Arrow had ever seen in his life. When Luco gave the word that they were safe, their bravery grew and they moved around the village, talking, laughing, shouting, pointing. Soon they were running across the field, stomping up steps, jumping into the huts.

Arrow's heart tapped, tapped, tapped at the sight of so many creatures who were like him. Big, small, muscled, skinny, with skin in all different shades from as dark as coffee seeds roasted in the sun to as light as the flowers left in the coffee tree's leaves. They had black hair and brown hair and yellow hair and red. They were tall and short, young and older.

For Arrow, these were the first humans who looked more like him. His age. And he couldn't look away.

He watched as they explored the buildings. He watched closer as they pulled items out of containers and carts. He watched even closer as they unwrapped packages and laughed.

With each laugh, Arrow's heart beat faster. As they kicked a ball, his toes twitched. When they shouted and screamed and pranced, he huddled behind the branch—but his eyes stayed on them all. Especially the girl, Petari, the closest one to his size.

And when the sun was about to set and Curly was tugging, tugging, tugging at his sleeve to go back home, he resisted for just a few breaths longer. He watched as Luco and Storma gathered the herd into a circle and handed out food.

Sadness flowed from him then, and I knew what he was thinking. How it reminded him of seeing Curly and her brothers and sisters when their parents would give them food. When he'd seen the older sloths sit with their babies. Even the birds, feeding their children in their nests. He had been a part of their circles but always outside, too.

Now the forest held humans like him, but he couldn't be with them, either. It was humans who had abandoned him at the curtain in the north. Maybe not these particular ones, but they were all the same. They were just like the Imposters from rings ago, and we couldn't trust that they wouldn't destroy us.

I had to make sure Arrow understood.

WEST OF THE RIVER, THE ROOTS OF TWO BOUGAINVILLEA
BUSHES SOAKED UP WHAT THE SOIL WAS DELIVERING, THEN
WITHERED AND BROWNED. THE BUSH WILTED, ITS PETALS FALLING
TO THE GROUND, SCATTERING THE FEEDING BUTTERFLIES.

Arrow was filled with questions that evening. His feet carved a path in the earth around me, excitement seeping into the soil.

But his feelings met urgency in my roots.

"We must make a plan," I said, but Arrow wasn't paying attention to me. He acted like my words were butterflies, flitting away.

"There are so many of the humans," he said. "And they've got so many things. Do you think they're going to stay at the village? They're going to live there?"

Arrow's emotions spun around him, happy, scared, sad, excited. It made it difficult to tell how he felt about this invasion. Curly was anxious. She paced behind Arrow, stopped, groomed, paced.

Curly was a mirror of the rest of the forest. The root network was abuzz with jitters about a return from the Kiskadee Man. I had already passed nutrients to help dying trees. And now this. . . .

"It does look like they plan to live there," I told Arrow. "It will be hard to get rid of the humans now. The forest has been found. We must do whatever we can to protect it."

"They haven't come any farther into the forest," Arrow said. "Maybe they won't harm anything."

"They are like the Imposters." I could hear the bitterness in my own words. "They will push and push and push, until they've made it all their own."

Arrow slowed for a breath, then picked up his pacing again. "I'll make sure they don't come any farther south. The river is wide there."

"Yes, but the bridge is—"

"I know. It's overgrown there, but I'll make sure they don't find it. And when we mend the Anima, you can move the curtain to just before the bridge, so they'll never come south of the river."

"That would sacrifice some of the forest." I hated to do that.

"Yes, that's sad. But it means the humans will never know we're here." He patted my trunk. "All this thinking has made me hungry."

As he and Curly collected berries and nuts, Arrow continued to talk about the humans.

"They were so loud for humans so small."

"What was that stuff they were eating?"

"Do you think they like acai berries?"

"Do you think they like the forest? Of course they like it."

"Do you think they play a lot of games?"

"Do you think they like strangers?"

That last question slipped over his tongue as though it had escaped. This was his quandary: his head knew he had to keep the humans out, but his heart wanted to be accepted by them.

The shadows grew thick, and Arrow and Curly climbed to their nest and lay down, but it was a long time before sleep slowed Arrow's breathing. When it finally took him, the boy tossed and turned while the moon crawled across the sky. I hoped his nightmares weren't too terrifying.

He was quiet the next morning, too, sliding out of my branches with barely a word.

"Remember," I shouted after him, "don't let them see you."

"I know," he called back, but I could feel the unrest in every footstep.

When Arrow and Curly got to the abandoned village, they first went to the hidden branch in the tree, the outlook from where they could see the human herd below. The young humans had stuck together, sleeping in clumps within one of the bigger structures. They had dragged most of their belongings into huts as well. So when Arrow and Curly crouched on the branch, they couldn't see any of the humans, just the small items they had left scattered on the ground outside.

"Did they leave?" Arrow whispered. Curly tutted back, and Arrow nodded. "Yeah, the Guardian would've said. If they're in the huts, I can go down and get a look at those things they left out."

He grinned and started down the trunk. *No. Bad idea.* Curly must've thought the same. She screeched and pulled Arrow's arm back up.

"I'll only be a few breaths," he said, pulling out of Curly's reach.

I wished the village weren't so far that Arrow couldn't hear my words. I liked that the boy was brave, but bravery comes with a price. He took too many chances, just like he had with the Kiskadee Man. But this time, there were more humans, and they wouldn't be whisked away by a flying bullfrog.

A swarm of bees sent me images: Arrow weaving through trunks to the edge of the clearing. Arrow watching, careful, then stepping onto the grass. Arrow stealing to the side of a hut, pausing, peering, then creeping nearer. He crouched low, examining something I could not see. I asked the bees to move closer.

Around the hut, the herd had placed a shiny vine of some sort of metal. It wove up the stairs, across the bottom of the door, then back down to the ground, where it connected with what looked like a thin metal trunk covered in scraps. They seemed to be parts of the tools the Imposters had used to eat: spoons, forks, and blunt knives. Arrow reached up to touch the vine, and I stilled my leaves. *Careful! Careful!* His finger gently pulled it—and a *TINK* rang out. Then another. And another! The momentum Arrow had started migrated along the vine to the metal trunk and onto the scraps, causing them to swing and hit each other with loud noises.

Arrow put his palm against the vine, trying to stop the sound, but that made it worse.

*DING.*

*TINK.*

*TING.*

Suddenly he tensed. He dove under the fern leaves nearby just as a head poked out of the hole in the hut's wall. Luco glanced around, stretching his neck to see what had disturbed the vine. Storma's head appeared next to his. They exchanged words, but none came to me. After the tools had silenced, Luco shook his head, then he and Storma ducked back into the hut.

Arrow's heartbeat raced against the soil. He had almost been caught by their trap. He watched and watched, but there was no more movement. I hoped he understood the danger he had put himself in. I hoped he would flee back to Curly, back to safety.

But when he emerged from under the fern leaves, Arrow didn't turn back. His curiosity had taken over. His feet carried him into the clearing. Keeping an eye on the herd's hut, Arrow hurried to one of the metal carts that had been filled with containers during their journey the day before. Now it sat empty, discarded on a patch of soil.

Arrow stood a few steps away from it, eyeing the box and wheels it sat upon. I'd seen carts with wheels like this a long time ago, in one of the Imposter camps before the Forest Dwellers were pushed out, before I hid the forest. But it was new to Arrow.

Cautiously he stepped closer, then closer, reaching out the fingertips of his right hand to touch its surface. Satisfied that it was safe, he moved next to the cart and pushed it back and forth.

There was a squeak, and he froze. He glanced at the huts.

Was there movement in the structures? It was too difficult to tell with their floors raised off the ground. Arrow was so close to where the humans slept now. Even though I knew he could be quiet, he was in the open and could easily be seen.

Arrow must've felt comfortable, because he continued to inspect the cart. Then he turned to the other items the herders had left on the ground: metal tubes, containers that glinted in the sun. Arrow got lost in these foreign wares, and when the sky opened and rain pelted down, he paid it no mind.

Until the scream.

It came from inside the biggest structure. One scream, then another, then shouts. The humans were awake. And scared.

*Run, Arrow!*

He couldn't hear my words, but he knew. He ran for the trees, but he was so close to the huts. His legs wouldn't be fast enough. He was going to be seen!

The door flung open, pushing aside the metal vine with a *TINK, TING, DING*, and the herd streamed outside.

Arrow scrambled away, but he was still far from the tree. Far from safety.

Suddenly he changed direction. *No, Arrow! What are you doing?* He threw himself onto the ground, right in the middle of a patch of tall grasses. Ahh, smart boy. The grasses would hide him.

As long as the humans didn't get close.

But they weren't paying attention to him. They were shouting and jumping and twirling. Arrow was right—they held so much noise in those small bodies.

"It's raining!" Petari screamed. She opened her mouth to let the water run onto her tongue. "It's raining!"

"It was so loud in there." Val glanced between the structure and the sky.

"I thought someone was shooting at us." Luco gave a shaky laugh. He lifted his arms, welcoming the water. "I've never heard rain on a roof before."

"I can't even remember the last time I saw any rain." Storma peered at the sky, the drops drenching her face.

"We need to collect it," Mercou said, picking a metal tube off the ground and holding it up.

Arrow stayed still, watching, frowning. Confusion soaked onto the ground beneath him, but he used their distraction to his advantage. With eyes on the herd, he crawled backward, his knees and elbows digging into the dirt as he stayed hidden in the grasses. His pulse thump, thump, thumped into the soil.

A short human shouted, "Woo-hoo!" and Arrow froze.

But none of their eyes were on him. Their attention was still on the rain. The drops hitting their noses, plinking onto the huts, splashing into the mud.

Arrow crawled and crawled and crawled. Finally he was within bushes, hidden enough to run back toward the tree. Far in the forest, my roots began to relax.

Curly scurried down the trunk and slapped Arrow's hand for going out there, but Arrow didn't care.

"Did you see how they were acting? Why are they so excited about some rain?"

The monkey shrugged, then pointed at the river.

Arrow nodded. "Oh yeah. Let's get to work while they're busy looking up at the sky."

As the herd cheered and danced and played under the raindrops, Curly kept watch from beneath the long leaves of a fern. Arrow gathered leaves that had fallen from some of the palm trees close by. Just like in so many other places in the forest, more leaves than normal littered the ground. I pushed away my worry; the bigger harvest meant Arrow had plenty to use. Carefully and quietly, he placed them within the bushes and between the trunks, thickening the trees to the south of the village. From far away, the tree line already looked dark, but we couldn't chance one of the humans catching a glimpse of something if they got close. We had to make sure they wouldn't be tempted to explore farther.

Arrow worked quickly, but it was a big task. Too soon, the rain stopped, and he no longer had the sound or distraction as cover. He slowed, listened. The humans were still laughing and talking, but none were near him. He continued to place branches, stopping when Curly made a warning noise, then starting again when he was sure he wouldn't be seen.

Finally all the downed palm leaves and branches were propped up, thickening the brush. It wasn't as good a mask as a magical curtain of rock, but it was hopefully enough to keep away humans who got distracted when water fell from the sky. Arrow ran through more bushes, east, west, east, west, until he finally returned to the tree line. I couldn't tell what he was doing, but I trusted it would keep the humans out.

After a quick check of his work, Arrow grinned at Curly. The monkey nodded then led Arrow back in my direction and away from the village. The job was done, and they had not been seen. Good. With any luck, the boy's work had given us enough time to fix the magic and go back into hiding before the humans decided to venture farther south.

Arrow followed Curly toward the river, until his feet stopped walking. His footsteps turned back to the village. Arrow stepped, stepped, stepped . . .

What was he doing? Why was he going back?

Curly must've not realized at first. She hurried in my direction for many breaths before turning back toward Arrow.

I reached out to the bees, asked them to send me the sounds and images of the village. At once I knew what the magnet was. A sound neither Arrow nor Curly would recognize.

A sound that hadn't echoed within the forest for close to twelve rings.

"What's that noise, Curly?" Arrow whispered, as the monkey pawed at the boy's leg to keep him walking. "It's not any animal I've heard before."

Curly shook her head at Arrow, anticipating the boy's thoughts.

"Just a peek," Arrow said. "Aren't you a little bit curious?"

Curly shook her head harder, pointing back toward the deep of the forest. Back toward me. But Arrow grinned.

"One look, then we'll go home."

That was what I had been afraid of.

Arrow ran on light feet past the trees and bushes he'd thickened. Curly followed but kept her distance. At the far end, where the trunks thinned, Arrow crawled behind a heliconia bush, beckoning for Curly to join him. She glared his way but finally skittered beneath the leaves as well.

They were close to the biggest structure in the village, where the herd had chosen to sleep. The humans were beyond it, in the open field in the middle of the huts, most of which Arrow and Curly could see from their hiding spot.

"I don't hear the noise anymore, but I was sure it was coming from this direction," Arrow whispered. The monkey frowned.

They watched as the humans ran and laughed and shrieked. One was the aggressor, chasing the others, reaching with toes dug into the ground to increase his length. The others chanted and jeered as they curved their torsos so that they were just out of his grasp.

"They're playing catch like we do with your brothers and sisters." Arrow smiled.

Curly motioned to her mouth.

"Yeah, I don't see one with food. Maybe they play differently." His head tilted. "There! It's the noise again. Where is it coming from?"

His eyes stopped on each of the humans. But it wasn't coming from any of the ones he could see. It was closer to where he and Curly were hiding. It was coming from the big hut, where the humans had slept.

Arrow stiffened, craned his neck to see the source, but the humans who were chasing one another didn't slow down. They continued their shouts and jeers and laughter.

Not all of the herd was there, though. Petari was missing. Had she made her way south and I'd missed it? No, another noise pounded from inside the structure, feet striding across the wooden floor.

Arrow pulled back, Curly tucking herself under his arm.

The pounding got to the door, and Petari emerged, a crying bundle in her arms.

"Hey," she called, "isn't someone going to help?"

There was no response. The other humans were enjoying their game.

Petari sat on the top step and lifted the bundle in front of her face.

Arrow gasped. Curly pinched his arm. He waved her warning away but placed his hand over his mouth to show he wouldn't make noise. Then he leaned in closer to the monkey's ear and whispered, "It's a baby."

He had seen plenty of babies in his life—monkey babies, sloth babies, capybara babies—but this was the first time he was seeing a human baby. The first time he was seeing how small he'd once been.

"Guys!" Petari shouted. "We've got to do something about Ruthie. She's really hot."

A boy with eyes as soft as a sloth's left the herd and walked up then, a frown planted on his face.

"Does she have a fever?" the boy asked.

Petari nodded. "Feel her." She held the baby toward him. "I'm worried, Rosaman."

The boy, Rosaman, put his hand onto the baby's forehead, and his frown deepened.

"Luco," he called out, and the older male looked over. "We've got to get her some medicine."

Luco picked himself up off the ground and strode over. "We're out."

"I haven't seen anything in raids for a while," Storma said from where she sat on the grass, pulling what looked like tools out of some sort of sky-colored carrying hammock. "You were with me in the last raid, Ros. You know."

Rosaman's head hung low.

"We have to do something," Petari said.

"She wasn't this bad before we came in here," Rosaman said, anxiety swirling around him. "Maybe we should take her back to the Barbs."

"That's where she got sick." Petari peered at the baby, who was still releasing a pained scream. "The bananas helped her when we first came in."

"Get her some more bananas, then," Storma said, wiping sweat off her brow.

"We tried that. She's not eating now." Petari hugged the baby closer. "Shhh, shhh."

Luco patted Rosaman on the shoulder. "We can go back to the Barbs for a raid tomorrow. Maybe we'll find something. Right, Storma?"

"I doubt it. I just tol—"

Luco glared at Storma. "We'll find something tomorrow, right?"

The girl side-eyed Luco, her red hair flaring bright in the sun. "Sure. We'll find something tomorrow." Her words didn't sound like they could be believed, but still, she turned to Rosaman and said, "We'll take care of your sister. Don't worry."

Rosaman nodded. "Okay."

"Let's try the bananas again," Luco said. "I bet I can get her to eat them."

Petari sighed. "We can try."

"Everyone," Luco shouted to the group, "let's see what other food we can find. We'll fill up one of these buildings with food, right?"

The others responded with cheers and "Yay"s. Storma shoved the tools back into the sky-colored carrying hammock. Then the group left Petari and the baby and headed toward the trees to the north of the village. The way they'd come in. The way they knew. Good.

The baby's crying didn't stop. Petari hugged her close.

"It's okay, Ruthie," Petari said, her voice as soft as an orchid petal. "We're going to be okay. I promise."

She lifted the baby again, then rocked her. Inside the heliconia bush, Arrow jumped back. He could see the other side of the baby now. One of her arms was wrapped in white material and pointed at the end.

Petari kissed the forehead of the screaming baby, winced, then laid little Ruthie back on the blanket on the top step.

"Where were the bananas again?" The shout came from Luco at the other side of the clearing.

"To the left," Petari called back.

"We can't find them."

Petari's eyes rolled in her head. "What about Ruthie?"

Luco pushed a girl whose brown hair stood up like a kingfisher's feathers back into the field. She looked maybe eleven rings. "Delora will keep watch. Come on."

Petari turned to the baby. "Ruthie, these people would be dead without me. But a banana might make you feel better. You stay in your bed. I'll be right back."

She picked up the crying bundle, carried her into the hut, then left, closing the door protectively behind.

She ran to Luco, calling out, "You'd get lost in a shopping cart, you know."

"What am I supposed to do?" Delora lifted her arms.

"Stay with Ruthie and keep an eye out," Luco returned.

61

"For what?" The girl looked around, but Luco and Petari had disappeared into the trees. Delora sighed, then trudged to the structure, her eyes darting toward the tree line. The shouts and laughter of the rest of the herd echoed out of the forest, and I could feel her jealousy sinking into the ground below her.

Arrow watched, watched, watched, then lifted onto his toes.

*No, Arrow. Don't go!*

Curly must've had the same thought. She grabbed his ankle to keep it in place. But Arrow picked her up, said, "Shhh," then slipped out from under the bush.

Large ferns were dotted between him and the structure, and he slunk from one to the next, all the while keeping an eye on Delora, who was approaching the hut. By the time she trod up the steps, he was only a few strides away. As soon as she went inside, he dashed for the wall, Curly clinging to his arm.

His feet were light over the grass. He ran quickly, then flattened himself against the back of the hut. His pulse thudded out from his soles, and he gulped air into his lungs. He was used to playing hide-and-find with Curly and the other monkeys—he was even used to hiding from the more dangerous creatures in the forest—but he didn't know humans and couldn't predict their actions.

"It's okay, Ruthie." Delora hummed a melody, and her

62

voice drifted through the hole cut into the wall above Arrow's head. He glanced up at the sound and smiled.

Arrow whispered something into Curly's ear, but the bees that were showing me the images were too far to hear. Curly glared at Arrow, then shook her head definitively. I didn't know what Arrow was up to, but it didn't look good. I liked Curly's answer.

But Arrow bent close to her again, whispered more words, and this time his mouth twitched up into a mischievous grin. No, I didn't like this at all.

Curly suddenly jumped from Arrow's arm and into the open field beyond the hut. She leaped over to the cart and started banging on it hard. *Curly!*

It must've had the desired effect, because when Delora came running out, shouting, "Hey! Don't touch that," Arrow took the stairs fast, pushed open the door, and entered.

My leaves froze. What was he doing? He was taking too many chances. He might be discovered!

He was in the hut for only a flap of a butterfly's wings before he scurried out and into the ferns.

My leaves exhaled in relief, but he didn't head my way or climb to the safety of the canopy. Instead he waited until Delora was turned away from him, then did his best impression of a macaw. Curly glanced his way long enough to see Arrow spin his hand in the air. He was telling the monkey to continue. I'd have to have words with them if they survived!

Curly jumped into the cart and picked up something. It looked like a spoon. She waved it in the air, leaped back out of the cart, and ran around the field, a yelling Delora chasing after her. From the hut, Arrow ran into the trees to the south, then pounded west. His arms brushed away branches, fingers searched leaves. Until he stopped, paused, turned, and ran back.

What was he doing?

When he got to the wall of the hut this time, he first peered into the field. Delora was laughing and running, but Curly was good at shifting direction to evade the girl's hands.

Arrow dashed up the stairs, heart pounding, and back inside the hut. I could no longer feel his weight, and there were no bees inside to send me images of what he was doing.

But I could feel footsteps approaching—fast. It was the herd, and they were weighted down. They must've found more fruit. They crashed through the bushes and into the field, arms laden.

*Get back, Arrow. Get back!*

Finally Arrow slid out the door. One glance at the herd told him he had to hurry. Instead of taking the steps, he jumped down and flattened himself in the shadow of the hut.

"Look at this little guy," Delora called out as the herd came back.

"How cute!" This was Petari. "What is he doing?"

Curly glared at the humans, no doubt for being mistaken

as a boy, then ran west as quickly as she could, tearing around the other huts and into the far edge of the forest. *Thank you, Curly, for not heading south.*

"Hey, don't go!" Delora shouted to the monkey.

But Luco said, "Ah, let it go. We probably scared it. Besides, we don't want the monkey getting any of this. Look!" He held up the bananas in his hands.

Arrow had been peering around the side of the hut. *Go, Arrow! Go!* But his eyes were fixed on the humans chatting and laughing.

"Where's Ruthie?" Rosaman asked.

"In the house," Delora said, rummaging through the prize the herd had brought back.

"I'll get her," Petari said, and jogged toward the structure. Toward Arrow!

The boy jumped—finally—and ran back to the cover of the ferns. He crawled under a bunch of large leaves, just as Petari stomped up the stairs.

*All right, Arrow. You've seen. You've done. Now come back.*

But he stayed. The baby's crying had stopped, and Arrow peeked through the long leaves as Petari appeared on the top step, the bundle in her arms.

"Delora, what did you put on Ruthie?"

Delora looked up. "Huh?"

Petari lifted the baby.

"I didn't touch her. I promise," Delora said.

Arrow shrugged farther into the fern, his eyes still on the girl and the baby, his heart drumming into the ground.

Petari pulled the baby into the crook of her arm and inspected the chubby arms and legs. The bees showed me now that Arrow had placed mulched malva leaves on the baby's skin. Petari's fingers rubbed at them, and a quizzical frown etched into her forehead.

"Then how . . . ?"

Arrow smiled and backed away, out from under the fern and into the trees behind, where Curly was waiting.

Suddenly Petari glanced up, out. Her eyes darted between the bushes. Explored the forest to the south. Looking for someone who could have given this gift.

Looking for Arrow.

DEEP IN THE EAST OF THE FOREST, THE YOUNGEST SLOTH
REACHED FOR A SHINY, NEW LEAF ON A CECROPIA TREE. IT
WAS GREEN, BRIGHT, AND LOOKED DELICIOUS. BUT JUST AS
THE SLOTH'S NAILS TOUCHED THE LEAF, IT DRIED UP AND BLEW
AWAY, LEAVING THE SLOTH'S BELLY RUMBLING.

I t was getting dark by the time Arrow and Curly strolled
back to me, but I didn't need the sight from the ants to
know the boy was pleased with himself. Every one of his
steps held a smile within it.

"You are proud of yourself," I said as he and Curly jumped
into the nest, pulling a hammock of berries and nuts they'd
collected onto his lap.

"Yes, I am." Arrow grinned as he handed Curly a palm
nut. "It's just a few malva leaves. I think we can spare them."

"Aren't you scared they will find you?" I asked, as he laughed at his joke.

"No one knows I was there. I am light as a feather. Quick as a hummingbird. As invisible as the wind." He giggled around the acai berry he was chewing.

"Is that so?" In that moment, I was jealous of the human ability to sigh.

Arrow swallowed. "I just wanted to help that baby. She . . . She's like me." He glanced at the pointed end of his arm.

"Is that why you helped her?"

"No." But he was too quick to answer. He paused, holding another acai berry in front of his lips. "I don't know. Maybe it was. But she's sick and she was crying. I didn't want her to be in pain."

"You are kindhearted, Arrow. It's a good thing. But you must be cautious with the human herd. They are not like us. You understand?"

He nodded, pulling an almond out of its shell. "Yes. Okay." He was getting frustrated with my constant reminders, but we couldn't let down our guard. I had been scanning the air for the telltale *tum, tum, tum* of the return of the Kiskadee Man. So far there had been nothing, but that didn't mean he wouldn't come back. Still, I knew Arrow needed a break, so I changed the topic to something he would enjoy telling me.

"How did you get Curly to distract them?"

Arrow laughed again. "I reminded her about the time I plucked the stinging caterpillar off her and got stung. She had to help me after that."

Curly slapped Arrow's hand, knocking out the berry he had just picked up, then popped it into her own mouth with a satisfied smirk.

Arrow was perhaps too smart for his own good. "The girl, the one they call Petari, she could tell the others that someone was there. They could come after you."

"Has she?" he asked, playing tug with Curly over the last banana.

"Not yet, but it's early. Arrow, you know what could happen if humans come farther in before we mend the Anima. We must protect the forest."

"I know. I know. It's just . . ."

"What?"

Arrow released the banana to Curly, then lay back in his nest. "They're not like I thought they'd be." Curly scampered to a higher branch, chittering in delight that she had won.

"What do you mean?"

"They're happy and friendly. They're like . . ." He paused, as though he were deciding on the right word. Finally he whispered, "A family."

A longing spilled from him as he said the word, but he swallowed it down.

"They might look happy and friendly," I told him, "but

the jaguars look soft and cuddly before they eat you. Don't forget what the humans did to you. Don't forget what they can do to the forest."

"I know. I know." He turned onto his side. Finished with her banana, Curly climbed on top of Arrow's head and picked at dirt in his hair. "They won't come this way. I made sure of that."

"Thickening the brush was a good idea, but it will not keep them out for too long."

Arrow smiled. "That's why I put a horde of stink bugs in the leaves and some fruit for them to eat so they'll stay. If the humans disturb any of them, there's going to be a horrible smell."

Arrow yawned, his eyes closing, ready for the welcoming arms of sleep.

"Smart boy," I said, my leaves fluttering at the thought of the herd's reaction. "Thank you. Tomorrow we'll do whatever we must to mend the Anima, then hide before they even know we're here."

Arrow nodded and snuggled into his nest, but it took many breaths before sleep was able to hug him. Emotions rolled off him in waves: excitement, confusion, doubt, fear. It wasn't until Curly pulled Arrow's tightly held arms apart and curled up next to him that the boy began to relax and allow sleep to sweep him away.

As they slept, I kept guard over the forest. I gave nutrients to help other plants where I could. I shrunk the tears I could find in the curtain and hoped it would hold. And I kept watch of the human herd. They huddled in the biggest hut again, carrying their food inside with them, as though worried it might be taken in the dark of night, and placing their trap around the hut door. Their precaution was wise. The forest animals were staying clear of the newcomers in the light of day, but the braver monkeys might've snuck in for an easy meal while none of the humans were around.

But no animals visited the village as the moon watched. They had not yet decided whether they could trust these two-legged visitors. And when the moon was replaced by the sun, the humans awoke with renewed enthusiasm for their newfound home. Luco emerged from the hut first, pulling away the metal vine and scanning for predators. Once he'd stepped outside, though, the rest of the herd ran out with screams and hollers.

If only Arrow had put stink bugs inside the huts, too. Then, maybe, the herd would've run screaming for their old, dry world.

Petari not only seemed secure in the village—she seemed eager to discover more. Too eager. Holding the baby closely, Petari kept scanning the trees to the south, where Arrow had disappeared. Had she seen him run off the day before? Could she tell his direction? I hoped that if she did go looking, the stink bugs would do their job.

It didn't take long before her curiosity became a flood she could no longer ignore. As Arrow and Curly sat near my roots, spitting the seeds of their passion fruit breakfast at each other, Petari carried Ruthie to Luco and Storma, who were passing out pieces of food.

"So no one did anything to help Ruthie yesterday, right? No one's going to own up to it?" She stood with one hip stuck out as a ledge for the now-smiling baby.

Her questions received silence, until Luco said, "You know what they say about gift horses," and that made the others laugh.

"I'm serious. Doesn't anyone think it's strange that she had some kind of mucky paste on her and suddenly got better?"

Val watched her but didn't respond.

"She probably got it on her when we came in." Luco shrugged, handing Delora a dry square they had brought from the outside world. "All kinds of stuff was coming off those trees. I'm surprised no one picked up anything poisonous."

"There's poisonous stuff in here?" asked a younger girl as wide-eyed as a lemur.

"Could be," Storma said, making her voice deeper for effect. She lifted her arms like claws and hunched over the child. "That's why you must stay away from the trees."

I liked her thinking.

"Don't tease Faive." Luco turned to another girl who was laughing close by. She must've been between Storma's and Arrow's rings and had a long thin nose like the giant ant-eater. "Safa, keep Faive busy, will you?"

"I'm helping Storma," the thin-nosed girl, Safa, said. But after Storma gave her a tight nod, Safa huffed, then led the young Faive away.

"This is important," Petari said, shifting the baby on her hip. "I think someone else lives here and they helped Ruthie yesterday."

I sucked air into my leaves, waiting for their answer. Some of the others giggled, but Storma silenced them with a hiss like an anaconda. She glanced around at the trees bordering the village's savanna, as did Luco.

"The only problem with your theory," Storma said, as she brought her own dry square of food to her mouth, "is that if someone else was in this forest, they would not help us."

"Yeah," said Mercou. "You think people in the forest will be any different from the Barbs?"

Anger radiated from Petari. "There are some good people in the Barbs. Maybe they're here, too. We can get their help."

Storma stood taller then. "No one helps us. That's why we're here. And if there is someone else in this forest, we need to stay far away from them. They'll be just like everyone else in the Barbs and the Stilts. They won't want us here any more than we want them."

"But—" Petari began, but Luco interrupted.

"Your job is to take care of Ruthie. We'll worry about other groups."

"But I—"

"She'll take care of Ruthie." Val hurried up to his sister. "Won't you, Petari?" He spat out the last words as though each had its own muscle.

"Thanks," Luco said, as Val spun his sister away from the older children.

Then Luco turned back to Storma and spoke in a lowered voice. "I'll set up watches. Maybe we should have someone on the trail in case other groups have found that hole in the rock."

As Val pushed his sister closer to the main hut, Petari twisted out of her brother's grip. "I don't want to stay here and look after the baby."

"You love Ruthie." Val glanced back at Luco and Storma talking.

"So? Doesn't mean I want to look after her all the time." Petari frowned. "I could help her more if I explore. I found this place and the bananas, didn't I?"

"You're safer staying with the group," Val said. "I don't want you exploring without me. If I hadn't been with you when we came in here, who knows if you would've made it back."

Petari rolled her eyes. "Stop babying me, Val."

"It's for your own good," her brother said. "Now stay here. I'm going to see if Luco needs help setting up traps." Val strode away, and Petari sat on the step of the hut with a huff. She bounced the cooing baby on her knee, but all the while, her eyes were on the tree line. After a few breaths, she stopped, glanced at the other children in the village, then stood up, holding Ruthie close. She hurried over to the boy with the sloth eyes and presented him with the baby.

"Rosaman, I need you to look after your sister for a little while," Petari said.

The boy looked surprised but said, "Oh, sure," then took Ruthie into his arms.

Val had been lurking behind Luco, but he rushed over to his sister when he saw what she was doing. "Petari!"

"Do what you want. I'm going to explore," she said.

Val glanced between Luco and his sister, regret ripping into the soil beneath him. After a few breaths, he said, "Fine, but I'm going with you."

Petari smiled, then waved Val to the tree line south of the village.

Butterflies showed me what they saw. Arrow had done a good job of weaving the loose palms and branches into the living ones to make that section of forest seem impenetrable. Petari still ran over to it, and I braced myself for the moment they realized it wasn't as thick as it looked.

"They are testing your fence," I told Arrow, who had

finished his passion fruit and gone to the river's nearby finger to wash his face.

He stood up, alert. "Did they get through?"

"Two of them are going there now. It's Petari. I told you her curiosity was big."

I turned my attention back to the village, where Petari was dangerously close, her brother only a few reluctant steps behind. Just branches and leaves stood between them and our secret. I held my leaves still as I waited.

"It's really thick. We're going to get scraped to bits in there," Val said.

"Now who's being a baby?" She smirked at him.

"I'm being practical. You heard what Storma said. We don't have medicine. We need to stay safe."

"It'll be fine," Petari said, then stepped up to the forest brush.

*Don't come through,* I warned, even though they would never hear my voice. *Stay back.*

Petari raised her arm, grabbed hold of a branch, and pushed it aside. "Whoa, this isn't even part of the tree. Look, it's just sitting here. But—"

"WHAT is that SMELL?" Val ran back a few steps, plugging his nose.

Petari followed, her nose crinkled to ward off the offending scent.

"What did you do?" Val shouted.

"Nothing, I just—"

"You did something. It wasn't like that before." He coughed, like the horrible smell had crawled down his throat. "Forget it. We're better off right here."

He dragged his sister back toward the others.

I released my leaves, spread out my roots. Said a silent "Thank you" to the stink bugs.

"That was close, Arrow," I told him.

"The stink bugs worked?"

"They did."

"Yes!" Arrow grinned, as Curly danced around his feet.

"But you know what this means, don't you?"

"I know," he said, his voice tired. "I have to stay away from the humans."

"Yes. And we have to mend the Anima right now."

IN THE FAR SOUTH, NEAR THE MOUTH OF THE WATERFALL,
A FLURRY OF HUMMINGBIRDS SUPPED AT A BRIGHT HELICONIA BUSH.
UNTIL THE FLOWERS SUDDENLY DROOPED, SHRIVELED, AND TURNED TO
DUST. THE HUMMINGBIRDS FLEW AWAY IN SEARCH OF MORE NECTAR.

The human herd stayed clear of the south side of the village after the smell rose. Arrow had placed so many of the bugs there, the stink they made after they were disturbed even drove the agouti away.

"We don't have to worry about the humans for a while," I told Arrow, "but they won't stay away for long."

"What are they doing now?" he asked, tucking in errant palm fronds within his nest. His words were light, but the uptick of his heartbeat told me it was more than curiosity. He liked learning about them. I understood. The herders were his own kind. But they were too dangerous to get close to.

"They've taken refuge near the smaller huts on the north side of the village, away from the stink."

Arrow breathed in deeply. "Then we can try to fix the magic again. Did you see the palms near the village? They're so bare. I'm worried about them."

"I know. The Anima's weakness is affecting the whole forest. I've been passing on nutrients when I can, but it's not enough. We must get the magic fixed, for them and the curtain."

The boy sighed. "I don't know if I can. I feel like I've tried everything, but nothing has worked."

"We just haven't found the right way for you to access the Anima yet. We will." It is easy to give up when thoughts turn to futility. I had seen it before with humans. But I needed Arrow to keep his belief strong.

Arrow nodded, even though cold uncertainty pulsed from his fingers.

"Okay," he said, straightening. "I've tried digging deep in the soil, like you said the Forest Dwellers would tell their children to do. I've tried digging near the river and near the villages where they lived. I've even tried dancing while I dig with my toes. What else can I try?"

"When the magic is plentiful, I only have to dig deeper with my roots and I can feel it tingle up," I explained. "From there, I picture what it is that's needed and ask its help. But it was easy when the Anima was strong."

"Is there a place the Forest Dwellers found the magic stronger than anywhere else?"

"I don't believe so. They would connect with it wherever they were, even in the village."

"Oh no." Arrow frowned. "What if that herd finds the magic there by accident?" He swiped at Curly, who was bouncing on one of my thinner branches.

"If we can't find it with all we are doing, they won't either," I said, trying to appease him. "But even if they did, the Anima could never be used for something bad. It is the life of the forest. It can only be used to strengthen us."

"That's good. But we still need to fix it fast."

"Yes. Then we can hide and make the forest healthy again."

A thin thread of sorrow leaked out from Arrow, but it was cut off quickly when Curly's tail poked the top of his head from the branch above. He pushed her away.

"Not now, Curly. I have to think."

She chattered her annoyance, then scampered down to the ground. Arrow's eyes followed her and he shook his head. He leaned back in his nest, deep in thought. Then he sat up, looked over the side, and swung onto the branch below.

"Maybe if I hold on to your root, like I used to when you taught me things in the daydreams." He climbed down quickly and jumped onto the mossy soil. "You can do the digging for me. That way we can dig even deeper together."

We hadn't done this for a long while. But when the boy was young, I used to show him all the wonders of the forest this way. How to spot a black caiman gliding through the river. How to track the trail of a jaguar. How to avoid antagonizing a giant otter. The images given to me by the dragonflies and birds had helped me teach Arrow where to find food and which foods he should avoid. But it took a lot of energy to share these dream images with Arrow, and once the magic had started to drain, I had to preserve it.

"It might work," I told him. "It's worth a try."

At the base of my trunk, Arrow dug a shallow hole, exposing a thick root. He pushed aside the dirt, and I wriggled the root to loosen it. Curly helped too, scrabbling in the soil with two paws until there was enough space for Arrow to get a good hold.

"I'm ready," Arrow said. "I reach out for the Anima and picture what I want, yes?"

"And ask for it to happen," I told him.

"Okay."

He glanced up at the orchid that was no longer blooming above his nest, then grasped the root, closed his eyes, and wished. And wished. And wished.

I wished too, digging deep with the soil, feeling for the tingle that usually accompanied the magic.

Curly patted Arrow's knee with a paw, and the boy slowly opened one eye and gazed up at the orchid. It was the same. Just leaves and roots; no pink blossoms. A large leaf on the palm tree in front of Arrow turned yellow. As he watched, it bent in surrender, then tumbled to the ground.

"It's not working," he whispered.

Feeling his sadness, Curly scrambled in the dirt to go even deeper. But that sharpened Arrow's pain.

"Maybe it's because I have one hand instead of two." His words were quiet, barely a whisper.

"No, Arrow, it's—"

"Did the Forest Dwellers who got the magic have one hand?"

I paused, knowing my answer would not help. But I had to be honest. "They all had two."

A tear soaked the ground beneath him, and I quickly tried to comfort him. "I've always told you, Arrow, your differences make you who you are. They make you unique, just like Curly is unique from all her brothers and sisters. Differences are to be celebrated, not condemned."

The boy shook his head. "This is why I was abandoned."

"We don't know why you were abandoned. Perhaps the person was sick. Perhaps they had no food. Whatever their reason doesn't matter. This is your home. One hand or two, you can do whatever you want to do, and you know that to be true. You have learned to climb the trees just as well as any of the monkeys, and they even have tails."

He did not respond to my attempt at a joke.

"Let's try again, Arrow. We will find what is missing."

He stood up, pushing the dirt and leaves off his arms and feet. "No. I told you I can't do it. I told you." Frustration and sadness poured off him.

"Arrow . . ."

"I'm never going to be able to do it. I'm not like the Forest Dwellers. I can't help the forest. I can't help you."

His voice was thick with tears.

"You have to beli—"

"I'm going to the Shimmer," he said, then stalked off to the south, Curly scampering after him.

"Arrow! We must not give up!" I called, but he was already on a liana flying toward the cave.

The Shimmer was his favorite place in the forest. Whenever he felt bad, he went there for comfort, just as the Forest Dwellers had done rings ago. Gazing at the many colors and shiny stones that permeated the walls gave them a calm they didn't seem to get anywhere else. Some of the great Forest Dwellers had gained inspiration and insight while they marveled at the Shimmer. I hoped Arrow would find that too.

I had seen the cave once in a dream sent by one of the Forest Dweller leaders of old. The breath taken in while he stood outside looking into the blackness. The call he threw in to scare off any predator. Then, once he knew it was safe, the steps he had taken inside, one drenched in sunlight and the next drowned in dark.

His heart had quickened here, just a bit. There is fear in the dark, the unknown, what cannot be seen, but when the other senses begin to ignite, the dark closes in like a hug. The Forest Dweller had breathed in deeply, letting the warm scents of the earth fill his lungs. Then, running his fingertips across the rock, he'd gone deeper, deeper, deeper, until, finally, light had returned and he could see the Shimmer.

Arrow had described it to me many times. A rocky sky that shimmered with color, illuminated by two thin holes that beckoned light from outside. After that light struggled through the tiny holes, it rejoiced in its freedom by touching every jagged edge of the cave surface. The rock of the curved walls and ceiling were different from the rocks by the river's edge. These were dark but speckled with bits of Shimmer that caught the dancing light and twinkled in joy.

It was hard to be sad in such a place. Arrow's face lit up when he talked about it, filled with wonder.

Like when he saw the magic . . . when the magic had worked.

My leaves dipped. If we could not mend the Anima, I worried for the forest and everything and everyone within it. We were already dying. All over the forest, trees and plants were shriveling. Animals were withering for lack of food. Even the root network was breaking down; the fungi that connected us all was ripping in places, making it harder for us to share. And now we had the threat of humans again.

How would we survive if we didn't mend the Anima, make it stronger? Perhaps Arrow would find inspiration in the Shimmer. Perhaps he would discover something the Forest Dwellers had left behind that could help us. I could only ho—

Footsteps! Twigs snapping! Leaves ripping!

One of the humans was breaking through Arrow's barrier to the south of the village. I reached out to the area, and a gecko provided me the picture. It was the girl. The nosy girl. The curious, unstoppable girl.

Petari.

I shook my leaves. I had been so busy focusing on Arrow and the Shimmer and the magic, I had not paid attention to the young human herd. And now, the girl was pushing through the dense brush, through the smell of the stink bugs, and coming our way.

The rest of the herd were playing some sort of game in the open field. I could feel the baby in the soil near them, crying again as Rosaman tried to soothe her.

None of them watched Petari, and in only a few seconds, she was on the other side.

Arrow needed to know about this, but my voice didn't

stretch to the Shimmer Cave. It was moments like this when I wished Arrow were an animal or insect; then perhaps I could've reached him at a distance like I could the rest of the forest's residents. One call out to the butterflies, and my message would be passed from butterfly to butterfly, sending it to the farthest trees and bushes. But humans were different. Not all of them heard my call. And even if they did, Arrow was the only one who knew me in the forest now.

I asked flies to buzz his head, hoping he would understand it was a message from me. But he was too sad. He waved them away.

Perhaps I could keep the girl back myself.

Petari pushed past branches, clambered over roots. She took the wrong direction, but then found her way. She was good at exploring, at finding a path, even one not often taken.

She was headed right for the thick copse of trees. Right for the connection between the village and the river.

I had to stop her.

I called for help, and the dragonflies were closest. A swarm swung around and headed her way. The girl stepped closer, and the dragonflies surrounded her.

Petari lifted her arms to shield her head. "Go away!" They torpedoed her face and back and arms, but the girl kept trudging south.

She was close to the river now, so I begged frogs to stop her. Few were this far north. They had spawned in the south, where the water ran cleaner. Those that responded leaped up, one catching her shoulder, another her arm, but she squirmed out of their grasp with an "Eeewwwww!"

But her disgust didn't stop her. It pushed her even closer to the crop of trees that grew from the lip of the water, the barrier to stop unwanted visitors from seeing what was hidden beyond the bend of the river. The area had become more overgrown with each passing ring, but it had thinned recently as trees had lost leaves and limbs. It didn't slow Petari. And neither did the frogs. She took a few more steps and . . .

She saw . . .

She gasped . . .

She knew there was more . . .

I could feel the excitement spark in her energy. Holding her breath, she pushed on, shoving leaves and twigs out of her way. Petari drove through the copse, then caught her breath when she came out on the other side.

"Wow!"

There would be no keeping her away now.

ON THE FAR SIDE OF THE RIVER, THE FLOWER BUDS AND
LEAVES OF A YOUNG MALVA BUSH CURLED UP AND DROPPED
OFF ONE BY ONE, UNTIL BARE TWIGS REMAINED. BUTTERFLIES THAT
HAD BEEN ATTRACTED TO THE BUDS CHANGED DIRECTION.

Petari had found our secret.

"Is this where you come from?" she whispered.

She must've meant Arrow. Yes, she was trying to find him. My boy, who had been too reckless when he had helped her.

Petari stepped cautiously up to the tree roots that rose out of the soil. Some twisted up, braiding into a railing; others reached out, weaving a tongue that stretched over the water. Up and across, up and across, until they clasped the roots from trees on the other side of the river. A living bridge that had not been made for her.

Tentative fingertips touched the rough surface of the roots.

*Perhaps she wouldn't like the bridge.*

She ran her palms over the crisscross weaving.

*Perhaps she would be scared.*

She put her toe on the tongue of roots that spread out from the river's edge.

*Perhaps she would give up.*

But I knew better. The girl tested the bridge's strength, held her breath, and stepped, stepped, stepped.

Holding tight to the railing of roots, Petari peered at the surface of the water beneath her. The bubbles and movement of something swimming under the surface didn't scare her. Her fear had turned to excitement, soaking into the bark as she touched each strand that knotted and dove and curled around its neighbor. Eyes widening, she marveled at the living tapestry that had formed this pathway over the water.

I wondered how quickly she would reveal it to the rest of her herd.

Another step, then she was on the other side. Our side. Her foot pressed down on the rich soil, the downed leaves, the moss.

"Arrow!" I called. I needed him now. The forest needed

him now. But there was no answer. He was still in the Shimmer Cave, away from my reach.

The trees were larger on this side of the river, denser, and reeds lined the water's edge. Petari ran her fingers through the reeds and walked north until she rounded the curve in the water's path that hid the bridge from the village. Here she could look across the river and see the huts and the rest of her herd. She could shout out and wave her arms and get their attention, point to the curve and the copse and the bridge beyond. She could tell them how to get to us.

I could have called to the forest's bigger predators to stop her. But Claw would have found her a tasty meal. I wanted the herd gone, but I was not like the Imposters. A life was too big a price. I had to find another way.

My leaves stilled as I waited, felt her footsteps on the soil, watched her from a fly buzzing over the water.

But she didn't alert her herd. She stopped and gazed at them but stayed hidden behind the tall grasses. Then she turned back toward the trees and entered the forest.

"Arrow!" I wished he would hurry back. I wished he could hear me.

Much like the day she and her brother had first walked through the hole in the curtain, I could feel Petari's wonder and thrill. It emanated in her every step, in the way she touched the leaves and rubbed the bark of each tree she passed. She never stopped looking and gaping. As the thick forest closed off sight of the bridge behind her, her breath quickened, but she wasn't to be dissuaded. She snapped twigs at the ends of branches, making each point in a direction. I was sure she wouldn't like me snapping the ends of her fingers, but I understood what she was doing: marking her path so she could find her way back.

Smart.

And she didn't show signs of going back anytime soon.

Not until she'd found what she was looking for.

"Arrow!" I called out. "Hurry!" I could finally feel his soles on the sun-kissed soil again. He and Curly were on their way. And just in time. Arrow was the only one who could stop Petari now.

"I haven't got any more ideas," he said when he heard my call.

"We can't worry about the Anima now, Arrow. The girl found the bridge."

"She did? She got through all those stink bugs?"

"I told you she was determined. Be quick before she gets too far. You must make her go back to the village and tell her herd to leave."

"I should've used more stink bugs, or put sap all over the trees, or moved in golden orb weavers to spin big webs," Arrow said, running to the kapok tree. "How am I going to get her out now?"

"I don't know." I hated the words I was going to say next,

but I could think of nothing else. "You might have to show yourself. You might have to talk to her."

Arrow froze. "Talk to her?"

"It might be your only choice. Tell her the dangers of the forest, Arrow. Tell her she must go back to the village. In fact, perhaps this is an opportunity. An opportunity I would've preferred to avoid, but still. When you explain how dangerous the forest is, tell her that she and her herd must leave, go through the curtain and never come back. Convince her."

The boy gulped. "Where is she now?"

"She's by the Crooked Rock and heading this way."

"Come on, Curly," he said, climbing to the liana vine attached high on the trunk.

"And, Arrow," I said, "tell her to keep you a secret. Don't tell her anything about you or me or the forest. If the others find out about you, they might come looking."

Nervousness dripped from Arrow as he pulled the hemp rope from around his waist. But he nodded, hiked the rope around his body and over the liana. Then, with Curly tucked onto his shoulder, he pushed off the trunk and flew. He connected with another tree and another liana, zipped past branches and squawking parrots. Finally, when he was just south of the Crooked Rock, he pulled himself onto a thick tree limb and hurried down.

I had hoped he would get in front of the girl, but she

had moved through the forest quickly. Quicker than I had thought she could.

Arrow's heel connected with something soft. Something that said, "OW!"

The surprise made Arrow jump, and he missed his next step. His toes slipped on the bark, sending his body sprawling onto the dead leaves, pushing Petari down with him. Curly chattered her annoyance from a branch above.

Arrow sat up and rubbed his head. "You mus—" He was ready, the words telling her to leave on the tip of his tongue. But as soon as their eyes locked, his voice left him.

*No, Arrow. This is not the time to stay silent!*

Petari glared at the boy and scrambled backward. "I knew I'd seen someone. It was you, wasn't it? You were the one in our home."

*"Your home?"* Emotions curled around Arrow. Anger mixing with anticipation mixing with curiosity.

"What did you do to her?" Petari stood up slowly, her narrowed eyes a warning.

A thrum of fear whipped through the boy, but he swallowed it back. It was his first time talking to his own kind, and even though he knew he had to make her leave, his interest in Petari made Arrow hesitant. He peered at her just like he had peered at Claw the first time he had seen the oldest jaguar in the forest. Then, I was glad he ran. Now I wished he would be more forceful.

"What did you do to Ruthie, the baby?" Petari repeated, her voice harsher.

Arrow straightened, swallowed, tried to find his voice. "You shouldn't be here," he croaked.

"What?" She crinkled her nose.

"It's not safe here." His voice was stronger now. "You have to leave. You all have to leave."

She glanced around quickly, picked up a stick, and raised it in front of her body. "Not safe from what?"

"From everything." Arrow pointed in the direction of the village. "Go back. Get all of your herd and leave."

"Herd?" Her brow furrowed, and I wondered if she understood English as well as I had thought.

Arrow gulped. "I'll get you out safely. But then you must leave the forest and never come back."

He started to stride toward the bridge, but Petari stepped into his path.

"Hold it. I'm not going anywhere until you tell me what you did to Ruthie." Her eyes roamed over him, his bare feet, his bare arms, his worn shirt the color of the night sky and shorts the color of twigs.

Arrow eyed her for a breath but kept his lips tightly shut.

"Someone came into our village and put some kind of muck on the baby," Petari continued. "It was you, wasn't it?"

Curly squealed in the tree, and Arrow glanced around the forest. "I told you. You have to leave."

The girl planted her feet firmly on the ground. "I'm not going anywhere until you answer my question. What did you do to the baby?"

She was not making this easy for Arrow.

He sighed. *Don't tell her anything.*

"I put mashed malva leaves on her skin. It heals rashes."

*Did he listen to nothing I said?*

"How did you know she had a rash?" Petari demanded.

"Didn't you see her? It was obvious."

Petari stamped her foot. "I mean why were you watching us?"

Arrow waved a fly off his arm, then noticed the girl gazing at his arrow arm.

"What?" he asked, as doubt seeped from him.

Petari backed up one step, turned away, and said, "Nothing."

There was a lightness to her word, but Arrow's doubt thickened. He glanced around again. "I told you, you and your herd have to go. The forest doesn't just have trees in it, and most residents aren't as friendly as me."

"You don't seem that friendly either. Answer my question!" Petari waved her stick at him, and Curly shook her fist at the girl.

Arrow narrowed his eyes. "Fine, you don't want my help. Get eaten. It's not like I didn't warn you." Then he turned, said, "Come on, Curly," and strolled in my direction.

I couldn't believe he was just leaving her. I had told him

to get rid of the girl, to make sure she went back to the village and left this forest for good. He knew how important this was.

He stepped away, but Petari didn't move, just stood there with her stick raised high.

*Go back.* I wished Arrow could hear. *Go back and make her leave.*

But then . . .

"Wait!" Petari lowered the stick and ran after Arrow. "What do you mean I'll get eaten?"

AN ACAI PALM NEAR THE CROOKED ROCK COMPLAINED OF A
BAD TASTE IN THE SOIL. THEN ITS TRUNK BENT IN TWO, AND ITS ROOTS
PULLED AWAY FROM THE EARTH.

Arrow's tales of hungry cats, sharp-toothed caimans, and striking anacondas convinced Petari she
should go back to the village, and the boy's thin
smile told me he had known she would. Smart boy. Maybe
he understood humans better than I'd thought.

He led the way quickly, dashing past trunks and jumping
over roots, making a show of looking for the dangers.

Petari was not as fast. She soon fell behind, and Arrow
had to stop and call to her to "Hurry! If you're not quick, the
animals will smell you and hunt you down."

The girl scowled but tried to go faster. It was not easy for her on the unfamiliar terrain. Finally she stopped and put her hands on her hips.

"I didn't see any animals when I came in here. I think you're bluffing."

"Bluffing?" Arrow didn't know this word. Neither did I, so it was not one I could have taught him.

"There aren't really any animals in here," Petari said, her voice sharp as a harpy eagle's talon. "You're lying to get me to leave."

"Lying?" Arrow did not know this word either, although I'd heard it before, about the Imposters so many rings ago. "You have to leave," Arrow continued, ignoring the strange word. "I told you it's too dangerous in here."

Petari pushed out her chin. "I haven't seen anything dangerous."

Frustration piled around Arrow's toes. "Just because you can't see it, doesn't mean it's not there. Come. I'm taking you out." He moved to grab her arm, to pull her away, but the girl stepped back.

"No. I won't go. Not until you tell me who you are." Her eyes drilled into him. "I've never seen you in the Barbs. How long have you been here? When did you find that hole? How did you learn about those leaves? Where's your group?"

"You ask a lot of questions," Arrow said, his annoyance rising.

"Of course I do," she said. "How else am I supposed to find out stuff? Now tell me—"

A twig snapped behind the girl, and Arrow's eyes widened. "Freeze!"

"What?" Petari swung around, then screamed. "AAAAAHHHHH!"

"Get behind me." Arrow pulled her behind him, and this time she didn't stop him. "That's Goldy. You're lucky. He's not the biggest of the anacondas in the forest."

"Not the biggest?" Petari started to shake, and I could understand why. Goldy was longer than the girl was tall, and his head was as big as Petari's fist. He looked menacing as he slithered slowly down from the branch ahead of them.

"Nope. But he'll still bite you," Arrow said. "Told you the forest was dangerous."

Petari screamed again, then turned and ran for the village. But her fear had her disoriented. Her feet took her deeper into the forest.

"Not that way," Arrow called after her.

She slipped, stumbled, fell onto the leafy floor. Arrow grabbed her elbow and quickly helped her up, glancing around to see if Goldy had followed. The snake had found a rodent to chase and was slithering in another direction.

"This way," Arrow said. "Follow me and stay close this time."

Petari nodded, hurrying after the boy. At last.

Her eyes glanced in every direction as they dashed toward the village. Even through her shoes, I could feel the rattle of her heartbeat. She was scared.

Good. Perhaps that would make her want to go.

She stayed silent for their harried walk back, and it wasn't until the root bridge came into view that her breath became less ragged.

"I'll walk you to the edge of the village," Arrow said. "But after that, you have to get your friends and leave the forest."

"Fine!" Petari huffed out the word, then started to follow Arrow. I could feel the relief rolling off the boy.

But after a few steps, Petari stopped. "Wait, why don't you want us here?"

"I told you, it's dangerous. Even in this area, there are lots of things that can kill you. Do you know which type of frog is poisonous? You don't want to guess."

"You know that stuff?" Petari's eyes widened. "Huh, I guess that makes sense since you knew which leaves would help Ruthie. But why would you care what happens to us?"

Arrow shrugged. "Because I do, okay? You don't belong here. Tell your friends to stay away, or next time, they'll face something worse than a smell."

Petari turned on him. "*You* made those trees stink like that when we walked up?"

Arrow grinned. She sounded impressed, and he was proud of himself.

"How did you do it?"

Arrow glanced at Curly, perhaps wondering if he should give away his secret. The monkey chuckled. "Stink bugs on the leaves. They don't like to be disturbed," Arrow said finally. A thrill of excitement whirled from him as he gave away this small secret. Then, as though he remembered his mission, he added, "And neither does anything else around here. So pack up your stuff and go."

He started to walk away, back toward the forest. I hoped this would be the end, that the girl would tell the rest of the herd about the anaconda and they'd return to the north.

Perched backward on Arrow's shoulder, Curly stuck out her tongue at the girl. But Petari ran after them.

"Wait. I walked through those stink bugs for a reason. And they were rank, thank you very much."

Arrow turned to face her. "They were meant to be." His toe twitched on the top of the soil. He was anxious. He had done what he had come to do; the girl was going to take her herd and leave. So why was she still talking to him?

"What I mean is, I had a big reason for coming to find you. I need more of that muck you put on Ruthie. Those leaves worked but not for long. She's getting bad again."

Arrow narrowed his eyes. The boy had a softness for

the baby. I couldn't blame him. I had felt the same when I'd brought Arrow into the forest.

He gazed at his toes for a few breaths, and I waited to hear his answer. We were so close to being rid of the humans.

Finally he looked up again. "Okay, you know the line of trees with the stink bugs?"

Petari nodded.

"Walk south. You'll see a big kapok tree. Turn east, then—"

Petari put up her hands. "I don't know what a kapok tree is. I'm not going to be able to find it. I don't even know what the leaves look like. You have to show me."

Arrow glanced back, in my direction. The longer he was with this girl, the more nervous he got, but I knew he wanted to help. His kind heart always got him into trouble.

"Ruthie's just a baby, and I have to help her," Petari said. "I don't want her to get worse. She's so young. She might die."

Arrow watched the girl. Tears welled in her eyes, and from the sorrow swimming around her, I knew they were genuine.

"Please. We can't get medicine anymore. If I can get those leaves, I won't have to worry about Ruthie being hurt."

"If I show you," Arrow said, "will you promise to get all your friends out of the forest and never come back?"

Now it was Petari's turn to think, but she nodded. "All right."

Good, but we weren't rid of them yet.

"Okay," Arrow said. Curly chattered angrily at them both, but Arrow ignored her. "Follow me."

He ran along the tree line, then turned south, past the kapok tree to the malva bush.

"This is it," he said. He pulled off some leaves, whispered a "Thank you" to the bush, and held them out to Petari. "Look for those yellow flowers. See how the shape of the leaf is like a three-fingered hand? Use a smooth stone to mulch the leaves. Water can help too. I usually spit on it if I don't have any. Then you carefully rub it on the skin. That's all you have to do."

Petari took the leaves and peered at the bush.

"I can spit. Mercou hasn't got a filter working for the river," she said.

"What's a filter?" Arrow asked.

"You know, to make the water safe to drink."

Arrow laughed. "You can drink the water in the river."

"You can?" Petari looked dubious.

"Of course you can. I drink it all the time. You just have to watch out for the caimans."

"Caimans?"

"Long, buggy eyes, big teeth." Arrow snapped his arms together like they were caiman jaws.

"You mean alligators?" Petari's eyes widened. "They're in here too?"

"Yes. I told you, lots of dangerous things. There are nice things too, like the pink dolphins and the giant otters and—"

Curly slapped Arrow's head, making the boy jump. His pride for his home had filled him up. He quickly dropped his smile and continued, "Like I said, lots of dangerous animals. Pick all the malva leaves you need, then go back to the village and get out of the forest like you promised. Got it?"

Petari was looking at Arrow strangely now. The fear was gone from her eyes.

Arrow added, "And don't tell anyone I'm here." He turned to go, but Petari put her hand on his arm to stop him.

"No."

"What do you mean, no?"

She shuffled her feet. "You're not trying to keep us safe. You don't care if that gator or giant snake or any other thing eats every one of us."

Arrow frowned. "Yes, I do."

Petari shook her head. "Maybe. But mostly you want us to leave for another reason. You're hiding something."

This girl was smart. Too smart.

Arrow didn't reply, just watched her.

"So," she continued, "I'll keep your secret on two conditions." She held up a finger. "One, my friends and I stay in the village. We won't go over the bridge and into your precious forest, but at least let us stay there. There's more food in the trees than we've seen in years. We need this place."

Arrow's eyes dropped to the ground. He knew I wouldn't like them staying, but they were humans—his kind—and they needed help. He didn't know what the world outside was like, but how could he refuse?

"And two," Petari said, holding up another finger, "you tell me everything you know about this stuff." She held up the leaves.

"About the malva leaves?"

"Yes. And more," Petari said. "If you know about this mulchy stuff and stink bugs and snakes, you must know other things too."

Arrow's toes dug into the soil. He was feeling something I couldn't quite make out. Uncertainty? Delight? Pride? I could tell that he liked this idea. He wanted to help them. And perhaps he wanted her to see how useful he was.

"I . . ." Arrow's voice trailed off, as though he knew what he should be saying but couldn't get the words out.

"You want us to leave, but we're not safe out there. In here, you've got things that can help us." Petari must've been able to tell how soft Arrow's heart really was. "That baby needs you. We all need you."

Arrow glanced in my direction again and said, "I can't." Good. "You should leave. I told you, it's too dangerous."

"It's not too dangerous for you," Petari said, then quickly put her hand to her mouth. "Oh! Is that how you lost your hand, to one of those cats or caimans or something?"

Arrow glanced at the point of his arm, then shoved it behind his back. "I was born like this."

"You were?" Petari took this in, then smiled. "There you go, then. You haven't been eaten in the forest, so I won't be either."

Arrow narrowed his eyes but didn't say anything. He didn't like where this was heading any more than I did.

"And besides," Petari said, "if I bring the rest of my group into the forest with me, it won't be as dangerous. All those people, trampling around in the trees. I don't think anything will harm that big a group."

"That's what you think," Arrow muttered, his nerves making a pool in the soil beneath him. He thought for a few breaths, then looked at her again. "If I show you, you have to keep the others away."

Petari couldn't contain her smile. "Got it."

"And after I've shown you, you can take whatever you need, then leave."

"We could just stay in the village," Petari said, her voice small.

"You have to leave," Arrow replied, more forceful.

Petari tucked her hands behind her back. "Okay. Okay. You teach me all about the food and leaves and stuff, then I'll get everyone to go. It's a deal." She grinned at Arrow as she twisted two of her fingers together.

I didn't understand her movement, but there was something about her energy I did not like.

Relief flooded the soil around Arrow. Even though he knew Petari and the herd had to leave, he was excited to show one of his own what he could do.

"We'll start tomorrow," he said, turning back toward the village.

"Great." She followed. "I'll tell the others I'm going on a run to the Barbs."

"The Barbs?"

"Yeah, you know, out there." She motioned vaguely north. Perhaps she was talking about the outside world.

"Yeah . . ." Arrow frowned but didn't ask again. "I'll meet you south of the tree line when the sun's ray is like this." He tilted his forearm to a diagonal.

Petari gave a short laugh. "What is that? Like nine o'clock?"

Arrow eyed her quizzically.

"Okaaaay," she said. "Like that it is." She copied his arm movement and grinned. "Oh, I'm Petari, by the way. If we're going to be friends, we should probably know each other's names."

"Friends?" Arrow's heartbeat raced.

"Sure. Friends hang out and show each other stuff, so we're kinda like friends. Don't you think?"

Friends on conditions, but I doubted Arrow saw it like that.

"Petari." Arrow rolled her name around his mouth.

"So, what's your name?" she asked. "You have a name, don't you?"

Arrow paused. He knew names are important. They have power. You protect them. I had taught him this, and no doubt it was going through his mind right now. But this was also new to him. He had never been asked his name before by another human. He had never even talked to another human.

"I'm Arrow," he said at last.

"Arrow. Like a stick with a point at the end?"

Arrow glanced at his arm and straightened his shoulders. "Yeah."

"I like it. Okay, Arrow, see you tomorrow at . . ." She tilted her arm the way Arrow had.

He smiled. They had reached the edge of the tree line, and the huts of the village were within sight. "Remember our deal," he said. "Don't tell them anything."

"I know."

Arrow nodded, then turned toward me. He took off over the roots. Curly waved an angry fist at Petari from his shoulder, but a thrill was in Arrow's every step.

A smile drifted onto Petari's face as she watched him go. Once he had disappeared into the trees, she slipped inside the village.

"I know what you're going to say," Arrow said when he and Curly got back to me.

"She tricked you into showing her more. You do know that, don't you?" I said.

Arrow sighed, swinging a tired Curly down from his shoulder. "Remember what you told me when I had that fight with Dark Brow?"

"That old howler monkey didn't like you pulling his hair."

A smirk swept across Arrow's face at the memory. "Yeah, but you said if I treated him with respect, he'd do the same for me. And you were right. Dark Brow and I became friends."

Friends. Some of the Forest Dwellers had thought the Imposters were friends. Humans seemed to have trouble living up to that word. But it was what Arrow wanted. While I understood his actions, I didn't want him to be disappointed.

"Do you think that will happen with the human girl?" I asked.

Arrow grabbed some acai berries and nuts and put them in the hemp hammock he kept hanging down from the branch by his nest.

"I don't know," he said, pulling himself up to his nest. He hoisted up the hammock and took a bite of berry. "We've at least started to be friends now. And as my friend, she'll respect me and keep the herd out of the forest like I asked."

"We'll see. But you must have caution. She's still from the outside world. She cannot be trusted."

He sighed. "I know."

That night, as Arrow slept with a small smile on his face, I kept a close watch on the human herd. The girl had said she would keep the others out of the forest, keep Arrow and the bridge secret, but I was not convinced.

Cockroaches lent me their eyes, sending images of the village. What they sent was blurry, but I could tell no one ventured south of the huts.

I listened, too, through the vibrations in the air. The conversations were light, filled with laughter. Joy and contentment soaked into the land, and I had to admit it was nice to feel so much human energy in the forest again. They teased one another, talked of plans, of ones they'd left behind. Sadness mixed with the happiness then, and some anger.

But one human stayed away from the rest of the herd. The only time she talked was to ask Mercou what time the sun's rays would be at the angle Arrow had shown her. After he calculated it, estimating around eight o'clock in the morning, Mercou asked why, and Petari said she was figuring out when shade would hit a section of the village because she wanted to plant a seed she'd found. After that, Petari lay on her back, gazing up at the stars, excitement pooling beneath her.

Good girl.

IN A CROP OF BANANA TREES NEAR THE CENTER OF THE FOREST,
ONE STRUGGLED TO BRING FORTH ITS FRUIT FOR THE MONKEYS
THAT LIVED NEARBY. IT TRIED, TRIED, TRIED, BUT NONE
WOULD GROW. THE MONKEYS MOVED ON.

While Arrow and the rest of the diurnal forest slept, I kept watch. Only the night hunters, beetles, and moths were awake, as well as the human called Luco, who sat on the steps of the village's main hut, his eyes alert to every flash of a firefly. Eventually the lullaby of the crickets weighed on his eyelids too. Then I reached out to the root network, satisfied that we were safe from the young herd until the sun was in the sky.

I poked at the places that hadn't communicated for a few moons, but still no reply was returned. Dead patches in the fungi that bridged the roots were more plentiful every day, and it was becoming harder and harder to connect with every part of my home.

But there was something unusual: The sickly taste in the earth of the Burnt Circle was getting thicker. I reached through the root network to the soil there. I needed to know for myself what was disturbing the ground.

That taste had sunk deeper into the earth, but I couldn't see any reason why, until something plopped onto the surface, and the taste deepened even more. I waited, waited, waited, but nothing happened. I was about to investigate another area when the plop came again. This time, I expected it to return, and when it did, it was the flitter of a hummingbird's wing sooner. With each plop, the sickly taste spread.

The rainbow liquid.

The seal Arrow had made in the metal bird must've weakened. Perhaps the liquid had eaten through the sap. We could not have the rainbow liquid in the forest.

"The metal bird is bleeding again," I told Arrow when he had woken. He and Curly were already preparing to meet Petari.

Arrow froze, his leaf-colored shirt halfway over his head. "In the same place?"

"Close to there, yes."

Arrow pulled his shirt completely on, then shook his

head. "I should've put more sap on it. Do you think it will catch on fire?"

"I don't know, but it's dangerous."

Curly squealed, pointing at the sun. Arrow glanced up, and nervousness escaped from him. "I don't have time to go and fix it now. I've got to get to the meeting place. If I don't show up, I'm worried Petari will tell the others in her group about me."

"That would be bad." I ruffled my leaves. "There are too many dangers in the forest right now."

Arrow nodded. "How badly is the rainbow liquid leaking?"

"It's a slow drip but getting faster."

"Okay." He frowned in thought. "I'll go and meet Petari, show her the things she wants to see, and make sure she gets her group to leave. Then I'll go to the Burnt Circle."

"That's a good plan."

I didn't tell Arrow I was worried the human herd would not want to leave, even if the girl said they would. This is what Imposters did, made promises they did not keep. This girl did not speak for the herd, and it was easy to see they all liked the forest. Why wouldn't they want to stay?

"I'll monitor the rainbow liquid, but hurry. We don't want it to spread too far."

"I will," Arrow said, as he and Curly jogged away.

Petari was already at the tree line when Arrow and Curly walked up. Eagerness radiated from the girl, and a nervous joy came from Arrow, too. Even though he knew he had to get the humans to leave, they were like magnets. He wanted to learn more about them, and in turn, perhaps learn more about where he had come from. I hoped he wouldn't be disappointed.

The only one who wasn't happy about their meeting was Curly, who pouted at Petari from Arrow's shoulder, not liking the competition for his attention.

"I'm here." Arrow glanced around, making sure they were alone.

"Hey," Petari replied. "Don't worry, my brother thinks I'm with Luco and his team, who've gone to find supplies. And they think I'm going to visit Mrs. Shalla in the Barbs. I could spend hours at Mrs. Shalla's place, and no one ever wants to come with me."

Arrow looked at her quizzically, and I knew he wanted to ask who Mrs. Shalla in the Barbs was, but he had more important things on his mind. He had to push his curiosity down deep.

"Good," he said. "Let's go. I can't be long."

"You're in a hurry," Petari said, stumbling after Arrow.

"There's a lot to show you," the boy said, keeping an eye on the movement of the sun above.

He took her first to a tall capirona tree and rubbed the bark with the fingers on his right hand. "These trees are all around here because they like being near the river. Feel how smooth their bark is."

Petari followed his lead. Her fingers were tentative at first, then pressed harder to get the full silky effect. "Wow."

"The bark changes color over time and sheds, like a snake's skin. See?" He lifted a piece of the shed bark from the forest floor and held it out to Petari.

"Eww." She shivered, but still took it.

Arrow smiled. "If you have a cut, you can boil the bark, and it helps to stop bleeding. But if you need something quicker, you can use the blood leaf."

He started off again, but Petari said, "Wait. I have to get this down."

She swung a gray lump from her back, tugged on what looked like a thin metal leaf, and sliced the lump open with a *ziiiiiiiip* sound.

"Stop! What are you doing?" Arrow touched the lump, then pulled back his fingers. He looked surprised, as though the material felt strange. I had seen items like this with the Imposters, but this was a first for the boy.

"I'm opening my backpack." Petari frowned. "Don't you have a backpack?"

Ahh, that's what the girl Storma kept her tools in, a "backpack." Arrow shook his head, gaping at the unusual item.

"They're mega useful, especially in the Barbs. When you're scavenging, you've got to carry a lot, and the zipper makes it really easy." She closed the backpack's wound with

115

another *ziiiiiiiip*, then sliced it open again. "I found this one behind an old apartment building and cleaned it up. I think it used to be pink. Look." She showed him a small strip at the bottom that was the color of a tongue.

Arrow crouched down and took the metal leaf Petari had been pulling to open and close the backpack. Pressing on the backpack with the tip of his arrow arm as Petari had done with her hand, Arrow tugged the metal leaf and smiled when the *ziiiiiiiip* sound rang out.

"It's like a hammock that closes," he said, and I liked his comparison. I had taught him to weave small hammocks like the Forest Dwellers had done, so he could carry fruit and nuts back to his nest. It had been his idea to haul the hammock up with a hemp rope. Smart boy.

"What's a hammock?" Petari asked.

Arrow smiled. "It's kinda like this, but different. I'll show you one. . . ." He stopped, no doubt realizing that if he didn't show her today, he wouldn't get the chance. A thread of bitter sadness leaked into the air.

But it was lost on Petari, who had been too consumed with her own task to fully listen. She pulled out of her backpack something else I had not seen since the Imposters were here, a book, but this one looked different from the older ones. Its pages were thin on the edges and thicker in the middle. Next she retrieved a pencil, placed the bark carefully in front of her, and began to draw.

"What are you doing?" Arrow asked, kneeling next to the girl.

"I'm putting it in my notebook, so I'll remember everything later." She peered at Arrow, then at the book. "Oh, right, you're probably wondering why this book looks so weird. I painted over all the words on the pages so I could use the paper again. Mrs. Shalla said it wasn't one of her favorite stories and she had collected two copies anyway, so she let me have one. I write everything I want to remember; then when it's full, I read it again and again until I've remembered it all; then I paint the pages and start again." She grinned, proud of her own ingenuity. "The paint makes the pages thick in the middle, but it's worth it. Brill, right?"

Arrow blinked. "Brill."

"Have you seen Mrs. Shalla's library in the Barbs?"

The boy shook his head. He didn't even know what those things were.

"It's amazing. She's collected thousands of old books, some that were left behind when people died in the Barbs and some that were thrown out of the Stilts when they made everything digital." As she talked, Petari etched the likeness of the piece of bark onto her painted page, then scribbled words next to it. "The Stilters get to read whatever book they want, whenever they want, with a click of their finger. They're so lucky. But I like the paper books too."

She leaned back, gazing at Arrow. "You are from the Barbs, aren't you? You came here through the same hole we did?"

Arrow shook his head. Curly chattered. She didn't like where their conversation was going.

"Really?" Petari's nose wrinkled. "Huh. I thought everyone around here who wasn't from the Stilts was from the Barbs."

She picked up her drawing and showed it to Arrow. He lit up when he saw her rendition of the bark.

"That looks just like it."

"Not bad, eh? I haven't had any lessons either. Okay, what's next?" Petari carefully placed the book, pencil, and piece of bark into her backpack and stood up.

"Oh, yes." Arrow had been so interested in the girl's outside world, he had forgotten why they were here. "I'll show you the blood leaf. There's a bush this way."

Arrow led Petari to the leaf that helped heal cuts, then the pink-flowered shrub whose roots boost strength and energy. He climbed the towering tree whose spherical fruits can disinfect wounds, and showed her the anise with its tiny white flowers and long fruits that help stop flatulence, among other things. They both laughed at the idea of flatulence. It seems that all humans find that funny.

At each stop, Petari collected samples, drew more pictures, and made notes in her book. Arrow instructed her on thanking the plant for giving up its leaves. The girl frowned, perhaps not seeing the purpose, but she did it anyway.

"I'll show you some food now," Arrow said, eyeing the placement of the sun. He was worried about the bleeding bird. I was too. The drip was still small but growing.

Arrow took Petari deeper into the forest to a crop of acai trees and pulled off some of the ripe berries. "These are good. Try them."

Petari looked skeptical, but after carefully rubbing a berry on her shirt, she popped it into her mouth. Her smile grew wide.

"Eese ar ood," she said, around the fruit.

"Told you," Arrow said, eating some berries of his own and handing a few to Curly. Silence fell over them for a few breaths, but not the awkward silence that slices the air, the sweet silence that comes from busy mouths.

Finally Petari swallowed. "You're so lucky to know all this stuff. I'm a scavenger for our group, but I hate having to constantly find food and medicine. I hate depending on the same places over and over again. I want to be an explorer, like the bigger kids, and find new stuff, like this." She waved around the trees. "You don't have to worry about not finding stuff you need. You've got everything all around you."

Arrow's gaze fell. "For now," he whispered.

"Huh?"

119

Arrow opened his mouth to reply, and I hoped he wouldn't give too much away. But suddenly his eyes lit up and he turned west. "Follow me, quietly."

The girl did as she was told, following Arrow through the crop of trees. He pulled back a palm and pointed. A capybara and her babies were lying in the sun.

Petari gasped and stepped back.

"It's okay," Arrow whispered. "They're not dangerous. Cute, though, don't you think?"

The girl nodded as she crept closer again. "How did you know they were here?"

"I heard them. And smelled them." He grinned.

Petari looked surprised at his answer, but her focus was quickly drawn back to the animals. "They're incredible. I wish I had a camera."

"What's a camera?" Arrow asked, leading her back to the acai palm and her backpack.

"You know, to take their picture, so I can look at them even when I'm not here. My drawings work for the plants, but it would be brill to have a video of the animals." She picked up her backpack and glanced at him. "They don't have books or cameras where you're from?"

Arrow shook his head.

"Weird," Petari said.

Curly pulled on Arrow's earlobe. "Ow!"

"That monkey is mean," Petari said with a laugh.

"She's just . . . ," Arrow began, then saw Curly pointing at the sun again. It had moved lower. He needed to hurry. He was running out of time to stop the rainbow liquid and get home before the sun rested.

"I'll show you the camu camu berry next," he said. "They're a little sour, but I like them." He headed back toward the river, where the thin bushes that held the fruit enjoyed lapping up the water.

"Ooh, I like sour stuff too." Petari smiled.

As they walked, Arrow kept up their conversation about the outside world, his curiosity now too big to be contained. "Tell me about the camera where you can capture the movements of the animals."

"Oh," Petari said, shifting her backpack on her shoulder. "Truth is, I've never seen one. They only have those in the Stilts, and I've never been."

She ducked under a branch. "I've heard people talk about it, though. My dad worked there sometimes. He mostly went through the tunnels, but he told me he saw inside too. They have water that runs out of faucets whenever you want. Like you turn it, and the water comes out. Amazing. The Barbs have faucets, but water won't come out no matter how much you turn them. Believe me, I've tried. Do you have them where you're from?"

Arrow shook his head quickly. "What else do they have?"

"In the Stilts, they have everything." Petari flung her

arms out wide, as though she were presenting it all to him. "They have lots of food. More than you could ever eat! And clothes. Way better clothes than mine or yours." She eyed his worn coverings. "And they have all this brill tech, like things you can write on and draw on and read books and watch movies on."

"Movies?" Arrow asked. Even Curly was intrigued, climbing to the boy's other shoulder to be closer to the girl.

"Wow, you must not have anything where you're from," Petari said.

Arrow glanced at the trees and rocks. "We have things, just different things."

"You've definitely missed out with movies. Although, I haven't seen too many. You can see them whenever you want in the Stilts, but we don't have them in the Barbs." She gave a tight laugh. "Like we have anything in the Barbs. Anyway, years ago, this one woman who knows about this stuff found something that made the movies work. She had only a few, but she played them on the wall of the building next to ours. I loved it."

"But what is it?" Arrow asked.

"I'm getting to that," Petari said, sighing loudly. "Okay, so you know how books have stories?"

"Umm..." I hadn't told him about books, not really knowing what they contained. But he knew of stories, because I had told him the stories the Forest Dwellers would tell.

"Those kind of stories you can see in your head, right?" Petari continued. "Well, movies are stories you can see for real. These people act them out, and it's stored like a memory or a dream so you can watch it over and over again. It's . . ." She shrugged. "Magic."

My roots froze on that word. What kind of magic did this human girl know about? Was the Anima in the outside world?

Arrow must've had the same thoughts, as warm hope seeped from him. "This magic is in the Barbs, where you're from?"

Petari shook her head. "They don't have movies anymore. The tech stopped halfway through this one movie, and they couldn't get it working again. Now I'll never know if that Leia princess was in love with the Luke kid or the Han guy. I'm guessing the Han guy, but who knows."

So the magic had died in the Barbs. No wonder it was such a desolate place. If we couldn't mend the Anima here, that was what we'd become—dry, dusty, dead.

"But this magic is still in the Stilts?" Arrow asked. Good thinking.

They were at the river now, and Arrow lead the way back over the root bridge.

"Hey, we're back at the village," Petari said. "I thought you were taking me to the camu things."

"I am. They like being by the water, and the biggest ones

are on this side." Arrow pointed but kept his attention on the girl. "The magic. Is it still in the Stilts place?"

"Oh yeah. You can see movies and all kinds of stuff in the Stilts. That whole place is magical."

An entire place filled with magic!

Excitement sprang from Arrow, too, so much so that he stopped in his tracks.

Petari kept walking a few steps, not realizing Arrow was no longer moving. Not realizing he was deep in thought about the idea of a place with all the magic we needed. When she finally looked back, she said, "You okay? We going to this camu tree or what?"

Arrow glanced up at her, pulled out of his dreams. "Yes. Yeah." He glanced around. "Oh, we're here. This is the camu camu tree."

He walked her to the tree and plucked one of the plump berries. He handed it to Petari, but I could tell his mind was not on their lessons anymore. Wonder swirled around him, and he was ready to ask more questions.

The girl polished this berry on her shirt too, then popped it into her mouth. Immediately her nose scrunched up from the sour taste, but beneath it she had a big grin.

"Yum," she said, after she had swallowed. "Can I have more?"

Arrow smiled. "You can have as much as you want. These grow all around the forest."

Petari picked more berries from the tree, some for her mouth and some for her backpack.

"Tell me more about this magic," Arrow said, as Petari made her drawings and notes of the camu camu berries.

"Like what?" Petari paused her drawing and looked at the boy.

"Can you take me to it?"

"To the Stilts?" She shook her head. "I don't know. They keep the entrances guarded. They say they don't have enough for everyone, so they keep people out. But from what I've heard, everyone there has more than they need." She leaned closer and whispered, "But Luco has this guy who can—"

Suddenly she stopped talking and frowned. "Hey, you never answered my question from before."

"What question?" Arrow didn't want to answer questions of hers. Frustration swirled around him. He wanted to hear more about the magic and the Stilts. Me too!

"About who you are." Petari crossed her arms over her chest. "I can't be giving our secrets to some enemy group. Where are you from really? Where does your group live? Are they a nice group or a goon group?"

Curly slapped Arrow's shoulder. This time the boy didn't need Curly to point to the sun. He glanced up, and his shoulders drooped when he saw how far it had moved across the sky. He had to leave now if he was going to stop the rainbow liquid and make it home before the dangerous night hunters began to prowl. The dripping of the liquid was getting quicker, more and more of it soaking deeper into the soil. Arrow had to get it contained.

"I've got to go," he said, his heartbeat quickening.

"Oh no you don't. You owe me some answers."

"I can't. I have to—" He started to leave, but Petari blocked his path.

"Just tell me one thing now: Tell me you're not from some goon group that's going to come and kill my friends."

Arrow frowned. "I'm not going to kill anyone. I told you to leave so you'd be safe."

"Or so you could keep this forest all to yourself and your group."

She was right about that.

"If you're not from the Barbs but you still found the hole into this place, where are you from?" She tapped her toe impatiently.

Arrow gazed at the sun again, anxiety soaking into the ground beneath him. I wanted my boy home, and with the Anima so low, I could no longer light up the forest at night to keep him safe.

Arrow was silent for a long breath, perhaps wondering why it was so important to this girl from a Barb and a Stilt. Finally he said, "I'm from here, the forest."

"You grew up here?"

"Yes."

"That would explain you knowing so much about the trees. But who do you live with and where? A group, or your parents?"

"I don't have parents," Arrow said, his eyes cast down.

"Oh. Sorry. Val and me don't either. My mom died about a year after I was born. Then it was just me, Val, and Dad, but one day Dad went off to work and never came back."

"That's horrible," Arrow said.

Petari shrugged. "Val had seen Luco's group scouting the houses in our area, so we took up with them. It was nice of Luco and Storma to let us. Storma didn't want to at first, but Luco convinced her. I understood. Not many groups want to add others, but Luco even allowed Rosaman and Ruthie in, and no one wants to have babies around. You probably know about that, though. So you live with a group? Where?"

Arrow shook his head. "I don't have a group. I live with Curly and the Guardian. The Guardian taught me everything I know."

Pride danced around Arrow, and I felt it in my cells, too. But this girl wouldn't know who I was—and if Arrow told her, she wouldn't understand. I should've prepared him for questions like these.

"What Guardian?" Petari asked.

"The Guardian of the forest. The mother tree."

Petari's mouth opened, but no words came out. After many breaths, she finally said, "The mother tree?"

Arrow nodded. "Yes. The mother tree."

There was another pause, then the girl burst into laughter, shocking the parrots sitting on branches all around them. The birds flew into the air squawking and chattering so loudly, they could've been heard from far away.

And they were.

Footsteps came running. Two shoed feet, clomping heavily on the ground. I recognized their falls and wished I could warn Arrow, but he couldn't hear me from that distance.

Unaware of the approaching danger, Arrow's attention was only for Petari, and hurt had spilled from him after her laugh.

"Good one," the girl said. "Living with a monkey and a tree that teaches you stuff. Right." She breathed deeply. "But seriously, where—"

"Petari!"

Arrow and Petari whirled around.

Val glared at them. Rage spiked the earth beneath his feet.

IN THE SOUTHEAST, A PITCHER PLANT CAUGHT A BEETLE IN ONE
OF ITS BRIGHT, CURVED FLOWERS. NUTRIENTS HAD BEEN POOR IN THE
SOIL, AND THE NUTRIENTS IN THE BEETLE WOULD MAKE THE BUSH
STRONGER. BUT THE PITCHER PLANT WAS TOO WEAK. ITS ROOTS
SHRIVELED, THE TRUNK CRACKED, THE BRANCHES SHATTERED,
AND THE FLOWERS DISINTEGRATED. THE BEETLE ESCAPED.

"Get over here." Val waved for Petari to get behind
him, as he held out a small knife toward Arrow.
"Who are you? What are you doing here?"

Arrow froze, his eyes flicking between the boy and the
knife, glinting in the sunlight. He'd seen knives before. I'd
asked the monkeys to collect everything the Forest Dwellers
had left in the village, including pots and knives. But Arrow
had never seen one pointed at him. His nervousness dug into
the dirt. Curly shrieked, then twisted into a ball on Arrow's
shoulder.

"What are you doing here?" Val asked again. "Answer me."

"What are *you* doing here, Val?" Petari frowned at her brother. She still hadn't moved from her spot next to Arrow, but her brother pulled her behind him.

"Protecting you. Luco said you'd gone to Mrs. Shalla's. Do you know how worried I was when you didn't come back? I went looking for you, saw those birds fly up, and heard you laughing. How could you be such a dust munch? Do you know anything about this kid?"

"Yes! I know plenty. And I don't need you to protect—"

"Be quiet, Petari!" Val turned back to Arrow, his hand with the knife shaking a little. He didn't want to harm my boy, but that didn't mean he wouldn't. My roots dug in hard. "Are you a spy? Who are you with?"

"Val!" Petari ran between Arrow and her brother. "He's not a spy. He lives in the forest. He's the one who gave us the leaves that helped Ruthie."

Val glanced between the boy and the girl, finally landing on Arrow with a confused face. "That was you?"

"This is Arrow," Petari said, motioning to my boy. "Arrow, this is my dipster brother, Val."

"Hi, Val." Arrow's voice was shaky, making my leaves curl with worry.

Val didn't answer, but turned to Petari with a frown. "Just because he gave Ruthie that stuff doesn't mean he's nice. It doesn't mean we can trust him."

He did not trust either. Perhaps I had more in common with these humans than I knew. It seemed as though no one could trust another in this world.

Val leaned toward Arrow, who took a step backward. Curly unfurled a fist to shake at the herder.

Petari pushed Val back. "Stop treating me like I'm a baby who doesn't know anything. Arrow spent the day showing me other leaves and stuff that can help us. It's like medicine. And it's just growing here." She pulled her backpack around from her shoulder and opened it, showing him the bark and berries she had collected. "We don't need to go on raids anymore."

She saw the worth of this forest. Good, but I didn't know if I could trust her to use it well. To protect it. Her brother did not seem the type to keep our secrets. He had already ventured beyond the village. How long before he would find the bridge?

Val narrowed his eyes. "Luco and Storma should know about this. You're coming with us."

"I have . . ." Arrow glanced at the sun. It squatted low in the sky now. He wouldn't have time to fix the rainbow liquid today, and I worried how much more would spill overnight. Arrow barely had time to get home before darkness devoured the forest. He had to leave now. "I've got to go—"

Val thrust his shaking knife closer to my boy's heart. My roots curled tighter. "I'm not letting you tell your group where we are so they can hurt us. You're coming with me."

"Val!" Petari's voice pleaded with her brother. "Leave him alone."

"It's okay. I'll go to the village." Arrow stepped forward. What was he doing? Fear pounded the air around him, but also something else . . . hope.

But hope for what? I had no hope of good coming from this human herd.

Curly didn't like this either. She shrieked, running down Arrow's arm to the ground, then pulling at his ankle to follow her into a retreat.

"What's that monkey doing?" Val asked.

"That's Curly," said Petari. "She's cute. A bit testy when you first meet her, but she warms up."

Arrow crouched next to Curly.

"They know where I can get more magic," he whispered to the monkey.

Ahh, that was his plan. It had promise but was reckless. What if they didn't let him go? What if he couldn't get to the Burnt Circle to stop the flow of the rainbow liquid in the morning? What if he never came back?

Curly tugged harder, but Arrow held her paw gently. "Go home. I'll be back before the sun is down. Tell the Guardian to watch the Burnt Circle."

The monkey frowned, peering at the humans from around the side of Arrow. Then she turned and fled back toward me.

Arrow watched her go, his feet drowning in anxiety.

I didn't like this. Not him going with these humans nor him coming back in the dark.

"This way," Val said, motioning to the village. Petari laughed.

"Arrow knows this place better than you know the Barbs," she said, then followed her brother to the village.

The other humans were picking through backpacks like the one Petari carried, worry spiking in the air. They turned at the crunch of footsteps and shot up when they saw Arrow. Petari grabbed Arrow's hand and pulled him forward.

"This is Arrow," she said, smiling big. "He's the one who—"

But Petari didn't have a chance to finish her sentence. Storma stepped up to Arrow as the rest of the herd flocked behind her. "So we're not alone in this place after all. I knew it was too good to be true. Which group are you with? One of the goon squads? We don't allow goons with us."

Arrow opened his mouth to speak, but Petari beat him to it. "He's not a goon."

"How do you know?" Storma threw the words at Petari, then strode around Arrow, taking in every inch of him. "You don't look like you could be hiding weapons, but I've been duped before."

Petari exhaled loudly. "He's not hiding anything. If he wanted to hurt us, he could've killed us all last night while we were sleeping."

"Petari," Val said, his voice a warning.

The girl lowered her chin. "I just mean—"

"I don't want to hurt you," Arrow said, barely above a whisper. Nervousness radiated from him.

"See? Told you." Petari straightened a little. "He's the one who saved Ruthie. And today he helped me find all these mega things in the forest."

"That's where you were today?" Anger rode on Luco's words. "We have rules."

"I know. But taste this." She dropped her backpack onto the ground and opened it, tumbling out leaves and bark, flowers and fruits. She gave Luco an acai berry.

Luco peered at it, then glanced around at the other humans. His eyes landed on Storma, but she twisted her face as though she'd eaten something rotten.

"Fine. Here." Petari took the berry back and popped it into her mouth. "Mmmm."

Arrow chuckled nervously, which drew the eyes of the others and kept him quiet again.

"Give me that," Storma said, snatching another berry from Petari's hand. She sniffed it, brought it to her lips, then, after a deliberating pause, tossed it onto her tongue and clamped down. The others watched, all eyes glued to the older girl as fear and wonder circled them. After a few long breaths, Storma swallowed and grinned. "That was amazing. Give me another."

The other humans quickly followed, palms out, waiting for their try. All except Val, who stood back, arms crossed, forehead furrowed.

Luco turned to Arrow. "You found these?"

Arrow nodded. "They're acai berries. My favorite. You can find a lot around here, if you know where to look."

"They're great. You've got lots of other stuff too, huh?" Luco glanced at Petari's backpack.

"Yep. Pretty much all the food you could want," Petari said.

Luco's eyes flicked to Arrow's arms, then up to his eyes. "How'd you lose your hand?"

Arrow glanced down at his arrow arm, holding it up. "I was born this way."

"And he can climb trees and knows about plants and tracks animals. And before you ask . . ." Petari paused, and I wondered how many secrets she'd spill. Arrow eyed her too, nerves prickling the soil beneath his feet. Petari sucked in a breath, then said, "He found the hole a few months before us and has lived here by himself. He discovered all this stuff. Great, huh?"

Arrow's eyes narrowed. He didn't understand lies. There are no lies in the forest. No lies from the plants and trees. No lies from the animals and birds. The forest lives in truth.

I knew of lies, though. I had learned of them from the Imposters. And the hurt still ran deep.

But here was Petari telling a lie to protect our secrets.

"You've lived here alone for months?" Luco asked.

Arrow gazed at Petari, then nodded.

"How do we know you're really alone and your group isn't out there waiting to hurt us?" Storma asked, crossing her arms.

"Arrow took me all over, and I didn't see anyone," Petari said. "Not even a sign of another person."

Storma kept her focus on Arrow. "Where were you from before? The Barbs?"

"He can't remember anything," Petari said quickly. "I think he was attacked by one of the goon groups."

"That's rough. I've been caught by them too. Last time I go to the roof of a tall building, I can tell you." Storma's eyes bore into Arrow, and he stiffened. "But you must be pretty smart to have figured out how to survive in here."

"I am smart." Arrow smiled.

"So what, you want to be part of our group? Is that why you helped us?" Storma leaned back, straightening to her full height. "People don't give something unless they get something else in return."

"I made a deal that if he showed me the medicines in the forest"—Petari gulped—"we'd leave."

An uproar came from the herd. Arrow watched intently as the children shouted, "I'm not leaving." "He can't make us go." "Who made him king of the trees?" "I like it here." And

Petari answered, "He said it's dangerous to stay, but I wasn't really going to leave. We don't let danger stop us." That got cheers from the group, until Petari continued, "I just needed his help to get more medicine for Ruthie."

Just as I'd suspected. I hoped Arrow had another plan to make them go, but perhaps he had other ideas now that he'd heard about the magic.

"It doesn't matter anyway, because I've changed my mind," Arrow said. His voice was still hesitant but stronger. "I'll help you stay and show you how to be safe, but I do want something."

"What's that?" Luco asked.

"I want to go to the Stilts."

*That was his plan.* My roots ached to think of my boy going to the dry outside world, but if he could find their magic and bring some back, we'd be able to save the forest. Hide once again, maybe forever.

Confusion squirmed from the herd.

"Why do you want to go there?" Storma asked, an edge to her voice.

"He wants to see the movies. I told him about them," Petari said, then added, "I told you he doesn't remember anything about where he was from."

Arrow didn't offer an alternative answer, and Storma turned to Luco.

"Let's huddle," he said, then began to walk away from the group. The rest of the herd followed him, until Storma pointed to Petari.

"Not you. You stay and keep an eye on him. And if he runs off or does anything I don't like, you'll be sleeping out here tonight. Got it?"

Petari nodded quickly. "Got it."

The herd gathered a few feet away and talked in hushed tones. The beetle that was sending me the images and sounds wasn't close enough to hear.

Petari turned to Arrow. "Sorry we got caught. And sorry about me not really planning to leave. It's just . . ." Her eyes fell to the ground. "You don't know what it's like in the Barbs. It's not nice like here. There's not much food. And there're lots of people who will hurt you. I know you think it's dangerous here, but the Barbs are called 'the Barbs' for a reason. It's like living with barbed wire."

"What's that?"

Petari grinned. "You don't know anything, do you?"

"Yes, I do, just what's in the forest."

Petari nudged Arrow with her elbow, making him look at her quizzically. "I'm kidding. You don't want to know what barbed wire is. It's prickly, and it hurts."

"Oh, like the stinging tree," Arrow said. "You don't want to get tangled in the stinging tree. It hurts for moons."

Petari raised her eyebrows at the word "moons," then leaned in closer. "Tell me where you really come from."

Arrow frowned. "I told you. I grew up in the forest with the monkeys and the Guardian."

"But this Guardian person, it's not really a tree with a trunk and leaves and stuff, right?"

Arrow nodded, although his eyes narrowed. He didn't like her tone, and neither did I. "Yes. She's the mother tree."

Petari glanced at the rest of the herd, who were still in a group talking. Before she could speak again, Arrow interrupted her.

"The Guardian is the mother tree for the entire forest. She talks to us, keeps us together, and protects everything inside."

"But—"

"Okay." Luco's loud voice broke into their conversation. The herd had separated and were crowding around Petari and Arrow again. Petari swallowed back the rest of her sentence.

"We've made our decision," Luco continued. "You can stay with us, as long as you help us with these medicines and food from the forest."

Petari grinned.

"What about the Stilts?" Arrow asked, anxiety building beneath him.

Luco glanced back at Storma.

"We'll try to get you in," Storma said, a strange smile on her face.

Arrow was pleased, warm happiness surrounding him. But I wasn't sure. I had seen that same smile on the Imposters, and it wasn't good.

"Let's get food on," Luco commanded. "I'm famished. Rosaman and Delora, you're on food duty. See what you can do with Petari's haul."

The boy and girl grabbed the berries and nuts Petari had collected.

Petari beamed with pride, but Arrow gazed at the sky and looked worried. The treetops were darkening. The sun would soon say good night.

"What's wrong?" Petari whispered to him.

"I've stayed too long. There's more danger in the forest at night. You can't see the predators until it's too late, and I still have to get home."

"Arrow, Luco and Storma just said you can stay with us. That means you can sleep here."

Arrow's eyes roamed the herd, then peered at the tree barrier south of the village. Fear and sadness dripped from his soles, but he knew this was his only option now.

For the first night since I had brought him into the forest, Arrow would not sleep within my branches. I felt his absence deep within my roots. I didn't trust that these

140

humans would care for him. My only solace was that they needed him.

But I could not deny the sliver of warmth that had begun to swirl around the boy. He had always been curious about his kind, and so far, he seemed to like what he saw.

I could only hope he wouldn't be proven wrong.

DEEP IN A SWAMP TO THE NORTH, A FROG HOPPED ACROSS
THE SURFACE OF A GIANT WATER LILY, UNTIL ITS BACK LEGS LANDED
IN WATER. THE FROG STRUGGLED AND STRUGGLED, THEN PULLED ITS
BACKSIDE UP AND HOPPED AWAY. A RIP HAD OPENED IN THE LILY. IT
GREW AND GREW, TEARING THE LEAF INTO TINY PIECES
THAT SILENTLY SLIPPED BELOW THE WATER.

With Arrow's help, the human herd feasted that night on a meal of camu camu berries, nuts, soursop, mangoes, aguaje, acai berries, and bananas. But there was not a moment of silent enjoyment. Each chew was interrupted with another question for Arrow.

"What kinds of animals live here?"

"Are there flowers?"

"You've really drunk that water?"

"And you're not dead?"

"What other kinds of animals live here?"

As each question was thrown out, Petari served it up with an introduction of the inquisitor.

"That's Delora. She's on food duty with Rosaman." She pointed at each of the children as she identified them. "That's Safa. She's older. She joined the group long before us. She's one of the scouts, which is what I want to be. That's . . ."

Arrow gazed from face to face, a nervous energy sinking deep into the ground at his feet. But the more he answered their questions and talked about the forest, the more his fear began to dissipate. When Petari brought the baby, Arrow gave her a big smile. Ruthie's skin was getting better.

His shoulders dropped when he saw her arm, which was no longer covered and now boasted a chubby hand at the end. For a breath, sadness etched into the soil beneath him— sadness that he was still alone, still different. But Arrow's smile grew even bigger when Petari put the baby in his arms and she gurgled.

The only human who stayed away was Val. He kept on the outskirts of the group, never close enough to join in, but always near enough to hear.

Soon the feast they had foraged ran out, but Delora brought out a backpack with food stuffed into metal tubes called "cans," bars slid from skins called "wrappers," and water and other drinks poured from bottles called "plastic."

"Not too much," Luco said. "That's got to last."

The herd devoured what they opened, sharing the insides

143

between them and Arrow, then tossing the cans and wrappers and plastics into the grasses and tree lines near them. Just like the Imposters. My roots stiffened.

Arrow didn't seem to trust the food that had been squeezed into containers. He sniffed at something called "peaches in syrup" before taking a bigger piece. Storma and Val watched him closely.

While Arrow and Petari told stories about their day— like when Petari had tried to pick up a stick before it slithered off—Storma broke off from the group, sidling up to the sulking Val.

"You're not much of a fan, are you?" she said quietly.

Val's jaw stiffened. "I don't trust him. We'd been scavenging that rock wall for months and never saw that hole. How did he find it? And how'd he figure out all this stuff so quickly?"

Storma nodded slowly. "He is too good to be true, isn't he?"

So much suspicion. I wasn't surprised. This herd had come from that outside world of unfeeling metal and stone. But I worried for Arrow. I hoped he'd be safe. I hoped he'd be able to protect himself from them and their ways. Petari seemed different, open to adventure and new possibilities. That's what had brought them all to the forest in the first place. But the older ones . . .

I never understood why imagination and belief dwindled

the more rings a human had lived through. It was as though with each passing moon, they turned from sponge to rock.

Storma turned to Val. "You and I will keep an eye on him. Yeah?"

Val nodded.

A sneer flitted across Storma's mouth, and she patted Val on the shoulder as though the two had just made some secret pact, before she joined the others.

I didn't like how that sounded.

Arrow was oblivious to their suspicion. He seemed to enjoy the rapt attention of the rest of the herd.

When the questions died out, Arrow jumped on the opportunity to find out more about the magic. Good boy. "How far is this Stilts place?"

"It's a hike," Luco said, wiping his mouth. "You have to go through the Barbs. Then there's the Moat."

"That's what we call the dead land between the Barbs and the Stilts," Safa said. "I'm surprised you don't remember. It's not like anyone can forget that area." She gave a hollow laugh.

Petari gave Arrow a sideways glance, perhaps noting his confused expression. "It's a place where no one lives, not even many animals."

"It's supposed to keep the scum like us out," Safa said, tearing into something they called "a fruit bar." "But that never stopped us." She grinned.

145

"The whole place is designed to keep us out." Luco turned to Arrow. "After the Moat, then there are the tunnels. We call the city 'the Stilts' because it's built on stilts, high up so no one can get to it."

"So they can look down on all us common folk." Safa's words rode on an edge as sharp as caiman teeth.

"Actually, it was built like that to maximize resources in as small an area as possible," said Mercou. He leaned forward so everyone could hear. "It was an interesting design cho—"

"No one cares, science boy," Safa said. She laughed, but quickly stopped when she saw Luco glaring at her.

He turned back to Arrow. "The point is, the city is built high up. And underneath it run a bunch of tunnels. That's where the workers enter and move around. That's where we get in."

"Can we go tomorrow?" Arrow asked.

Luco shook his head. "It's heavily guarded. I've got connections, but it takes planning. We've got to meet them tomorrow for a supplies handover, so I'll see about getting you in."

Relief flooded the soil around Arrow. This was a good sign. If we could get the magic back in a few moons, we'd be able to hide again before more humans found us.

Petari presented Arrow with a can of pink contents. "You've got to try this."

He scrunched up his nose. "What is it?"

"Spam. I don't know what it's made of. Some kind of ham, I think. Try it."

He pinched off a small piece and put it into his mouth. Still scrunching his nose, he chewed, chewed, chewed, then swallowed. I waited for him to ask what this "ham" was, a word I thought I had heard before but couldn't place. Arrow didn't ask, though. He gave a small smile and nod, trying to make these herders believe he was like them.

Petari grinned. "Brill, huh?" She took the can from him, pinched a piece for herself, then handed the can to Mercou.

"Has anyone ever been in the Stilts? I mean like really inside?" Delora pushed back her brown kingfisher-feather hair.

A murmur of "no"s and "only the tunnels" went through the herd.

"I heard that everyone's wishes come true there," Delora said.

"I heard you can get any kind of food you want," Rosaman said.

"I heard—"

"I've been in the Stilts," Storma said.

"You have?" Delora's eyes lit up.

"Before my mom died, she took me. She was doing a delivery there."

"What was it like?" Delora asked.

"It was even more beautiful than you can imagine." Storma smiled, a wistful look on her face as though she were

147

seeing it in front of her now. "Everything was clean. All these shiny glass buildings. And there were gold statues in the streets."

Arrow placed his hand on his belly. Thick, bitter pain began to twist from him.

"And the smells," Storma continued. "The whole place smelled like flowers and baked cookies and all the best smells."

"Wow," said Delora.

Arrow pressed down on his belly to stop the hurt.

"What was your mother delivering to those people for?" Luco asked, a bitter taste to his words.

"They're the only ones who can afford to pay anything," Storma said with a smirk. "We ate well that week."

"Uhh!" Arrow suddenly bent to the side. His stomach rejected every item the humans had given him to eat, and it all streamed back out of his mouth and onto the ground.

"Eww!" shrieked Delora.

"Gross!" exclaimed Rosaman.

"He's wasting the food," cried Faive.

Arrow swayed and held his belly. "I'm sorry."

Luco laughed. "Now you're truly initiated into life in the Barbs."

"Remember when we found that milk carton that had expired and Mercou said it was cheese?" Delora giggled.

"It tasted okay going down," Mercou said.

The other humans laughed, then launched into more

stories as Arrow clutched his belly and listened. He stayed quiet for the rest of the meal, taking in their every word. I did too, hoping, waiting, but the humans' talk didn't give any clues of where to find and harness the magic in the Stilts.

Once darkness fell, the humans didn't stay outdoors. They hurried into the large hut as they had the previous nights.

"You coming?" Luco shouted to Arrow, who gazed out at the forest. "We put up traps to keep everyone safe." He carefully unwound the metal vine and pulled it across the front of the hut, like it had been when Arrow had touched it.

Arrow glanced at the hut, then back out to the forest. I wondered if he missed me.

I missed him. His warmth in my branches. His tossing and turning in his nest. This day had been eye-opening for Arrow. He had talked to more humans than ever before, and from the smile that had lit up his face, I knew he had enjoyed it.

But how would he fare in the dark?

Arrow shook his head finally. "I'll stay out here."

"Nope. That's not going to happen. I can't trust that you're not going to run off and tell whoever you're with that we're here." Luco finished securing his trap, then motioned to the door.

Arrow dropped his chin, glanced back at the forest, then followed the boy into the hut.

But as the moon rose higher, the door opened quietly,

and bare feet carefully stepped over the metal vine trap. Glancing around, Arrow walked to the patch of ferns he'd hidden beneath when he'd spied on Petari. He pulled the leaves down and settled on top of them, arms behind his head as he gazed at the stars.

*Sleep well, Arrow. Sleep well.*

Before sleep could come, there was more weight on the steps. Two covered feet padded lightly onto the ground, then Petari hurried over to the boy.

"What are you doing?" she whispered, glancing back at the building.

Arrow shrugged. "I can't sleep in there. Too closed in." He sat up. "Is that how you sleep in the Barbs?"

Petari settled onto the ferns next to him. "You mean in buildings? Yeah. You do everything in buildings. Some places even have different rooms for sleeping and cooking and other stuff. Although some are like this with one room where you do everything. Except the toilet. That's always in a separate room."

"Toilet?" Arrow asked.

Petari grinned. "It's where you pee and poop." She laughed, and Arrow smiled.

"These Barbs sound like a complicated place," he said. "Some areas you can go and others you can't. Some places you do one thing in and another for something else. There's a lot to remember."

Petari shrugged. "You get used to it. It's not like here,

though. There's nothing like here in the Barbs or the Stilts."

They sat there in silence for a few breaths, eyes on the stars, ears on the sounds. Crickets, owls, and frogs filled in the gaps of their speech. Finally Arrow broke their quiet.

"Your brother doesn't like me much."

Petari groaned. "He doesn't like anyone, except Luco. He wants to be just like him when he gets older, but Luco isn't nearly as suspicious as Val. Ever since Dad left, Val figured he had to step up and protect me, even though he's only three years older than I am."

"It's good that he wants to protect you," Arrow said.

"Eck. He's a dust munch. He acts like I'm a baby who can't do anything, but I can protect myself. I don't need anyone. I don't want to ever need anyone." She swallowed. "You want to know something funny about Val?"

Arrow nodded.

"His full name is Valvoline, but don't ever call him that. He hates it."

"Valvoline." Arrow let each part of the word sit on his tongue. "Why doesn't he like it?"

"It's the name of an oil company."

"What's oil?" Arrow asked.

"It's this stuff you have to put in machines. My mom was a mechanic. She loved old cars, and cars use oil. When Val was born, my mom liked the word, so they named my brother Valvoline."

Arrow chuckled. "What does your name mean?"

"My name doesn't have a meaning. Val actually named me. Because he hated Valvoline so much, he told my parents he could name me something better than they could, so they let him. He named me after this old game console my mom had found in salvage and fixed up. It's supposed to be Atari, but Val was only three and he said it as Petari, so that became my name."

"A game console?"

Petari waved her hand. "You've got a lot to learn." She grinned. "Who named you Arrow?"

"The Guardian Tree." Arrow glanced at Petari, but this time the girl didn't laugh.

My roots relaxed into the daydream as Arrow said, "The Forest Dwellers used to use identifiers as names, something unique about you. So the Guardian called me Arrow because of my arm. She said it's like an arrow." He lifted his pointed arm to show her. "She told me that arrows can hurt things, and I have to be careful that I don't. But they also stay true, and that's what I am." He paused, then said, "I miss her."

My leaves fluttered.

"I'm sorry you couldn't go back to your home tonight," Petari said. "But I wouldn't want to walk through the forest in the dark with all those scary things."

Arrow sighed. "I used to be able to go all over at night. Everything would light up wherever I went."

Yes. The forest was glorious. The animals savored it. Not the predators, but they had their darker times.

"What do you mean?" Petari asked.

Arrow sat up, breathing in the memory. "The orchids in the trees would light up. The flowers on the water lilies would shine. The fungi on the ground and low on the trunks would glow. Even some of the grubs in the soil, and the fireflies and butterflies, of course. There would be all different colors, and the Guardian would ask them to light up wherever Curly and I went. We would run through the trails of light weaving throughout the forest every night. It was beautiful."

"The tree would make things in the forest light up at night? Really?"

"Not *make*. The Guardian can't make a creature do something. She'd ask. But who wouldn't want to glow?" He smiled.

"I didn't know flowers and orchids and stuff lit up."

Arrow laughed. "The Guardian gave them help."

"That's mega." She paused. "I'm sorry I laughed when you told me about the Guardian. It's just a little unbelievable. There's nothing like the Guardian out in the rest of the world."

"What do you mean?"

"No one makes sure everyone's okay. The people in the Stilts have more than they could want, and the people in the Barbs have to fight over whatever they can get." Petari thinned her lips. "When I was little, I wanted so much to live in the Stilts, so we wouldn't have to worry about food or anything anymore."

"And now?"

She gazed around. "I like living here, in the forest." She looked back at Arrow. "Why doesn't the Guardian Tree light up the forest now so you can go home?"

Arrow's eyes lowered. "She's too weak. She hasn't had the strength to do that for many moons."

Petari leaned forward. "That's sad." She fiddled with the strings on her shoes. "I'd love to meet her."

"You would?"

"Of course. Who wouldn't?"

Arrow glanced at her. "I wasn't sure if you really believed me."

"This is normal for you, but where I lived before, trees don't talk or make flowers glow or take care of people and animals."

"Maybe they do, but you can't hear them."

"Maybe." She sighed. "Out there, even if I could hear them, it'd be difficult. There are hardly any trees and there's lots of noise, with all the cars and trucks and people. It's better in here."

Arrow lay back down and placed his palm on the soil like he used to when he was far from me, playing with the monkeys, and wanted some comfort. I would send nutrients to the soil beneath him, ask the grubs to move quickly, to heat up the earth in that spot. Arrow would giggle, lift his palm, then put it back on the ground for more.

"The Guardian doesn't trust humans now," he told Petari. "Except me."

This was the truth, but I wondered why he was telling her. Then he continued, "But I can ask her if you can come, if you'd like. I need to go anyway."

The rainbow liquid was on his mind. Good.

Petari sat straight up. "You'd do that? Do you think she'll let me?"

Arrow dug his fingertips into the soil, and I understood. He was asking now. He was hoping I'd send him an answer.

But what answer should I send? The girl had tricked him into helping her, caring more about what she needed than him. But when her brother had been aggressive, she had defended Arrow. She had lied to her brother and friends, too. But it was to protect Arrow and me. Plus, she knew of the magic in the Stilts.

Was she good? Could she be good? I had trusted before and lost almost everything. I couldn't make that mistake again. But if she could help us mend the Anima, I could rebuild the curtain, move it closer, shut out all the humans forever.

Arrow's fingertips wriggled in the dirt.

I reached out to the grubs beneath them and gave them

my request. Soon the earth began to warm, and a smile spread across Arrow's face.

He turned to the girl. "I'll take you to meet the Guardian tomorrow."

"You will?" Petari squealed, then slapped her hands over her mouth. She glanced at the hut, but the door didn't open. She hadn't been heard. "This is the best. We should go early, before the others are up. I'll leave them a note saying we're going to get more plants and stuff. That way, they won't follow."

"I know some plants we can bring back. Some more food, too." Arrow was getting excited, although I didn't know if it was because he'd see me or because he was bringing the girl. "You're going to love the Guardian," he told her.

"I can't wait," she said. "Thank you." She gave him a quick smile, then disappeared inside the hut with the rest of her herd.

Arrow settled back onto the fern leaves, curled onto his side, palm on the soil. "See you tomorrow, Guardian," he whispered.

Maybe he did miss me after all.

NUTRIENTS IN THE WATER FLOWING THROUGH THE BARK OF AN OLD
LUPUNA TREE IN THE EAST TURNED BITTER. THE BARK CRACKED, AND
TWO LIANAS HANGING ON THE TRUNK SHRIVELED AND SLIPPED TO
THE RAINFOREST FLOOR. *THUMP. THUMP.*

In the night, the rainbow liquid soaked more of the earth at the Burnt Circle. It wasn't coming out of the metal bird in drops anymore but in a thin stream.

Arrow had to hurry.

True to their plans, he and Petari snuck out of the village just after the sun's rays were reaching across the sky. Petari had her "note" ready, the ripped edge of a page from her book with scribbles on it.

"How do those scratches work?" Arrow asked as they ran across the root bridge.

"You mean writing?" Petari hoisted her backpack higher on her shoulders. "I have to teach you about writing and reading. It's the most brill thing there is. You know how I'm saying a sentence to you now and you can understand it?"

Arrow nodded.

"That's like writing. You put down the words that you would say if you were there, but it means someone else can read them later when you're not there. Like I told them we were going to the east to get more food."

"Good idea to tell them we were going in the opposite direction," Arrow said.

He was starting to get used to the idea of lies. I wasn't sure if that was good or bad.

As quietly as they could, they hurried over the root bridge and into the forest. Arrow moved through the trees swiftly. Petari tried to keep up, but she didn't know the terrain like him, and her feet tripped on roots and rocks.

"We'll go slower," Arrow said, but the girl shook her head.

"Don't worry about me. I'm fine." And she raced ahead, a thread of irritation streaming behind her. The girl did not like being told she couldn't do something.

Eventually, though, Arrow slowed, seeing that Petari was having trouble. But this time he didn't talk about it, just stopped to pick some acai berries, then continued on at a less brisk pace.

I hoped bringing her to me would be worth the time. There was still no sign of the Kiskadee Man or other humans, but the curtain continued to tear. The dangers were growing for the forest.

Whether Petari noticed Arrow slowing, she didn't say. Instead she picked up her questions from the night before.

"So when did your parents die?"

Arrow glanced at her. "What do you mean?"

"They brought you to the forest then died, didn't they? Isn't that how you got in here?" She pressed her lips into a thin line. "I read a book like that once."

Arrow frowned. "I don't know who my parents are."

"Then how did you get into the forest?"

Petari had had difficulty believing I was real and could talk to Arrow. How would she react to this story? Perhaps it would be better to keep it secret, but it was up to Arrow now.

He was silent for a few breaths, then said, "You know where you came in, through those rocks?"

Petari nodded.

"I was left near there when I was a baby."

"Someone just left you there? That's horrible. Why would anyone do that to a baby?"

Arrow shrugged, but he pulled his pointed arm protectively into his chest. Petari noticed and said, "Never mind. Go on."

"The trees in the forest had heard my crying. I'd been there for half of the sun's path, crying loudly, and the human had not come back. So the Guardian asked the nearest tree to bring me inside. I was carried in by the tree's roots. That tree passed me to the next tree, and the next, until I was at the roots of the Guardian." He sighed. "I don't remember it, of course. I was too young."

And there it was. Our truth was out.

Arrow glanced at Petari, whose eyes had grown as big as the sun. "You have to admit it sounds strange," she said.

"Not to me it doesn't." Hurt spilled from him.

But Petari said, "Oh right. I guess it wouldn't."

"You were actually the first human I spoke to."

"I was?" Petari's brow lifted, and excitement danced around her. But it was laced with something else, something dense. She still wasn't sure if she could trust what Arrow was saying.

And I was still not sure if we could trust her.

"So how'd you learn to talk like this?" Petari asked, perhaps testing the boy. "How come you can understand me?"

"I told you, the Guardian learned from the Forest Dwellers," Arrow said. "Actually, she learned from all the humans who came here, and she taught me all the words she learned. Sometimes you say words I don't know, but it's not too hard to figure them out. And if you're wondering about my clothes, the birds bring them every year, probably from where you come from. And the Guardian asked the monkeys to help me eat when I was younger. And—"

"All right, all right." Petari put up her hands. "I get it."

Arrow narrowed his eyes. "You still don't believe me."

"I . . . I'm just trying to understand. That's all. But it sounds—"

She stopped talking when a large drop of water smacked her forehead, then another on her arm, and another on her cheek. Petari gazed up and gasped.

"It's raining! Again!"

Arrow peered at the drops, coming down faster. "It does that a lot." He pursed his lips. "But not as much as it used to. It used to rain almost every moon, but now moon after moon after moon goes by before the rain comes again."

Petari's eyes widened. "It NEVER rains in the Barbs. Like NEVER."

"Never rains?"

"Okay, not never, but it's probably rained maybe three times since I was born, and since I've been in the forest, it's already rained twice!" She twirled in the raindrops, letting the water soak every part of her. "It's incredible."

Then the drops stopped.

Petari raised her arms to the sky, glancing between the canopy leaves for more. "Wait! Don't go. Where'd it go?"

Arrow frowned. "First there are fewer rainstorms; now the storms are just drips. This isn't good."

Movement caught the corner of his eye, and he put his arm out to stop Petari.

A jaguar skulked through the trees ahead, turned their way, sniffed, then trod on.

When the creature was gone, Petari let out her breath in a rush. "That's a . . . That's a . . . That's . . ." A shaky finger pointed in the jaguar's direction.

"Yeah, that's Claw. She's old and she can be ornery sometimes, depending on her mood. Best to leave her alone."

Eyes wide, Petari nodded. "Yeah. I'll do that."

"Come on." Arrow pulled her forward, back on their journey.

Soon the trees opened to a small gap in the forest, and Petari blinked in the bright sun.

"Wow," she said. "Look at those flowers. They're bigger than my head."

She ran toward them, but Arrow shouted, "Stop!"

Petari's feet sloshed in water, and she quickly stepped back again. "What? It's just a puddle."

"It's deeper than it looks. It's one of the river's fingers."

"It can't be too deep. It's got flowers growing on it."

"Those are giant water lilies. Their stalks go down into the water at least twice as tall as me."

Petari stepped back farther. "That deep? I can't go across there. I can't swim."

He looked at her quizzically. "You can't swim?"

She crossed her arms over her chest. "There's no need where I come from. All the pools are dried up, and any riverbed that has water in it is too polluted to go in."

Arrow shook this horrible idea out of his head. "Don't worry, you don't want to swim in this water anyway. Dangerous things could be hiding under the leaves."

"What kind of dangerous things?" Petari's mouth curled.

"Caimans and anacondas, stuff like that."

"Those giant snakes are in the water?" Petari stepped back even farther.

"It's okay." Arrow touched her arm lightly. "As long as we're on the surface, we'll see them before they get to us."

Petari shook her head. "Maybe I don't need to meet this tree. I can't get across this water."

"Yes, you can. We'll go across on the lily leaves."

"What leaves? Those leaves?" She pointed at the giant green circles on the water's surface. "You must be kidding. Those will flip us into the water. With the anacondas!"

"No, they won't. Come on."

Petari didn't move.

"Come on," Arrow said again. "Giant water lily leaves are really strong." He walked to the edge of the river and reached for the closest one. "And they've got these spikes underneath. See?" He lifted the edge so she could see. Petari stepped forward, carefully putting a finger on the tip of one of the long spikes that dripped with water.

"Wow."

"That keeps snakes and other predators from coming up too fast from the water. And all those ribs under the leaf . . ." He nodded toward it, still holding up the edge. "That makes it sturdy. I've seen small jaguars walk on these things."

"Really?"

Arrow nodded. "They hold better if you're flat, though, so do like I do." He crawled onto the surface of the leaf and lay down, looking back at her. "Get on that one," he said, pointing at the leaf next to him.

"I don't know." She glanced around, probably for anacondas and jaguars. Whether he had meant to or not, Arrow had scared her.

"Come on. It's fun." Arrow flipped onto his back, grinning. "I might not know about books and movies, but I know about this."

Petari smiled too, uneasily, but she smiled nevertheless. "Will you get me if I fall in?"

"Yes, but I'm going to be right next to you anyway." He paddled his leaf closer and took hold of the edge of her leaf. "Here, give me your backpack."

She clutched the straps. "What if you drop it?"

"I won't. Trust me. Put it there." He nodded to the space next to him. Petari swung her backpack off her shoulders, then gingerly placed it on the leaf by Arrow.

"Jump on." He nodded to the leaf he was still holding for her.

Taking in a deep breath, she jumped and landed flat with a *thwump*. The leaf bowed a bit with the sudden weight, and Petari gave a small shriek, but just like Arrow had told her it would, the leaf stayed steady on the surface of the water. It was so large around, she could fit on it completely, without her feet dangling off the side.

"This is brill," she said.

Arrow smiled. "Told you. Come on."

He pulled her leaf up to another so Petari could grab it. Then he got hold of his next leaf and crawled across, being careful not to push down the edges. He pulled her backpack behind him. Petari did the same, again and again. As she crossed between leaves, she eyed the water. I could feel her pulse pound down the stalks of the lilies into the riverbed.

"I see fish," she said.

"Yeah but keep watching the surface. Hurry."

Arrow pushed his leaf along the water until the stalk was tight but he could capture the next leaf. He crawled on, Petari following, until they got to the other side of the river and she stepped onto solid ground again.

Petari grinned. "That was fun."

"You should be here at night when the flowers start to smell," Arrow said as Petari reached for her backpack. "You'll never want to leave." He laughed, but I was not amused. I didn't want him giving her any ideas.

When they finally got near to me, Arrow slowed. Calm was returning to his heartbeat, and his steps grew lighter. Curly had been with me since Arrow had gone into the village with the herd, but hearing her friend now, she swung from branch to branch until she plopped onto his shoulders.

"Curly!" he shouted, hugging her close.

Curly nuzzled his neck, then peered at Petari with an angry look.

"Hi, Curly," the girl said cheerily.

The monkey chattered in her direction, then curled in the crook of Arrow's shoulder again.

Arrow laughed. "She's picky. But come . . ."

They rounded a tree trunk, and he beamed at Petari.

"This is the Guardian," he said, pointing at me. "The mother tree of the forest."

Petari held tight to the strap of her backpack as her eyes followed my trunk into the sky.

I sucked air into my leaves, plumping them up. I hadn't met another human for many, many rings before Arrow came into the forest, and none since. I found myself nervous, questioning why I had allowed this visit, how I could have hoped it would help. Petari was a girl, a child, but still a human child of the Imposters. I didn't know what she would think—or do.

"She's a beaut," the girl said, a buzz of anticipation whirling around her.

"Isn't she wonderful?" Arrow beamed at me. "Guardian, this is Petari."

Excitement flooded from him, and I got the urge to warn him to have caution again. This was his first time dealing with humans. He wasn't used to being let down by them the way I was.

"Hello, Petari," I said to her.

The girl ogled me, walked around my trunk, then turned back to Arrow.

"She said 'hello,'" Arrow told her.

"She did?" Disappointment dripped from Petari as she gazed at my trunk. "I couldn't hear anything." She narrowed her eyes, and I could tell that the thrill she had of meeting me was fading fast. I was afraid my instincts about her were correct. I only hoped bringing her here wouldn't prove a mistake.

"Say it again, Guardian." Arrow patted my trunk. His smile was still broad.

"I warned you of this, Arrow. She's from a different world, and those humans don't know how to listen to trees. They will not help us. We'll get them out of the forest, but first we must stop the spread of the rainbow liquid."

"Is it worse?"

"A lot worse."

Arrow pressed his lips together, then talked to me more quietly, as if trying to hide the words from the girl. "I'll fix it after I've taken her back to the village, but she could help us. Try talking to her again."

"All right. Once more. Hello, Petari," I said, louder this time.

The girl looked from me to Arrow to me and back to Arrow, her face full of hope.

"Did you hear her?" Arrow asked.

Petari shook her head slowly. "Where's her face? Maybe if I can see her mouth moving . . ."

"She doesn't have a face like we do."

"So how does she talk without a mouth?"

Arrow shrugged. "I don't know. Not with a mouth, like us, but I can hear her just like I can hear you."

"Oh. It must be amazing to hear her talk." She sounded discouraged.

"The Guardian says all animals and humans can hear, but some don't listen, especially the humans. But the other humans that were here, a long time ago, the Forest Dwellers, some of them could hear the trees. I'm sure you'll be able to. Maybe you need to come up to my nest. Then you'll be able to hear her."

"What nest?"

"That's my home. See?" He pointed to his nest, high in my branches.

"You sleep up there? Wow." Petari's eyes grew wide as she peered up at the nest. "You think I'll be able to hear her from there?"

"Sure. Come on."

Petari watched as Arrow wrapped a liana around his wrist, then scaled my trunk to the first branch. Next he grabbed a higher branch with his hand and crooked another with the bend of his pointed arm. Curly showed off, jumping off Arrow's shoulder and swinging from tree limb to tree limb until she chittered from the nest up above. After a few steps, Arrow looked down at Petari.

"You coming?"

Petari bit her lip. "Yeah." Nervousness swam around her, but also pride. She didn't want to admit she was scared.

"Use the liana first. I can help pull you up." He reached out his hand.

"I can do it," she said. Stubborn, this one. But a few more tries, and she was in my branches, sitting next to Arrow's nest. She brushed her fingertips across the leaves.

"What is this?"

"Curly and I weaved it from hemp leaves. They're really strong. And it's very comfortable. Try it." He motioned for her to step inside.

"Are you sure it won't fall?"

"Here." He tumbled into the nest, then jumped and

rolled. When she was laughing, Arrow climbed back onto the branch and beckoned for her to try.

Petari poked the nest with her finger, then grabbed the material and shook it. Pressing her lips together, she took in a deep breath, then she slid off her branch into Arrow's nest.

"Mmmm." She was stiff at first, but then snuggled in. "You're right, this is comfy." She peered over the side. "And you can see a lot up here." She gasped. "What's that?" She pointed and Arrow's eyes followed.

He laughed. "That's Hanger. He's a sloth. He likes to—"

"Hang?"

Arrow nodded. "Yep, upside down. He's funny. But don't worry, he's perfectly safe. And look at this."

He showed her the arrow in my bark. "I didn't understand what an arrow was, so the Guardian told me what to carve. I thought it would hurt her, but she said only for a moment. She said anytime I didn't know who I was, I could look at this. Right, Guardian?"

"That's right," I said.

"Talk to Petari again, Guardian," he instructed.

Petari gazed at him expectantly, then looked at my trunk once more as though hoping a mouth would open up.

"One more time, Arrow. Then we must give up and stop the rainbow liquid." I reached out to the girl. "Hello, Petari. Welcome to the forest."

Arrow watched the girl, and the girl watched Arrow.

"Well?" he said.

Petari's eyes dropped and she climbed out of his nest. "I should go." She started back to the ground.

Arrow climbed down after her. "Are you okay?"

Petari jumped from the liana to the ground, then swung her backpack onto her shoulder.

She gazed up at Arrow, sorrow written in her eyes. "The Guardian is really nice. But . . ." She paused, her fingertips carefully touching my bark. "Arrow, I wanted to believe. I really did. But trees don't talk or bring babies to a forest or help them grow up."

My roots curled. Just as I had suspected, she was too closed to listen. Sad for one so young.

Arrow didn't seem sad, though. A thread of anger wormed out of him. "This one did." He hopped onto a low branch.

Petari looked back up at the boy. "Arrow . . ." Her voice was soft, kind at least. "This tree isn't talking to you and didn't bring you in here. It's impossible."

Arrow's anger grew thicker. "No, it's not. The Guardian takes care of me."

Petari sighed. "I don't know how you got into the forest, and maybe you really don't remember. It doesn't matter. What counts is that you learned all that brill stuff on your own."

"I'm not alone!" His anger grew into rage, twisting around the air between them.

171

"Arrow, most humans won't believe," I reminded him. "Even when it's the truth, even if they heard my voice, they'd think it was something else, a trick or imagination."

He grabbed the liana, jumped to the ground, then turned to me. "Can you show her?"

Behind him, Petari looked down and shuffled her feet. I could guess the thoughts in her head, that Arrow had been in the forest without other humans for too long, that he was hearing voices that weren't there, that he needed help.

"I'd have to use some of the Anima," I told Arrow. "We have to protect what's left."

He leaned his head against my bark. "I know," he whispered, "but I'm going to need help to get the magic, and she's the only one I think will help me."

"Arrow . . . ," I began, not sure what to do.

A long breath rolled out, and when nothing happened, the boy slowly turned back to Petari. "She's weak," he said.

Petari nodded. "Yeah. Sure. Look, I love your nest and everything, and this adventure has been brill, but I should get back."

She hoisted her backpack higher on her shoulder, stepped away, then stepped again.

Sadness drained from Arrow, and I suspected it wasn't just because he wanted her help to get the magic. He wanted her to believe him. He wanted to share me with her.

I had told Arrow he could bring her. I had been curious

about this human who made Arrow smile. Was it possible that she was different from the Imposters? It was hard to believe she or any of these humans could be. But what if Arrow was right, and she was key to fixing our Anima with the magic in the Stilts? I didn't like depending on a human from outside, but we were running out of options. Perhaps it was worth a small amount of Anima to open up to her.

Steadying myself, I dug deep and pulled a drop of magic from the earth.

Petari's feet halted. Her mouth gaped open. Her breath left.

EAST OF THE RIVER, A BRANCH OF THE SAPODILLA TREE, LADEN
WITH FRUIT, BLISTERED IN THE WIND AND CRUMBLED INTO DUST.
HOWLER MONKEYS CRIED OUT, THEN WENT TO SEARCH FOR MORE.

Orchids sprouted and bloomed in the arms of the trees ahead of Petari. Fungi glowed yellow and pink and purple and blue on the ground. Beneath her the earth shook, and thick roots twirled upward, toward the sky.

I couldn't keep it for long, only a few seconds, but she saw.

"What was that?" she asked, as the flowers died out, the light dissipated, and the roots fell under the soil once more.

"I told you." Arrow grinned.

"But that wasn't there just now." Petari dropped her backpack and glanced around. Her eyes were as wide as passion fruit blossoms. "Flowers don't bloom that quickly. And that glowing stuff . . ."

"That was fungi."

"Yeah, the fungi. So many colors. And the roots . . ."

"The Guardian's not as strong as she used to be," Arrow said. "But I can tell she likes you. The orchids were a special touch."

Petari smiled. "Tell her I like her, too."

"She knows. I told you, she knows everything that happens in the forest."

Petari turned to Arrow. "I'm sorry I said—"

He waved his arm. "Now you know." He turned back to me, hugged my trunk, and whispered, "Thank you." I felt the warmth of gratitude radiate from within him.

Looking at Petari now, he couldn't keep back his smile. "Will you help me get to the Stilts?"

"I don't know why you want to leave here." Petari twirled around. Her eyes were seeing the forest in a new way. "I liked it before, but now . . ."

"I told you," Arrow said. "The Guardian is weak. She needs help, and I think the help is in the Stilts."

"You do? Why?"

Arrow nodded. "All the things you talked about. If the people in the Stilts can do all those things, they must have ways of helping the forest."

Petari frowned. "I don't know. They don't have many

trees, but . . ." She glanced around her as if she could still see the Anima working. "I'll do whatever I can to help you."

Arrow beamed, relief spilling out around him. "Thank you. I'll take you back to the village now. You can make the plan like Luco talked about. I have to do something in the forest, but when I get back, we'll go to the Stilts. Okay?"

"Okay." Petari picked up her backpack. "What do you have to do?"

Arrow didn't waste time explaining about the rainbow liquid. Instead he said, "Just something for the Guardian. I won't be long. Come on, we don't want to lose sunlight. We'll be back soon, Guardian." Arrow smiled at me and whispered, "I'm going to fix everything." He started walking. "Curly, you coming?"

The monkey chattered but swung down and plopped onto the ground beside them.

Petari gazed at where the orchids had been as she murmured, "They were there, then they were gone." The thrill of seeing the Anima still swarmed around her. I must admit, I liked it. I hoped she would prove me wrong about being cautious.

During their journey back to the herd, they collected food as Petari had promised, but her mind wasn't on it. She talked excitedly about what she had seen.

"I've never seen flowers like that.

"The colors were so bright.

"Those roots just lifted out of the soil!

"We have to show the others."

Arrow laughed. "We will, as soon as the Guardian is better."

When Arrow and Petari arrived at the tree barrier to the village, Curly chattered nervously and jumped from Arrow's shoulder to a branch.

"The humans will like you," Arrow said, but Curly didn't agree. She shook her fist at the boy and stayed put.

Petari stifled a giggle, but Arrow sighed. "Fine. Stay here, but I'm going to help Petari take this food in."

"Hey." Petari grabbed Arrow's arm, stopping him before he walked through the trees. "Maybe we shouldn't tell them about the Guardian. Not yet, okay?"

Arrow glared at her. "Because they won't believe me, like you didn't?"

Petari shrugged. "We'll just tell them at the right time. Trust me."

I didn't. I hoped Arrow didn't either.

The rest of the herd were crowded around Storma and Luco when Arrow and Petari trod into the village. My attention had been on my boy and the girl, but now I noticed the thickness of worry and anger around the rest of the herd.

"What's going on?" Petari asked as they got closer.

177

Val turned quickly. "Where have you been?" He glanced at Arrow, brows furrowed, but quickly swept his eyes back to his sister.

"I told you in the note. We went to find more food." She lifted her laden backpack as Arrow placed what was in his arms on the ground. "Got a heap of it."

"You better have," Storma said. "We're going to need it."

"Why? What's happened?" Petari asked.

Luco straightened. "Safa and me just got back from the Stilts."

"The Stilts?" Arrow stepped forward. He was as eager as I was to learn more. Perhaps there would be word of the magic.

Luco continued. "Jom wasn't there. No one was."

"Who's Jom?" Arrow asked.

"My contact," said Luco. "His family works in the Stilts, so they've got permits to be there. He smuggles out food and other supplies for us."

"They never miss the meetings," Storma said, crossing her arms. "When they haven't been able to get food out in the past, they've still made the meeting to explain."

"Not this time," Safa said.

"What happened to them?" Petari asked.

Luco shook his head. "It can't be anything good."

"Unless they sold us out." Storma's voice was icy.

"Jom wouldn't do that. Not for anything." Luco shifted

his weight, and I recognized something else around him—streams of icy fear. "We tried to get into the Stilts ourselves through one of the back ways, but everything's closed up. It's like they've locked down the entire city and they're not letting anyone in or out."

Arrow stiffened.

"You tried every back way? The sewer's never too secure." This was Mercou, who held Ruthie in his arms.

Luco nodded. "That was the first place we tried. Then the old pipes by the dried-up river. Then the holes in the wall. All of them were closed off or had so much security, a rat couldn't scurry by."

"What does this mean?" Arrow asked.

The humans glanced at one another; then Storma spoke up. "It means the people in the Stilts are greedier than ever."

Anxiety swarmed around Arrow. "So we can't go there? We can't get in?"

Luco shook his head.

Arrow glanced at Petari. If they couldn't get into the Stilts, they couldn't get to the magic. They couldn't save the forest.

"But you promised." Arrow turned back to Luco. "I help you get food and show you how to be safe in the forest, and you get me to the Stilts. That was the deal."

"No one promised anything." Storma gave a dry laugh. "Things don't turn out the way you want all the time. You haven't learned that yet?"

"But I have to go. You have to try again," Arrow said. "The Guardian needs it."

"Who's the Guardian?" Storma's voice rang out strong, and a hush fell over all the humans.

Petari froze. Arrow's eyes widened. His cold, sticky fear sank into the ground beneath him.

He had let out a secret.

Arrow looked at the herd. They were glowering at him now as someone they didn't know. Someone they couldn't trust.

Storma stepped forward, suspicion carved into her face. "You told us you lived here alone."

"He does—" Petari started, forcefully, but Val grabbed her arm and tugged her back.

Storma's eyes didn't leave Arrow. "If you live here alone, who's the Guardian?"

Arrow focused on the ground. He was probably trying to decide what to tell them. Petari hadn't believed him when he had told her about me. How would this group react? And how could he stop them from coming to find me, from coming south into the heart of the forest? These questions raced through me as well.

"Is there another group here?" Luco asked. "Is that why you don't want us to go anywhere?"

"We should find them before they attack us," Safa said. Agreement was murmured throughout the herd.

"Yeah. Maybe they've got batteries," Delora said.

"And more spam," Rosaman said.

"Maybe they're not the sharing types," Mercou said.

"We'll protect ourselves like we do in the Barbs." Storma turned on Arrow. "Where are they? Where's your little group hiding?"

Arrow shook his head quickly. "No! You don't understand."

"I understand perfectly." Storma's eyes bored into the boy. "You were a spy all along."

"That's not true," Petari shouted. "He—"

"Be quiet, Petari." Luco glared at her.

"Yeah," Val said, holding on to Petari's wrist. "You brought him here. This is your fault."

"But—" Petari squirmed in her brother's grip.

"There aren't any other humans in the forest," Arrow insisted. "I'm not what you said."

"Humans?" Rosaman echoed. "Who does he think he is?"

"Maybe he's an alien," said Faive.

"Whatever he is, he's not one of us," said Delora.

Twisted sadness sank from Arrow. He had joined them to get information about the magic, but I knew that being accepted by them the night before had begun to fill the hole inside him that I never could. But now . . .

"He's just a traitor, that's what he is." Safa spat on the ground in front of Arrow. "If his group comes here, we'll tear them apart."

"Yeah. Tear them apart!" said Delora.

"EEEE!" The shriek pierced the sky, drawing the attention of the herd.

"What the—" said Mercou, but Arrow knew immediately what had made the sound.

"CURLY!" He ran toward the cry. It had come from the tall grasses between the herd and the tree line. "Curly!" Arrow dashed from side to side until he found the monkey curled around her paw. She was whimpering, and the ground was stained with red splotches.

"What happened?" Arrow knelt down next to her. He slid his right hand under Curly's back and the tip of his arrow arm under her head, then carefully tucked the monkey into the crook of his left elbow.

The herd crowded around, even Luco, Storma, and Val.

"It's a monkey," Mercou said.

Petari gasped. "Curly! This is Arrow's friend."

"You're friends with a monkey?" Faive asked.

"Even weirder," Rosaman said.

"Is that blood?" Delora pointed to the specks of red on the ground.

Curly whined, and Arrow gently examined her paw. A gash was open in its side. "Oh no, Curly," Arrow said. "Petari, get the blood leaves."

Petari ran to the hut, where she'd stored the samples she had collected. A few breaths later she was back with the leaves.

"Here," Arrow said when she knelt beside him. "Take her."

Arrow gritted his teeth as he guided Curly onto Petari's open palms. She accepted the monkey into her hands, and Arrow pressed the leaves onto the cut. Curly shrieked and the others backed away.

"Come on, Curly. It's okay." Arrow smiled at her, tears clouding his eyes. He tore the leaves into strips with his teeth, then, holding the ends down with his elbow, wrapped them gently around the paw. He kept up the pressure until the bleeding stopped.

"How did this happen?" Arrow looked around and spotted a glint in the grass. The sliced-off top of a red-and-white can lay on the ground, its edges sharp. "What is this doing here?"

"It's just a can." Delora shrugged.

"It doesn't belong on the ground." Standing, Arrow gazed over the open field and saw more glints in the sun. "They're everywhere."

"What's the big deal?" Rosaman said.

I was right that these humans couldn't be trusted to protect the forest.

"Maybe the monkey should wear shoes," Delora said.

This brought laughter from the herd, all except Petari and Val.

"I'm sure your monkey friend's going to be just fine," Storma said. "Now tell us where we can find this Guardian."

Anger arched out from Arrow. "The Guardian isn't a

183

human. She's the mother tree of the forest. She warned me not to trust you, and she was right!"

My roots froze. He had told them about me. I was sure they'd have the same reaction as Petari. I couldn't waste Anima convincing them. It would not be worth it.

"A tree?" Storma asked. "What do you mean 'a tree'?"

"Are you kidding?" Safa turned to the rest of the herd. "Is he kidding? Did he just say he talks to a tree?"

Laughter rose up from the herd, louder and louder. So loud, it scared the parrots in the tree line. They flew away in a flurry.

Fresh tears sprang into Arrow's eyes. He leaned down and pulled Curly from Petari's hands.

"Are there fairies in the forest too?" Delora asked, igniting the laughter again.

"What about trolls?" said Rosaman. "Or goblins? Or gremlins?"

Their high-pitched squeals of laughter raced around Arrow, sharp and pointed.

He backed away, Curly crying softly in his hands.

"Stop!" Petari shouted to the herd, but no one paid her any attention.

"Maybe the animals talk to him too," Mercou said, tears from laughter running across his cheeks. "Can you ask them to get us some food?"

Arrow stepped back.

Back.

Back.

And ran.

He ran for the trees that bordered the village.

"Arrow!" Petari called out. Her footsteps followed, but Val pulled her back.

"Let him go," her brother said.

Petari shook her arm from his grip and shouted, "Arrow, come back!"

But the boy was gone. He fled through the trees, across the root bridge, and into the thick forest on the other side. When they got back to me, Arrow collapsed among my roots.

"I've failed," he said. "I thought they'd help me, but they won't. They're making the village dangerous and don't even care. Now I've told them about you, Curly's hurt, and all the time I was trying to help those horrible humans, I could've been stopping the rainbow liquid."

"Curly will heal," I told him as he gently brought the monkey up to his nest in a carrying hammock. That was the only thing I was sure of, even though I couldn't be sure of the future of Curly's and our home. I wished I could tell Arrow that everything would be all right, but at this point, I could only hope nothing would get worse before we could mend the Anima.

Arrow rubbed Curly's head gently, and the monkey nuzzled his hand. "I shouldn't have helped them."

Tears streamed down his face. So much disappointment and hurt wrapped around him.

How I wished he had listened to me. I should have been more forceful. I should not have let hope for humans sway me. All the humans from that outside world were the same. Liars who care only for themselves, just like the Imposters.

"All of the humans are bad, aren't they? All of my kind."

"Those humans are bad, Arrow. The Imposters, the humans from the outside world. Now you know why I've been saying we can't trust them." My roots curled. "But the Forest Dwellers were good. You are good. And . . ." I hated to admit what I was about to say, but it was the truth. "Petari did stand up for you. She might have good within her."

"Petari's no different. She's one of them." Arrow wiped his eyes. "But you're right about the Forest Dwellers. And since they were good, that has to mean that not all humans are bad. We just have to find the good ones."

He reached into the fold of the nest where he had hidden the golden disc and pulled it out, rubbing the rough surface.

"The Kiskadee Man didn't do anything bad when he was here," Arrow said, hope circling him.

"He wasn't in the forest long enough. He would've been just like the herd. I'm sure."

"No." Arrow shook his head. "I saved his life. He'd be

thankful. He'd see that we're good and want to help us, like the Forest Dwellers."

I didn't answer. I had been suspicious of the herd, and I was proved right. I longed for humans like the Forest Dwellers, but I didn't know if I'd ever find them again. If the Kiskadee Man was like all the other humans from the north, the best way he could thank Arrow was to not return. If only I could've fully plugged the rips in the curtain where the plane had crashed through before.

Arrow put the golden disc into his pocket, then laid Curly gently in the crook of the nest and climbed out. "Look after Curly, Guardian. I'll go and stop the metal bird from bleeding, then come back. We'll come up with a new plan, won't we?"

That was my boy, always seeing the sun. "We will," I told him. I hoped I was right.

Sadness trailing after him, Arrow scaled my branches and journeyed to the Burnt Circle. The rainbow liquid had drenched the soil there, and Arrow worried as he gathered more sap to plug the hole. No matter how much he placed over the wound, though, it quickly dappled with the rainbow liquid again.

Arrow sat back on his heels, glaring at the bird, at the Burnt Circle, at the rainbow-colored stain in the soil. Despair flooded from him, but then he stood up, reached into his pocket, and pulled out the golden disc. Hurrying over to the metal bird, he placed it over the hole. The disc covered the wound. Arrow collected more sap, but this time he used the substance to stick the disc over the bleeding part of the bird. He waited, waited, waited, but no more liquid came out. Good boy. The soil was still soaked, but at least the danger would grow no more. Worry swirled around Arrow, but he had done all he could do, so he journeyed back to me.

"I don't know how long it will hold. Keep watching it," he said as he climbed back into the nest. "How's Curly?" He had brought the monkey some bananas.

"Sleeping, but she'll enjoy those when she wakes up. You should rest too, Arrow. It has been a long day."

He curled around his small friend, stroking her soft black fur, and nodded. "We can wish for a better tomorrow, Guardian."

"Yes, a better tomorrow."

Reaching out to the root network, I monitored the Burnt Circle to the south and the herd to the north. Arrow was right about one thing: We needed help. The forest was in danger, but we were still no closer to mending the Anima.

I didn't know if any answers would present themselves after the moon had gone and the sun returned. Arrow hadn't failed, I had. I had put too much on his small shoulders. And now, with the forest dying and the magic disappearing faster, I began to lose sight of the possibility of us saving it. Perhaps this was an end. Perhaps there was no help. Perhaps I had lost us our home.

But, as the sun peeked over the horizon, Arrow woke with a start. A familiar sound rocketed through the canopy of the forest.

*Thrum.*

*Thrum.*

*Thrum.*

ON A ROCK IN A CLEARING NEAR THE ROOT BRIDGE, A
BROMELIAD STRETCHED OUT IN THE MORNING SUN, ITS STIFF PETALS
CATCHING EACH RAY. SUDDENLY ONE ROOT PULLED AWAY FROM
THE GROUND AND CURLED UP TIGHT. ANOTHER FOLLOWED. AND
ANOTHER. UNTIL THE WHOLE PLANT WAS PARCHED.

The thrum was only a far-off tickle in Arrow's ears,
but its disturbance might as well have been thunder
overhead. He sat up, rubbing his eyes, and looked in
the direction of the noise.

The sky through the leaves was a pale gray with a bright
yellow center, but he couldn't see the metal frog. Not yet.

He scrambled to higher branches and peered out over
the leaves. "There! They're coming back."

I had feared they would. But whether they would be like
the Forest Dwellers, the Imposters, or the herd, I did not
know.

"It's just like you said." Arrow started to climb down.

"What do you mean?"

"You said the answer would come in the morning, and look . . . the Kiskadee Man is coming back." Arrow grinned.

"That is not what I meant." And yet, the Forest Dwellers had talked of getting answers in dreams. Could I have been wrong about the Kiskadee Man? Was he the answer Arrow had asked for?

"He'll mend the Anima," Arrow said as he climbed back down. "He's not a kid like the herd. He's older, like the Forest Dwellers. He knows things. He can fly! He will bring the magic from the Stilts and fix everything. I know he will." He jumped onto the ground.

"You must listen to me, Arrow."

"I know I was wrong before, but I'll be more careful this time. I'll watch and learn." His feet were already hurrying south. "It's going to be different. It has to be. Look after Curly." He ran to the kapok tree, swung his belt around the liana, and slid off toward the Burnt Circle.

He was hidden in a tree before the wind picked up. Leaves and twigs battered his face, but he held on tight. The *Thrum, Thrum, Thrum* was louder now, and Arrow could see the machine hovering in the sky above him. It was another bullfrog, larger than the bird that had crashed. Holes were cut into its puffed-out belly, just like the metal bullfrog that had rescued the Kiskadee Man.

It screamed as it lowered, and the monkeys around Arrow scattered into the forest with their own screeches. But Arrow stayed.

Eyes squinting against the dust and ash swirling around him, Arrow watched as the bullfrog got lower and lower, bigger and bigger. Shouts came over the *THRUM, THRUM, THRUM*, and the bullfrog shifted forward and back, twisting until its long tail wouldn't catch on a tree. Finally it touched down with a *THWUMP*, and what was left of the ash on the ground flew up, covering the Burnt Circle in a thick cloud that was quickly dispatched into the forest by the giant arms rotating over the bullfrog's back.

Arrow huddled on the branch, his right hand holding on to the tree limb as his arrow arm shielded his eyes against the wind and dust. Finally the bullfrog's arms stopped spinning, and the forest fell silent.

The metal bullfrog had settled west of the bird's carcass. Piles of ash and leaves rested around its feet and at the edges of the clearing.

Voices drifted up to Arrow, then a head poked out the side of the frog's belly. It was difficult to tell if it was the Kiskadee Man. It disappeared, then another came, this time followed by a body. It jumped onto the ground, and Arrow squeezed the branch. He knew this one was different. It was a woman, tall and skinny like a walking anaconda. She had something black and shiny slung over her back. It looked familiar, but I couldn't place why. A man came out next, thick and short with a head as bald as a pink dolphin. Then another man, taller than the woman, and wider, too. He had the eyes of a jaguar.

Finally another man descended. His shirt was the color of a tupi bird instead of a kiskadee's belly, but Arrow still recognized the man who had fallen from the metal bird. The man he had given fruit.

Arrow sucked in a breath.

The Anaconda Woman heaved a box out of the frog's belly, then another, helped by the Jaguar Man. The Dolphin Man strode to the burnt carcass, then around the clearing, eyes out among the trees, looking, watching, anticipating. The humans talked among themselves, but Arrow couldn't hear them clearly, just the occasional word.

"Hand . . ."

"Lift . . ."

"Here . . ."

The Anaconda Woman and Jaguar Man unpacked a large swath of material as green as my leaves. They hoisted it up on poles under the long arms of the frog. A green roof for an open hut.

This new herd and their flying machines were here to stay.

Arrow remained in that tree for most of the day, watching the machiners. Metal was taken out of the boxes, pieces clamped together to construct other items. A table was set up under the green roof, things pulled from boxes and laid out neatly. These grown humans talked and laughed and jostled each other in a friendly way.

As the sun began its final drop, Arrow climbed down from the branch, feet skipping over the bark as his right hand and the elbow of his arrow arm levered him from tree limb to tree limb. But when he got to the bottom, his footsteps froze. Why wasn't he moving? I hoped he hadn't been seen. But when I received the view from the monkeys, I knew exactly why Arrow had stopped.

All around the Burnt Circle were domes—and they were glowing.

They didn't look like any flower or fungi I knew, but they glowed with the Anima all the same.

I reached out through the root network but couldn't feel anything new. The domes could be in the soil but not connected to other roots yet.

The biggest question was: How had they found that much magic?

Arrow must've been thinking the same thing. While most of the machiners investigated the carcass of the metal bird, pulling out anything salvageable, Arrow hid behind a wide ficus tree and peered at the domes.

"Stop!"

Arrow froze, fear drilling into the tree. After a few breaths, he chanced a glance around the trunk at the machiners.

They were gathered near the metal bird. The Kiskadee Man was crouched at its base, pointing at the wound Arrow had plugged. He leaned forward and plucked the golden disc from the hole. Rolling it over in his fingers, he smiled slightly.

"This is leaking oil." He nodded toward the Anaconda Woman. "Wiser, come and have a look. It's spread all over here. We need to clean this up. We can't have anything dangerous."

The Anaconda Woman, Wiser, hurried over. "Fratos, you got the tools out yet?"

"Yep, I'll bring them over. Give me a hand, Mora." The Dolphin Man, Fratos, strode to the green roof, followed by the Jaguar Man, Mora. They opened boxes and pulled out things I'd never seen before. Some were small enough to be held in a palm; others unfolded to be longer than an arm; others wrapped around their backs and seemed to make them stronger. Bit by bit, the machiners dismantled what was left of the bird's metal skin and innards, placing it all in the belly of the bullfrog. Then Mora carried a giant spoon to the rainbow-colored stain, scooped up the tinged soil, and placed it into a large box.

"Got all of it?" the Kiskadee Man asked, leaning over the area to inspect the work.

"As much as I can," Mora said. "But there are probably traces in the soil. It's hard to say how far it's spread."

"Okay. Great job." The Kiskadee Man patted Mora on his shoulder, then gazed out at the trees. "We need to take care of this place like it's a jewel."

Watching from behind the tree, Arrow smiled, and I had to admit, this pleased me, too. I didn't know if I could hope for help from these older humans. Children were usually the more trustworthy ones. But so far, these adults seemed more promising than the herd. Perhaps Arrow was right and it was only the adult Forest Dwellers who could work with the Anima. Perhaps we did need the Kiskadee Man after all.

The Kiskadee Man pulled the golden disc from his pocket, rubbing his fingers on its surface just like Arrow had done. Gazing out into the trees, he narrowed his eyes. Was he hoping to get a glimpse of the boy? This man was wise. He knew someone had helped him all those moons ago, and he knew someone had stuck that disc to the carcass to stop the bleeding.

True to his word, Arrow didn't show himself. He flattened his body against the backside of the ficus, still as a gecko waiting for a fly.

The Kiskadee Man pursed his lips, whistling a pretty tune. He paused, listened, waited. A few breaths, then the birds picked up his song, playing it back to him. The Kiskadee Man smiled. Slipping the disc back into his pocket, he turned away from the tree line and strode under the green roof. "Splendid. Let's make camp."

Arrow released the breath he had been holding, then

quickly ran to the kapok tree. He grabbed a vine that was hanging down, held it tight to his chest with his arrow arm, and pulled with his right hand as his feet climbed up the trunk. He got his hemp rope in place, then launched along the liana back home.

"Did you see them? Did you see?" Arrow's words came quickly when he was close. "Did you see the glowing lights? Did you see the magic?"

"Yes," I said. "But I can't feel any more Anima than before. I don't know where they're pulling it from."

"I don't know, but it was strong. Maybe they brought it from the Stilts, just like I thought." Arrow panted a little, running up to my trunk. "We're saved."

"We're not saved yet, Arrow." Although the lights did give me hope.

"The Kiskadee Man is nice, too. He cleaned up all the rainbow liquid. He called it, 'oil.' Oil," he said again, letting the word roll over his tongue. "He said the forest was a jewel that had to be protected."

"I heard."

His excitement streamed off him as Arrow pulled himself into my branches. His grin was even bigger.

"You think he will help us?" I asked.

Arrow nodded. "He'll help. I saved his life. Remember?"

"That you did." Perhaps this boy's kind heart would save us after all.

"How's Curly?"

The monkey peered over the side of the nest when she heard her name. Seeing Arrow, she chittered happily.

"Getting better," I said, as Arrow climbed into the nest beside Curly.

"Let me see." He lifted her paw. It was healing nicely, and to prove it, Curly clapped her paws together gently, then swung around the branch above him with her tail. Arrow laughed and leaned back.

"Everything's going to be all right, Guardian. You'll see. The Kiskadee Man likes the forest. He's brought the magic from the Stilts. I'll get him to show me how to access it. Soon everything will be back to normal, and you can put up an even bigger curtain to keep out all the rest of the humans."

His voice was light, yet as he talked of shutting out the humans, a drop of sadness fell onto the nest. He liked having more of his kind in his home, but the herd had hurt him. His feelings wove around one another into a confused knot that he tried to push away.

I understood well. I missed the Forest Dwellers, but the actions of the Imposters were still burned into my roots.

Arrow hadn't been alive when the Imposters had come. He hadn't seen the forest before, or the forest after. He hadn't felt the hurt. When he'd cried at the base of the curtain, I had hoped that a baby, one so young, could be brought up to be like the Forest Dwellers and leave the ways of the Imposters behind. He was exactly as I had hoped, with a kinder heart than I had seen from a human in many rings.

But these new humans, they had grown up in the outside world, just like the Imposters. The young herd had turned out to be as uncaring as I had expected. Could Arrow be right about these older ones?

Whether I trusted or not, we were running out of time. The forest was dying, and without help to build the Anima, I feared that we would not survive. Maybe this Kiskadee Man *was* our last hope.

THE PETALS ON THE ORCHIDS NEAR SHIMMER CAVE
WITHERED, THEN DIED. THE *EUGLOSSA* BEES THAT NEEDED THE
SCENT OF THE ORCHIDS LEFT TO FIND OTHERS. THEN THE NUTS ON
THE LARGE BRAZIL NUT TREE THERE, WHICH NEEDED THE BEES
FOR POLLINATION, STOPPED PRODUCING SEEDS.

As soon as the sun peeked above the horizon the next day, Arrow said goodbye to me and Curly, much to the monkey's protests, and journeyed south back to the Burnt Circle. He was hidden behind a wide ficus near the clearing before the machiners were awake.

The glowing domes were gone now, but Arrow peered around, hoping to spy them. Soon his attention was pulled away as the humans woke and crawled out of the fabric huts they had erected the night before. They stretched, talked, and ate food from their boxes.

Wiser seemed to be the leader. She barked out orders that Mora and Fratos followed with a "Yes, Wiser." They sorted through boxes, pulling out small items that I couldn't identify from the blurry images I received from the butterflies. The task kept the humans busy, and they didn't notice when the Kiskadee Man wandered into the trees.

He was cautious, watchful. He eyed the trees and bushes, glanced back often to look at his companions. Each time, he must've felt satisfied, because he stepped, stepped, stepped farther into the forest.

I sucked air into my leaves. He was heading right to where Arrow was hiding. I hoped the boy wouldn't be caught.

The man's hands were clasped around tiny clear tubes. He reached down and collected soil in one, then pulled a pen from a pocket on his chest and scratched on the tube like Petari had done in her notebook. After tucking the tube away, he collected leaves, then different leaves.

He had become so engrossed in his work, he did not notice Arrow as the boy skipped behind a closer trunk. I saw it, though, and fear raked through my roots.

But Arrow didn't show himself, just observed as the man moved from plant to plant, inspecting the leaves, the bark, the moss.

Until the man reached out to pluck an oval leaf.

"Don't touch that," Arrow said, stepping out from his hiding place.

My roots froze. I had wanted more time to watch these humans, and yet here was Arrow risking his own life to save the man again. I hoped the Kiskadee Man knew the gift he was being given.

He jumped, then narrowed his eyes at Arrow.

Arrow was still a distance away, but he was in sight, not in shadow. The man had seen the boy; the faster pitter-patter of his heart let me know.

"Those leaves will hurt you," Arrow said. "They've got hairs that'll put poison into your hand. It's very painful."

The man nodded in appreciation. "I definitely don't want that. Thank you."

A noise from the Burnt Circle drew their attention, and the man glanced back, but the other machiners were still paying him no mind. He didn't call for them. Instead he returned his gaze to Arrow.

"It's you, isn't it?" the Kiskadee Man said. "You're the one I saw, the kid who helped me."

The man stepped forward as he pulled the golden disc out of his pocket. "Ingenious using this to stop the leak. Did you think of that, or was it your parents?" He glanced behind Arrow as though looking for more humans.

"It was me," Arrow said quietly.

The Kiskadee Man smiled slightly as he took another step toward Arrow. "You're very smart. And lucky for me you are. I've been trying to get back to this place for days but couldn't find it. It's the strangest thing. This whole area looks like a mountain from up there." He pointed to the sky. "We flew around and around but couldn't see where I'd crashed at all. I knew I hadn't crashed into a mountain. Then finally the signal from this disc pinged back to life. And we found the site. It probably turned on when you attached it to my plane. It needed the metal on metal to give it some juice." The man gave Arrow a big smile. "I owe you a big debt, little man. Thank you."

Arrow frowned at the disc like he wasn't sure how something so small could be a guide to such a large metal bullfrog.

"It's strange that you can't see the mountain range from down here," the man continued, gazing up at the canopy.

The Kiskadee Man stepped closer again, but Arrow kept an arm's length away. He studied the man's chiseled face.

"Of course, I owe you from before, too. You saved my life." The man lifted the bottom of the blue fabric on his leg, revealing the splotches of scabs and burnt pink skin. "It's healing up nicely. I can't walk as fast as I used to, and it still hurts, but I'm alive. Thanks to you. You just keep saving me. I think that makes you my hero."

Arrow smiled.

"Would you like to keep it?" the man asked, holding out the disc. "A gift to show my thanks."

Arrow shook his head.

"Don't worry. We've got others set up around here now.

We'll never lose this place again." He winked, a sparkle glinting from his eye.

Arrow gaped at him. Perhaps he was wondering whether the machiners' never losing the forest would be good or bad. I definitely was.

Finally the Kiskadee Man put the disc back into his pocket. "You must live here," the man said. "With your family? A community? Got any brothers and sisters?" He smiled big, showing off large white teeth.

Arrow frowned. He was no doubt remembering the questions from the herd and their reaction when they'd heard about me. Arrow didn't answer this time. Good boy.

"Ah well, I hope your family doesn't mind that you're helping me. They're lucky to have a boy like you."

A sliver of warm happiness slipped from Arrow's soles. This human was nicer than the herd.

"What's your name?" the man asked.

"Arrow," he said slowly.

"Arrow. That's a splendid name. A strong name." He glanced at my boy's arrow arm, then smiled. "An apropos name for you."

Arrow's happiness grew. He didn't know all these words, but the man hadn't judged Arrow because he was different, like the herd had.

"My name is Crankas. Bosono Crankas, but everyone just calls me Crankas."

"What does that mean?" Arrow asked, which brought a laugh from the man.

"Absolutely nothing." The man leaned in, but not too close. "You know something? Ever since you helped me, I've been dreaming of those fruits you left."

"The mangoes?"

The man nodded.

"And bananas? And acai berries?"

"Yes, yes." The man's eyes lit up. "Do you think you could show me where I could find some more? It was the best food I've ever eaten."

"I can get you more." Arrow straightened.

"Would you take me? I'd love to see where it is for myself."

Arrow peeked around Crankas at the other humans. They were still sorting through their boxes.

"Don't worry about them," Crankas said. "They'll be busy for hours."

Arrow nodded but still didn't move. He was being cautious after the actions of the herd. Good. "You won't harm the forest, will you?"

Crankas let out a small laugh. "Harm it? It's the most wonderful place I've ever seen. Why would I want to harm it?"

His words sounded sweet, and I hoped they were real. Arrow seemed to think they were. He smiled and said, "This way."

He led the man through the forest, pointing to the best

foods. Like he had with Petari, he warned about the caimans and the jaguars and the anacondas, and he showed the man where the birds liked to nest, where the grubs sifted the soil, and where the sloths hung around. He wanted the man to like him.

The Kiskadee Man was a patient and rapt student, slower than Petari but just as enthusiastic. He put more samples into his small clear tubes. And he carefully marked the trees along every trail with a line he drew quickly across the trunks. He put corresponding markings on a small rectangle he pulled from his pocket, which he told Arrow would make a "map."

Arrow didn't ask about the magic, but as they walked back toward the Burnt Circle, fruit and nuts in their arms, the boy asked, "Do you like the forest?"

"Very much," Crankas said. "I haven't seen something this beautiful since I met my wife." He winked at Arrow. The boy wouldn't know what the word meant, but he didn't let it stop him.

"Good," Arrow said, halting before they got too close to the clearing. "Then you want to protect it, right?"

Crankas nodded. "Absolutely. A place this wonderful should be protected."

A twig snap startled Arrow.

Wiser strode into their space. I had felt her footsteps coming and wished I could have warned Arrow.

"What have we here?"

Arrow stiffened. But this woman with her big stride and strong arms had a warm smile, and it drew the boy in.

"Wiser, this is Arrow. Arrow, this is Wiser. She's the wisest person I know, so she takes after her name, like you."

"Nice to meet you, Arrow," Wiser said. "Crankas told me you saved his life. That's pretty incredible, and I'm very glad you did. I suppose a thank-you is in order."

Arrow swallowed but found his voice. He was getting more used to humans. "He needed help."

"That he did." Wiser's eyes had a twinkle to them.

"And he just helped me again," Crankas said. "Look at all this food. Wait until you eat it. Best you've ever tasted."

"Wow," Wiser said. "Fantastic."

"He's also been showing me where things are around here. Look." Crankas showed her his map and they shared a small smile, for what I couldn't guess.

"You're handy to have around," Wiser said. "I could use a kid like you on my team. You're more useful than those two put together." She smiled slyly, nodding at Fratos and Mora in the Burnt Circle.

"I know every inch of the forest," Arrow said.

The woman laughed. "Then you're the man who should be king around here."

"Wiser's in charge of the other folks at the camp," Crankas said.

"Not you?" Arrow asked.

"Nope," he said. "I'm here for the forest, and they're here to help. Wonderful, huh?"

Arrow nodded. That did sound promising.

"I know you're shy, but the lads are decent, and they'd love some of this fruit you've brought back. Mind sharing?" Wiser asked.

Arrow looked over her shoulder and noticed for the first time that they were being watched. The two men had gathered at the edge of the Burnt Circle and were patiently waiting. I didn't like this, but I couldn't read any bad feelings around them.

Arrow's emotions twitched from nervousness to excitement, but I knew he was comparing this encounter to when he'd first met Petari's brother. This time seemed more favorable. No one was angry with him; no one was shouting. No one was forcing him. And perhaps that's why he allowed them to lead him into their camp.

"Fratos," Wiser announced, pointing at the thick man. "Mora," she said toward the tall man. "Arrow." She nodded to the boy, and the two men smiled.

These humans were definitely different from the younger herd. No one stared at his arrow arm or his bare feet. They smiled big and laughed loud, showed him their tools and the metal bullfrog. They treated Arrow like he was one of them, like he belonged. Happiness radiated from the boy's every step, and I could understand why. They made him feel comfortable, wanted, special. All the things Arrow had never gotten from another human. All the things he felt he had lost because he had been abandoned.

I worried that he was starting to like the machiners too much. We had a mission. We wanted their help. But we still needed to hide the forest once the Anima was back. We had to leave them out.

As if he knew my worries, Arrow asked, "How do you make the magic?"

"Magic?" Crankas asked.

"I know you have it. I saw the glowing domes. I need to know how to get more."

"Oh, that. The magic." The man chuckled, and I wondered what was funny. "Yes, we'll get lots of magic in here."

He winked at Arrow, and the boy beamed.

"Actually," Crankas said, "you can help me with that. When I crashed here before and you rescued me, I discovered something so beautiful on the bottom of my shoe when I got home." Crankas narrowed his eyes above a broad smile. "Something in the soil. It sparkled like stars."

He reached into a pocket and pulled out a small clear container that looked as though it held some soil. Holding it up to the light, he moved it back and forth so that pieces of the soil glinted in the sunlight.

"You see that in the bag?" Crankas asked, glancing between his clear bag and Arrow. "You see the shine?"

Arrow nodded, a thrill twirling outward from him. "That's the Shimmer."

"The Shimmer?"

"Yeah. That's what I call it."

"The Shimmer," Crankas said again, rubbing the bag between his fingers. "Is there a lot of it in the forest?"

Arrow shrugged. "There's some, but most of it's in Shimmer Cave. I go there when I need to think sometimes."

Crankas smiled. "It sounds beautiful. I'd love to see it. Can you show me?"

Arrow glanced at the ground. Cool uncertainty dripped from his toes. "I need to get the magic," he said finally. Good boy.

"Oh, Arrow, that Shimmer of yours is going to give you all the magic you want."

Arrow narrowed his eyes. "The Shimmer makes the magic?"

Was that true? The Forest Dwellers hadn't pulled Anima from the Shimmer. Was that how the magic worked in the Stilts?

"Yes," Crankas said. "That Shimmer will give us *every-thing* we want. Let's go see it."

Arrow beamed. All his uncertainty was gone now; only joy soaked the earth beneath him.

I felt it too, but I was still apprehensive, the memories of the Imposters not letting me trust this human yet. Could it really be this easy?

"Let's go," Arrow said, then glanced at the man's injured leg. "It's far to walk, though."

"Then why don't we take my trike? I think you'll like it."

Crankas walked Arrow to some sort of vehicle, but it looked different from the vehicles the Imposters had. This one sat on what appeared to be two rows of balls, smaller at the front and larger at the back. Crankas sat on one side of a chair that stretched the length of the larger row and called Arrow to sit beside him. Then he held on to an arm in front that connected to the smaller row. After his fingers pressed into the arm, the trike roared to life and took off faster than jaguars could run.

"Woooooooo," Arrow screamed as the trike rushed between the trunks.

With a twist of the man's wrist, the trike leaned one way, then another, allowing it to quickly turn around the trees.

Arrow wasn't connected to the earth or forest so I couldn't feel his emotions, but a bird quickly showed him to me. Sitting on the trike, Arrow raised his arms high, grinning widely as wind rushed through his hair. He was probably going faster than he'd ever gone in his life, faster even than when he swooped along the lianas. Even I could feel the speed, as the trike kicked up the top layers of the soil, sending grubs spinning out of their homes.

He almost forgot to point out the path, and when they got close to the cave, Arrow had to shout, "It's there!" to make the man stop.

"That was amazing," he said, his hair a stiff cloud behind his head.

Crankas smiled, but after Arrow led the way off the path, into the cave's entrance and through to the Shimmer, he said, "No, Arrow. This is the most amazing thing of all."

He turned to the boy, that unsettling twinkle in his eye again. "We are going to do wonderful things here, you and I. Wonderful things."

"We're going to save the forest," Arrow said.

"Oh yes," Crankas said. "We're going to make this forest the most precious place on earth."

To me, it always had been.

SOIL IN THE WEST TURNED DRY, AND THE LEAVES ON A
CACAO TREE TURNED FROM GREEN TO BROWN. THE RED PODS
HANGING BETWEEN THE BRANCHES SHRUNK UNTIL THEY WERE
BARELY BUDS, LEAVING THE BATS AND MONKEYS HUNGRY.

That night, as he and Curly ate by my trunk, Arrow
could not wipe the smile from his face. He also could
not stop talking.

"The bullfrog is called a 'helicopter'. It was amazing. It's
much bigger up close. There were so many dials and knobs
and buttons. They all do different things. The humans knew
so much about it. And the woman, Wiser, she smelled nice.
Like flowers. They're all so big, so much bigger than Storma
and Luco. The herd thinks they're so much better than me,
but the humans in the Burnt Circle are so much better than

them. And that trike. It was incredible! I felt like I was riding on the backs of a thousand jaguars. Well, maybe not a thousand, but a lot of them. I could go—"

"Arrow . . . ," I said.

He paused. "What?"

"Take a breath."

He giggled, and Curly joined in.

"They're really nice, Guardian. They're not like the herd in the village at all. They have the magic, and they're going to help us get it too. You heard Crankas, didn't you?"

"Yes, Arrow, I heard. I just . . ."

"Guardian?" Arrow wiped mango juice from his chin.

I paused. How could I explain my fear to him after everything we had seen? "I want to trust, but the Imposters—"

Arrow sighed, long and loud. "You keep talking about them, but you saw those things glow. Crankas said he'd get us all the magic we want. He's going to protect the forest."

"I know they look promising, but we still have a lot to learn about these humans, Arrow. We must not completely trust them yet. You thought the herd was good, but they let you down."

The hurt refreshed in him, seeping into my bark. "They're different. They don't have the magic. They don't care about the forest. And they don't want to help us."

The boy pushed his toes against my trunk. "You're not

giving them a chance. Crankas came here by accident, but he came back because he loves it. What's wrong with that? I don't understand why you hate them so much."

I stilled my leaves. "I don't hate them, Arrow, but there are things you don't understand."

"Then tell me." He got to his feet. "You keep saying humans are bad because the Imposters were bad. Then tell me what they did."

"Arrow . . ."

"Please, Guardian. I'm not a baby anymore," Arrow said.

I could tell he wasn't going to stop asking. And perhaps he was right, perhaps I had protected him long enough. Perhaps it was time for him to know the whole truth.

"All right," I began, as Arrow tapped his foot impatiently. "The story I will tell you happened when there used to be many humans living in the forest. This was when the forest was much bigger than it is today. Much, much bigger. It spanned land from ocean to ocean—"

"What's an ocean?"

"Hmmm. I have left gaps in your education."

Arrow crossed his arms. "See?"

I shook my leaves at the boy. "An ocean is like a forest but made of water."

"Like the river?"

"Bigger. Much bigger. And as blue as the sky. Filled with the most amazing creatures, some so small, they could snuggle between your fingers. Others so big, they could block the mouth of the great waterfall."

Arrow's eyes grew as wide as a coconut, as he sank back down to sit. "So what happened?"

"Outside, in other lands, humans made machines that would help them do things they couldn't."

"Like the metal bird and bullfrog help them fly?"

"Yes, those are machines," I said. "And they brought machines here to help them cut and slice and dig deeper and faster than they could on their own."

Arrow jumped back up. "To dig deep for the magic?"

"No, the Imposters did not believe in the Anima. Those machines were created with good in mind, but good ideas can be easily corrupted."

Arrow began to pace around my trunk, his fingertips running over the bumps in the bark. Curly swung from branch to branch behind him.

"So these machines did bad things?" the boy asked, his voice low.

"Machines can only do what humans tell them," I said. "The machines made it easier for the humans to get more of what they wanted with less work and in less time. This might sound nice."

"It does!"

"But when something is easy, humans get used to wanting

more. Then more. Then more. But for more, there is always an end."

Arrow stopped. "So what did the machines do?"

"They harvested land. They cut down trees. They tore up the earth."

His pulse quickened, but his frown stayed firmly in place. "I don't understand."

This was the part I had been dreading. How could I make him know without upsetting him? But I couldn't hold back his curiosity any longer. And knowledge of the past was necessary to make sure it didn't happen again.

"I can show you, if you'd like, but only if you want to." I didn't want him to see horrors in his young life, but he had to know what we were facing.

He thought, then said, "You'll have to use some of the Anima again."

He was right, but . . . "This is important. I should've shown you the forest's history long ago. Even if the curtain deteriorates faster, you should see what happened for yourself."

Trepidation tilled the soil beneath him. "Okay."

"Grab my root."

He followed my instructions, and I wriggled my roots to loosen the soil. Slowly I raised the root to meet his palm.

"Now close your eyes."

His body stiffened as soon as the dream images came, but he quickly relaxed. I showed him the good images first, ones sent by birds who had flown around the world. Moving pictures of blue, then yellow, then green, then blue—oceans and lands and more oceans. Arrow gasped, joy bubbling from his heart, then let out a small yip when he saw the rainforest.

It loomed large, a giant blanket of green that covered the land as far as the bird's eye could see. A swath cut only where the river flowed. Millions of trees, patches swaying as wind barreled over their heads.

"It's so big," he whispered.

"Yes, much bigger than it is now."

Thousands of birds had sent images of the rainforest, and Arrow was treated to a handful of the best ones. All the different shades of green. All the different parts of growth. All the life.

Then came the Imposters.

Machines cut away at the edges. Wooded forest turned to flat farmland. Crop after crop turned the soil dry. Machines cut away more, deep ridges into the thicket.

In other parts, machines tore down trees to make way for cattle ranches, paved roads, giant pipes. The land the Imposters stole was never enough, so the machines scraped away more.

Arrow shuddered, hugged his knees, and pressed his back against my bark. But he didn't let go of the root.

Images collected for rings and rings flitted through his mind, each one showing a rapidly shrinking forest. His forest. Disappearing.

"Humans did this? They commanded the machines?"

"Yes. But not all humans. The Forest Dwellers saw what was happening. They understood the danger. They tried to stop it."

"What happened to them?"

"The Imposters drove them out."

Arrow shifted on the soil. "So the Imposters you've talked about . . ."

"They are the humans with the machines. They came from the cities. They told of nice things, help and prosperity that they were bringing. But they were not truthful. They pushed the Forest Dwellers out of their homes. It took a long time, many rings. The Forest Dwellers fought to stay, to protect their home, the forest. Even some of the humans from the outside fought to protect the forest too. They would come from all over the world. They would discover our home and all the wonders inside, and they knew immediately its importance, for them as well as us."

"But they didn't help either?"

"They tried, but they were battling the Imposters, with their bigger machines and bigger greed. And while I can't see too far beyond the borders of the forest, I heard talk of the land outside drying up. Less rain, less water, more desert.

When good land was in a shortage there, even the humans who wanted to protect the forest couldn't stop the Imposters. We were their last place to conquer. Eventually the Forest Dwellers were forced out, and we were left on our own. I had to do something. I had to protect us. I used all the magic I could muster from the earth, and I hid as large a part of the forest as I could."

Arrow sucked in a breath. "So that's why you put up the curtain."

"Yes. I put it around the part of the forest that didn't contain any humans so I could protect what was inside."

Arrow gulped.

"Now you see why it was so important then and is still so important now. Those Imposters talked to the Forest Dwellers with tongues as sweet as berries, but underneath, they were as poisonous as the dart frog. These humans now spill sweetness upon you, but for how long? How can we know for sure that they won't turn and destroy us, just like the Imposters tried to do?"

Tears sprang to Arrow's eyes, and he rubbed them away with his hand and the end of his arrow arm.

"We can't know for sure, but they're our only hope!" The words rushed out of the boy's mouth, riding on a harried breath. "I can't fix the magic by myself. I can't save you. I can't save the forest. So they have to. Don't you see?"

Ah, that was what had kept his fire of faith in them

burning. I hadn't seen. Even knowing his emotions, I hadn't truly understood that he was scared he would fail again. That he would let me and the forest down. That he wouldn't be able to save us.

"Arrow, I—"

"I've been trying for so long to dig deep, like you said, but nothing has worked. It's because I can't do it. My family abandoned me when I was a baby because they knew I couldn't do anything."

"Arrow, that's not—"

"It is true. The other humans are bigger and stronger, and they . . ." He looked at his pointed arm. "They're better."

I didn't like these words coming out of the boy. Still such a small boy. A small boy who didn't know his own power, and no matter how much I told him he could access the Anima just like the Forest Dwellers had done, he would not believe me.

"Arrow! You are every bit—"

He hugged my base, his arms so small against the bark. "I *am* going to mend the Anima and save you," he said. "But I can't do it the way you think I can. They've already got the magic working. I just have to make them share it with you. They won't be like the Imposters. You'll see."

Then he stepped away. He turned and ran.

"Arrow. Arrow!"

He ignored my shouts, running toward the kapok tree

on legs fueled with hope and fear. He scaled the tree quickly, swung his belt over the liana, and sped off toward the Burnt Circle.

"ARROW!"

But it was too late. He was too far to hear me now.

What had I done? I had tried to warn him, tried to show him. But instead I had pushed him away.

The sun was dying in the sky, and darkness was falling. This wasn't a good time for a boy to be out on his own.

And yet he was.

So he could save me.

Oh, Arrow.

What had I done?

TWO EPIPHYTES ON THE OLD WIMBA TREE NEAR THE
ABANDONED VILLAGE SHRIVELED UP AND FELL TO THE GROUND.
THEN TWO MORE. THEN TWO MORE. THEN . . .

A rrow spent the night curled into a corner of the
Shimmer Cave. I felt the thump of his pulse on the
ground like an echo of regret. I wished he would
come back. Curly shrieked in my branches and slapped my
bark. She wasn't happy he had left either.

The whine of the trike machine startled the boy awake
the next morning, but by the time he had scrambled outside,
it was heading back to the Burnt Circle.

Arrow started to head their way, but when his stomach
growled, he went north instead. I hoped he would come

home to me, but he stayed away. He didn't even get close enough to be able to hear me. Two liana slides, and he was in the part of the forest that had the most variety of foods. It was near the Crooked Rock, near where he had first met Petari, and I wondered if he was thinking of her. If he was, he didn't show it. Just a twinge of cold dripping into the earth gave away any stray hurt he was feeling. He had given himself a mission, and he was determined to do it.

First he went to the soursop tree, loaded up his bent arrow arm with the ripest fruit, and then placed it on the rock for safekeeping. Next he pulled acai berries from the palm, then shimmied up a banana tree, then over to the passion fruit vines. Before long, he had more fruit than he could carry, so his next trip was to a palla tree to harvest palm fronds.

Sitting cross-legged on the forest floor, he hitched the palm fronds under his arm as his fingers and toes weaved the ends together. Until he heard the *SNAP* and froze.

He curled smaller, his butt digging into the leaves and soil below him.

I had felt the steps coming his way, but his excitement, his need, had made him distracted. Fear thumped through his heart as he scoured the forest. He was usually more careful, more alert. Now his darting eyes told me he was wondering what had broken the twig. Monkey? Jaguar? Caiman?

And was it too late for him to hide?

He sniffed the air, then frowned. Dropping his woven

palm fronds, he stood and ran quickly to the intruder.

"What are you doing here?" he asked loudly when Petari was in sight.

The girl screamed and leaped into the air. Turning, she saw Arrow, his arms crossed tightly over his chest, his eyes boring into hers.

"You scared me to death," she said.

Arrow didn't understand what that meant, but he didn't question it. "You shouldn't be here."

"I was looking for you. How'd you know I was here, anyway? I know the twig made a noise, but I was silent after that. I've been practicing walking like you do, and I'm getting brill. There's no way you heard me."

"I didn't hear you. I smelled you."

"Smelled me?" Petari's toes twisted in the soil as she tried to see if she could smell herself too. "I don't smell. I just cleaned by the side of the river."

"Exactly," Arrow said. "I can smell the algae that builds up on the water between the lilies. It's probably stuck in your hair."

"Eww!" A stream of water pummeled the earth by Petari's feet as she wrung out her long hair. "I don't want that stuff living on me."

Arrow sighed. "I don't have time for this. Go back to your herd, Petari. And leave the forest for good."

He headed back to the hammock he was making. But the

girl wouldn't be stopped that easily. She hurried after him.

"Wait, that's why I came to see you. I'm really sorry about what happened. They shouldn't have been like that to you. I'll talk to them. I'll make it right."

Arrow's heart ticked up at her words, but he stayed silent and didn't look at Petari. He picked up his carrying hammock, then pulled the final set of fronds into a knot with his fingers and teeth.

"I wish you'd come back," Petari continued, her voice small.

Arrow placed his pile of fruit in the hammock, testing the strength after each load. "I've got things to do."

"Come on," Petari said. "We were having fun before. And I want to help fix the magic."

That stopped Arrow. He glanced at her.

"I know the Stilts are locked down," she said quickly, before he could stop listening, "but we'll find a way in somehow. We'll find the magic together."

Arrow's eyes stayed locked on hers for a breath, two, and I thought perhaps he was going to give her another chance. But he looked away, added one more mango to his hammock, then slung it over his shoulder. "I told you, I've got things to do."

Stubborn. This quality had served him well when he was younger, learning to walk, but sometimes I wished he'd outgrow it. I didn't trust the herd either, yet I had to admit there was something different about Petari.

"That's a lot of food in that bag. I thought you only picked enough for one meal. Is it for us?"

"In the carrying hammock? No."

"Yeah, the bag. Who's it for, then?"

Arrow glanced in the direction of the Burnt Circle. The sun was getting higher, and the stomachs of the machiners would be rolling by now. "It's no—"

The rest of his words were sliced up by a *ROAR* that ripped through the forest.

"What was that?" Petari's eyes were as wide as her mouth as she gazed past the tops of the trees.

*THRUM.*

*THRUM.*

*THRUM.*

More metal bullfrogs were descending on the forest, this time coming from the north instead of the south.

"Go back to the village," Arrow shouted over the noise.

"I'm not going anywhere," Petari said. "Those are copters. And they're close."

Arrow raised his eyes as another screamed overhead.

"You knew they were coming, didn't you?" she asked.

"I have to go," he shouted, and took off, his hammock of fruit slung over his shoulder.

"You're not leaving me behind!"

Petari followed. She didn't know this part of the forest at all, and wasn't as careful as Arrow, but she had gotten quicker and kept up with the boy. Crafting a strong vine into a harness like Arrow's, she followed him down the liana, and soon they could see the Burnt Circle.

The boxes and green roof had been moved to the side with the metal bullfrog, leaving space for more to land. Crankas and the other machiners stood by the side of the clearing, looking up.

Three more massive metal bullfrogs hovered above the trees.

One was descending.

THE PINK PETALS FROM THREE BOBINSANA SHRUBS
ON THE RIVERBANK DROPPED TO THE GROUND, FOLLOWED BY
THE SHRUBS THEMSELVES. THEY TOPPLED INTO THE WATER THEN
FLOATED DOWN TO THE WATERFALL.

As the bullfrog got closer, the ash that still lay on the ground sprang up to meet it. Dust swirled around, hazing the air. Arrow turned his back against it and grabbed Petari's arm to motion for her to do the same. He pulled her behind a trunk, shielding his eyes.

"You should've gone back," he shouted.

"I want to see." She was as stubborn as he, but I understood. I, too, wanted to know what they were doing.

Arrow pursed his lips, then led her to a tree on the far side of the Burnt Circle. It was the same tree where he had sat and watched Crankas all those moons ago, where the thick branches and leaves would keep them both protected. At the base of the trunk, he hung his bag on a low branch, then squatted so she could climb onto his shoulder, but Petari batted him away.

"I can reach."

"Fine," he said, and pulled himself up.

As the bullfrog lowered, Arrow and Petari climbed higher and higher, until Arrow motioned for her to squat on a thick branch and hold tight to the trunk. He perched next to her, his elbow crooked around an upward tree limb.

From their spot, they were hidden but had a view of the Burnt Circle through the branches and leaves. No animals or birds sat near them; all had fled at the sounds of the flying machines.

The massive bullfrog descended slowly, scattering more ash and dirt when it landed with a *THWOMP* in the clearing. On its side was the same picture of the head of the stinkbird that had been on Crankas's shirt when he had crashed here.

"Fenix!" Petari shouted over the noise.

"What?"

"Fenix, that symbol. They make all the power and water and everything for the Stilts."

Arrow turned back to the symbol as that section of the metal bullfrog's rigid skin opened from the top and flapped to the ground. It made an incline that connected the earth to the cavity within its belly. Another section at the back did the same, and humans trailed down them into the Burnt Circle.

They were all adults, like Crankas and the others, some female, some male. All looked big, strong, quick.

Shouts could be heard over the *THRUM, THRUM, THRUM* of the metal bullfrogs still in the air, but the arms of the one on the ground had stopped turning.

"What are they doing?" Petari whispered.

"Shh," Arrow replied.

"They can't hear me."

He glared at her, then turned back to the clearing. *CLANG*s and *BANG*s came from within the bullfrog.

Wiser ran to the end of the machine's inclined skin, peering inside. She beckoned to Mora and Fratos, who ran up too. Crankas stayed back, but his eyes watched every movement.

Then there was another *ROAR*, this time from inside the bullfrog's belly. The noise filled the Burnt Circle, and Arrow and Petari leaned forward for a better look.

A machine with four large wheels and a flat back rolled onto the inclined skin at the bullfrog's backside. Claws stuck out at the four corners, and cases were stacked on top. The machine rolled down the rear section of skin, over to the machiners' green roof, and stopped.

Petari gasped. "I've seen those in the Barbs."

"What is it?" Arrow whispered.

"It's a carrier. They're really strong and can carry stuff a far distance."

"What's it doing here?"

Petari frowned. "About to make trouble, I'd guess."

Arrow glared at her. "You sound like the Guardian."

"I do?" She grinned. "I like that."

I did too.

Arrow shook his head. "Ssshhh."

"You were talking too!"

Arrow waved her words off and drew his attention back to the Burnt Circle. The claws on the side of the carrier were extending, long tubes that thrust their snapping ends into the air. They grabbed the boxes the machine was carrying, pulled them down, and laid them gently on the ground under the green roof.

"How does it know what to do?" Arrow asked.

Petari pointed to Mora, who had placed some kind of stiff vine on his head. "He's giving it instructions."

Another *ROAR* came from the bullfrog's belly, and a second carrier rolled out laden with boxes. While this one was unloaded, the first carrier returned to the flying machine's cavity and emerged minutes later with more boxes.

Arrow and Petari glanced at each other, eyes wide.

A few breaths later, the arms atop the metal bullfrog started spinning. Dust rose, and Arrow grabbed Petari to keep her on the branch. The new humans in the Burnt Circle jumped back into the bullfrog, but two emerged again, this time with bags on their backs. Then the bullfrog rose, higher and higher, as the new humans clasped hands and arms with Crankas, Wiser, and the others.

"Do you know them?" Petari asked. "Are they your group?"

"I told you I don't have a group." Arrow sounded exasperated, but there was a hesitancy to his voice.

"Okay, fine. But you knew they were here, didn't you?"

"I only—"

He didn't finish his sentence. The rising bullfrog flew north, but the *THRUM, THRUM, THRUM* of the others got closer. Another was descending.

More dust and ash flew up as this metal bullfrog touched down. Just like the first, a section of its skin opened on its side and its rear, revealing the inside of its belly. More humans stepped out, men and women, shielding their eyes. More shouts. More *CLANG*s and *BANG*s. More *SCREECH*es. Then another box-laden carrier rolled out from the rear of the helicopter. Just like before, it was joined by another. They carried boxes of all different sizes. Flat, black cases and tall gray containers.

Again, the humans ran around, some getting back into

the bullfrog's belly and a few coming out with bags of their own. Once its skin was closed up, the bullfrog rose again, taking off for the north, as the final metal flyer took its place on the ground.

Arrow and Petari held on tight as the third one came down. It was larger than the first two, and the wind pushing out from its spinning arms rocked all the branches around the clearing.

After the side and rear opened, a new carrier emerged, but it was different. Instead of wheels it had six thin legs that sprouted from a flat square. A woman walked next to it, speaking into the stiff vine on her head. The machine looked like a strange giant beetle.

"I haven't seen one like that before," Petari said.

Arrow's eyes flicked in her direction, then back to the clearing below.

The woman stopped at the edge of the inclined strip of the bullfrog's skin, but this beetle machine kept going until it was under the green roof. It folded itself up as another large beetle machine strode out, then a rolling carrier unloading more boxes.

Finally the bullfrog rose again, above the tops of the trees, then took off north in the path of the rest of its flock.

The dust and ash began to settle. The echo of the spinning arms died out in the forest, but there was still plenty of noise. The Burnt Circle was a bustle of human chatter, boxes shoved into new homes, carriers squeaking as they rolled across the dirt.

"Did you know they were coming?" Petari whispered, turning to face Arrow.

"No, but . . ." Arrow's narrowed eyes stayed on the carriers below.

"But what?" Petari nudged him.

"Maybe those are the things that will help them save the forest."

Petari scrunched up her nose like she'd just smelled another stink bug. "What do you mean?"

"See that man with the sky-colored shirt?" Arrow pointed to Crankas. "He loves the forest just like me. He's going to help me save it."

"He said that?" Petari frowned.

Arrow ignored her expression and smiled. "Yep. And it looks like they're about to get started."

Petari scowled at the machiners below, moving boxes and bags, talking, laughing, and controlling those strange rolling and walking machines. She shook her head.

"I don't know, Arrow. This doesn't look too good to me."

"Trust me, it's good. Crankas, that's the man's name, he's already fixed the magic here. I've seen it. It's not as beautiful as the Guardian's, but it's still magic."

"I thought you lived alone in the forest." Confusion mixed with hurt radiated from Petari.

"I do." Arrow shifted so he faced the girl. "Crankas fell from the sky moons ago, and I saved his life. Now he's come back, and he's going to protect the forest."

"And you believe that?"

"I saw the magic, Petari. And the man promised. Not all humans lie like you and your group."

"Hey, I . . . ," Petari began, but then closed her mouth, perhaps not knowing how to respond. They fell into silence again, watching the activity below. Then Petari narrowed her eyes. "Remember I said that symbol on the side of the copters was for Fenix?"

"Yes."

"Fenix is a big company. Machines like that are used in the Barbs sometimes. I don't trust them."

"Those things are machines?" Arrow's ears pricked up at the word. His face clouded over, and I was sure he was thinking about the Imposters.

"Yeah, and they do whatever the people want them to do, which isn't always nice. Fenix is from the Stilts, and people in the Stilts don't help other people."

"Luco said some humans in the Stilts helped you."

Petari pressed her lips together. "That's different."

"How?"

"It just is."

The two studied each other. Finally Petari said, "Just don't trust those people, okay?"

236

Arrow glanced down for a breath, then back at the girl. "That's what the Guardian said about you."

"I . . ." Petari huffed. "Hey, I thought the Guardian liked me."

Hurt radiated from her, sparking and erratic.

"She does," Arrow said. "Well, did, until Curly was hurt."

"I'm so sorry, Arrow. I really am. I like Curly, even if she doesn't like me." Petari twisted her arms around her middle and pulled in tight. "I just . . . I want you to be careful, that's all."

Arrow sighed. "I know what I'm doing. I know you and your group think I'm strange and that I don't know the things you do—"

"No—" Petari began, but Arrow didn't let her finish.

"But I don't throw things on the ground so animals can get hurt. And I'm not mean to other humans." He nodded toward Crankas and the other machiners. "You think they're bad, but it's you that's bad, Petari. You and all your horrible group. Crankas wants to help me and the forest. He and his group want to make things better here. And I'm going to let them. I don't have another choice."

"Arrow . . . ," Petari began, thick waves of hurt washing around her. But the boy didn't listen. He started to climb down the tree, without looking her way.

"Go back to the village, Petari," he said. "I've got to save the forest."

Sadness etched into the bark where he touched, but he pushed it down and continued on.

I felt sadness for the boy too. Petari had been his first human friend, but like the Imposters had done to me, the children in the village had let him down.

It's difficult to soften a heart that's hardened from hurt.

AS A CORAL SNAKE SLITHERED ACROSS ONE OF THE BUTTRESS
ROOTS OF THE GIANT FICUS TO THE EAST, THE ROOT GREW DRY,
SHATTERED, AND DISSOLVED INTO THE GROUND. THE SNAKE
CARRIED ON, BUT THE FICUS STRUGGLED TO BREATHE.

When he got to the ground, Arrow retrieved his bag of fruit, then peered at the machiners' camp, all the humans as busy as flies around fresh dung. Boxes and bags were being opened, items displayed on tables, pieces clamped onto other pieces.

There were many more humans now, all much taller than the boy, and for a few breaths, nervousness radiated all around him. He inhaled deeply, gazed around for Crankas and Wiser, then approached them quietly.

"Two to three days tops," Wiser was telling Crankas

when my dragonfly got close. "We should get more light out that way, then we can start more shifts."

"Splendid," Crankas replied. "We'll—"

A hush grew over the other machiners. They froze in place, only the carrier continuing its journey. All eyes were on the skinny boy with bare feet and a palm-woven bag of fruit.

Suddenly the new machiners dropped their boxes. They grabbed shiny black metal tubes, like the one Wiser carried on her back. The machiners pointed the tubes at Arrow, and I finally recognized what they were. The Imposters had called them guns. They had pointed them at animals in the forest and at some Forest Dwellers. Sometimes the guns had made a *BANG* and whatever was before them had fallen to the ground, dead.

I feared for Arrow now more than ever before. He hadn't seen them in the images I'd given him of the Imposters. He didn't know the danger he was in.

But Petari knew. She had begun to climb down the tree after Arrow, but now terror soaked into the branch she perched on.

"Stay back," a man wearing gray clothes shouted.

"Stop!" cried a woman with a long tail of hair swinging from the top of her head.

"Whoa!" Crankas stepped in front of Arrow, who had frozen too. He had always liked shiny things, but he could tell from the way these humans were pointing the guns at him that something was wrong.

The machiners glanced from Arrow to Crankas, but they didn't lower the guns. Then Wiser laughed loudly.

"Are you guys scared of a little kid?" Her eyes rolled in her head. "Put your weapons away before you damage the equipment. And don't drop those boxes."

She waved Arrow forward. Pulse thumping wildly on the soil, the boy walked closer to Wiser, holding his bag toward her.

"What a haul!" She turned to Mora. "Put these out of the way, will you?"

Mora took the bag, patting Arrow on the shoulder. "You rock, kid."

Arrow smiled, even though I imagine he had no idea why he was like a rock. I certainly didn't.

"Look at all of this," Crankas said, strolling between Arrow and the machiners, who were once again as busy as flies, although they kept their eyes on the boy as well. "State-of-the-art tech, Arrow. All of the best that money can buy. We'll have everything up and running soon."

Arrow nodded, despite the uncertainty that swirled around him. He didn't understand money, or art, or tech. But the idea of things happening soon pleased him.

"You're using more of your magic for lights?" he asked.

Wiser glanced at Crankas, some message I couldn't translate hidden within her eyes.

Crankas nodded slightly, then turned to Arrow. "Yes, we're going to make the best magic right here. You wait and see."

"Can you show me how you get the magic?"

"We're a little busy right now," Wiser said. "Why don—"

"That's okay," Crankas said, sliding an arm around Arrow's shoulder. "I think the boy deserves a look. I'll show him."

Arrow's footsteps were lighter as he followed Crankas to one of the tables near their fabric huts. Joy swirled around him. He was finally going to see how they got the magic. *Perhaps I had been wrong about these humans. I had always known Arrow would save us, but I didn't think it would be this way.*

The table was covered with what looked like small black water lily pads, white bowls similar to ones the Forest Dwellers used to eat from, plus other small items of all different shapes that glinted in the morning rays.

Crankas picked up one of the bowls and one of the black lily pads. Holding up the pad, he said, "These panels connect to these domed lights with signals that go through the air."

"Like the one that helped you find us?"

"Well done, Arrow. You're a smart kid."

Arrow beamed, ready for more.

"The panels collect all the energy and send it to the domes so that they light up and will stay lit all through the night."

Arrow's eyes widened. "So you dig deep with the panel?"

As far as I knew, the Forest Dwellers hadn't used a panel, but could this have been what we were missing?

"No, no. We point it at the sun. Usually we can place them near the lights, but with all the trees here, we had to design something quite a bit taller. You see those poles next to the trees?" He gestured around the Burnt Circle, and Arrow noticed the poles for the first time. They were strapped high up onto the trunks of many trees, extending above the canopy and into the sky.

"Each one of those poles has a panel on the top," the man said, pride ringing in every word. "And they power the lights below."

Arrow frowned. "So where do you get the magic?"

Crankas laughed. "Well, it's not really magic, but I like to think that science is magical. The power comes from the sun. These panels take the sun's rays and transform them into electricity to power the lights."

The sun's rays. This was not how it worked. The humans were not harnessing the magic of the earth.

"But . . . But how . . ." Arrow couldn't get his mind or words around this information. "But that's not the real magic. That's not the *Anima*."

"Anima? What's that? Some sort of folklore magic? My boy, I told you, there's no real magic." The man leaned in close and narrowed his eyes. "Are there other people living here that you forgot to tell me about? Did they tell you this place has magic?"

"I . . . It's just . . ." Arrow swallowed. "You said you were going to save the forest."

"Of course I am!" Crankas raised his arms, like he was beckoning all the trees to come his way. "This forest is the reason I'm here. Of course I want to protect it. It's going to make me very rich."

My roots curled. The Imposters had used that word too.

"I don't understand." Arrow shifted from foot to foot. "How are you going to save it if you can't get the magic?"

"Oh, I've got big plans. Look here."

He pulled the small rectangle he had been making notes on from his pocket. Pressing it lightly, he tilted it toward an empty space on the tabletop, and a light shone down, illuminating a drawing like Petari's. Arrow's eyes widened. "That's the forest. Those are all the places I showed you." He traced his finger on the line that went from the Burnt Circle to the Shimmer Cave. More lines trailed to the pockets of food growing in the south part of the forest, a calm part of the river, and more. It also had the same squiggly lines Petari had written in her notebook, but Arrow couldn't read them.

"This is a map of everywhere you've taken me," Crankas said, squeezing Arrow's shoulder. "Without this map, I couldn't have gotten my plan underway so quickly. And I couldn't have made this map without you. I owe you a lot, young man."

Arrow smiled, but it wasn't big, and it wasn't pleasant. Something was bubbling within him. Something he didn't like.

"What does the map help you do?"

"It shows us what we have to do to make our dreams come true." He winked at Arrow. "The first step is that cave you showed me." He pointed at the Shimmer Cave on the map. "That place is a gold mine. Once we've got a clear path to that cave, we'll be able to harvest all the gems and get them back to the camp for export. I'll get a lot of money for what we pull out of that cave."

"Pull out of it?"

"Yes. Once we've broken it up and extracted the most precious pieces, I'll sell them in the city. People there won't be able to get enough of them. And they'll pay a lot."

Arrow's arms began to shake. "You're going to destroy the Shimmer Cave?"

"I know. It sounds bad. But it's not." Crankas turned Arrow away from the map and looked straight into the boy's eyes as though he were about to tell him something very important. "That money will be enough to bring in all the fertilizers and pesticides we need. We'll get rid of all those bugs and grubs on the trees so we can save them. I'll bet that's the problem you've been having with things dying.

Bugs will eat up a place like this fast, but we've got pesticides for that. And the fertilizers we use in the city will make an ordinary tomato grow to the size of a melon. Wait until you see how big your wonderful acai berries get then. They'll be as big as your head."

How I wished for more Anima. My biggest fears were coming true with every word he said.

"They're good the way they are now," Arrow said, worry streaming from him. "Their size is just enough."

The man didn't seem to hear. He had spent a lot of time formulating this plan of his and seemed to enjoy sharing its every detail. He pointed to another part of his map.

"We're going to need bumper crops of all the fruit. We'll plant more here. A whole area filled only with the most delicious fruit trees."

"But they like where they're growing now." Fear built up beneath Arrow's feet. Just as it built up within me. Arrow was trying to tell the man, to educate him about the forest, but Crankas wasn't listening.

"They're going to like this much better," he said. "The fertilizers and pesticides, remember? The trees won't need to fight off bugs. We'll do it for them."

He laughed again, louder. "While we're cleaning up this place, we'll start working on the second part of the plan."

He straightened his shoulders, growing taller. Arrow stiffened. "I'm going to build huge resorts with the best views and food around. We'll take out all those pesky reeds around the river, make it clearer so people can go swimming."

He can't. He can't!

"The reeds protect the soil." Arrow's voice got quieter with every word he uttered.

But it didn't matter. Crankas wasn't listening. He pointed at the circles on the map, then at the lines between them. "We'll build trails all through the forest so people can go hiking. We'll capture all the animals you've told us about. But don't worry, we won't hurt them. We'll build big cages . . . wait, that doesn't sound good. We'll build enclosed areas, but natural-looking. The animals won't know the difference. And best yet, they won't have to go hunting for their food; we'll give it to them so they'll stay nice and healthy. Don't want the people staying at the resort to see scraggly animals around, do we?"

Buildings. Roads. Cages. After everything I had done to protect our beautiful forest, this one human was going to destroy it.

Arrow's heart pounded, pounded, pounded. His hand pulled tight into a fist by his side.

"See that machine they're working on over there?" Crankas pointed at a group of the humans clamping items together. "That makes easy work of grinding up tree trunks once we've got them down."

Arrow glared at the man, a cold flood of confusion and despair rolling beneath him.

Crankas sighed, a contented smile on his face. "My dear Arrow, you have no idea what a treasure you've got here. I had read about places like this, seen them in old movies, but I didn't think they really existed anymore. And to think it was so close all the time, and I'd never even noticed."

How I wish he'd never noticed at all. Why did the magic have to fail me now?

Arrow was as stiff as a trunk. I wished I could rip my roots out of the ground and crash my full weight on top of that camp.

This was worse than I had imagined. This man was even more horrible than the Imposters. They had known they were destructive and hadn't cared. This man believed he was benefiting the forest, which would make him even harder to stop.

But how could they not see the damage this plan would cause? The animals needed to roam free, not be penned. The removal of the reeds by the river would change the delicate community of algae that feed the fish and plants. And hotels. Trails. Humans . . . Coming . . . Here . . . Where would they go? What would they destroy? Every part of the forest depended on the other parts. Kill one, and you kill more.

Arrow was silent. From the despair swimming around him, I knew he was too stunned to speak.

The man didn't notice, though. That's what you can always count on with arrogance—it doesn't see well.

Crankas clapped the boy's shoulder. "We've got a lot of work to do, you and me. We—"

A *ROAR* shook the Burnt Circle. All eyes darted in its direction, including Arrow's.

The images the dragonflies sent were blurred, but I could still understand why his fear had leaped.

Standing in the middle of the clearing was a shiny machine twice as tall as the biggest human. At its base were the six metal legs of the giant beetle. A tall tube had been built up high on the flat square of the machine's back. Arms sprouted from holes in the tube, each equipped with claws, clamps, knives, and more. In the center of the tube stood the human with the tail of hair flowing from the top of her head. She had a determined expression on her face.

The monster lifted its feet, six legs moving it forward, while the arms twisted and curled, slicing the air.

"Looks splendid, Oxsen," Crankas called.

The female inside the metal monster, Oxsen, waved.

"It'll look *splendid* when it's doing what it's supposed to," Wiser said from the other side of the Burnt Circle. She turned toward Oxsen and the machine. "Let's make sure everything's functioning properly."

Oxsen nodded, the focused expression back on her face. Her arms moved, although I couldn't see her hands behind the circular wall on the beetle's back.

The other machiners had stopped what they were doing and watched.

Arrow stepped forward to get a full view, curiosity and fear clouding the air above him.

The metal beetle's legs twitched, then lifted, front and back working in tandem. It scurried to the edge of the forest and stopped beside a tall palm tree.

Clawed arms wrapped around the middle of the trunk. Knived arms slashed the base. Legs dug into the ground, then pulled up.

In less than a breath, the palm was gone. Roots were dragged out of the soil.

Arrow gasped.

My roots shuddered.

The loss spread throughout the root network. Fungi retreated from the area. Communications were lost.

Crankas's hand tightened on the boy's shoulder. "Fantastic," he called to the monster.

Wiser raised her arm. "Don't congratulate her yet. There's more."

The metal beetle pulled the dying trunk to another machine on the far side of the Burnt Circle. A giant bucket had been built on the back of one of the wheeled carriers. The beetle hauled the trunk into the bucket, leaves flapping.

Fratos jumped onto a ledge on the side of the bucket machine. His fingers pressed against nodules; then another

*ROAR* reverberated around the Circle. The roar changed to a *CRUNCH*. The visible end of the palm shook violently as the trunk was pulled farther and farther inside, until it disappeared altogether. A few more breaths, and the crunch stopped. The man hit the nodules again. And the machiners slapped one another's hands in the air.

The palm was gone. Dead. Ground into dust before the soil had even settled.

"Unnh." The scream was strangled in Arrow's throat.

The root network twitched with the loss. My branches drooped.

"Excellent. Excellent!" Crankas shouted.

"That was quick, but we need them quicker," Wiser said. "We've got a lot to tear out in a short time. Hurry up and finish. I want everything ready to begin clearing in the morning."

A smile broadened across Crankas's face as he turned back to Arrow.

The boy, my boy, had slumped, gazing under a furrowed brow at the bucket that now held the ashes of the dead palm.

Perhaps the man noticed the color drained from the boy's face, because he said, "Don't worry, the forest won't miss a few trees."

But Arrow knew it would. I would.

I did.

Deep within the root network, the loss was felt. The palm

hadn't even had time to pass along its nutrients and knowledge to be used by others. A hole had been created. A useless hole for no purpose at all. My roots twitched with anger.

"We've got to clear away the stuff we don't need," Crankas said. "But soon we'll have roads all over the forest, and we'll be able to work much faster to save it then." His voice was light, joyful, excited, while anger and fear seeped from Arrow.

"Okay." Crankas slapped his hands together. "Let's go over the map again. I want you to make sure I'm not missing anything."

Arrow groaned. The guttural noise rose up from his heart and got stuck deep within his throat. I knew he wanted to scream, shout, but his fear was holding him back. He'd seen predators before, but never something that could eat an entire tree in one breath.

Crankas didn't understand. Didn't listen. "You hungry? We can get some food first. Come on. We've got some protein bars you'll love."

Arrow shook his head. He opened his mouth, but nothing came out.

I wished I could help him, offer him comfort, but even if Arrow could've heard me at the Burnt Circle, all the comfort I had had drained away.

Arrow no doubt wanted to tell this Crankas that his map should be burned like his plane was, that his plans stank more than a pile of capybara dung. But this was new for Arrow.

The introduction he had had to humans being dishonest and unkind was nothing compared to this. And worse, the man still treated Arrow like a treasured friend. Confusion wove within the thick fear around the boy's head.

Finally he stepped out of it.

"Uhhnn . . ." He held his belly. What was wrong? Worry snaked through my leaves. "I need to get some anise. My tummy's bad."

Crankas's eyes grew wide with concern. "Oh no. Let me get you some medicine. It'll clean you right up."

He began to walk toward another table of supplies, but Arrow said, "No. The anise is good. There's some close by. Ahhh."

He held his belly tighter and scrunched up his face as he had done many times when he had pain. But there wasn't pain in his energy, only a tiny sliver of hope. "I won't be long."

"Okay. Hurry back," Crankas said.

Arrow nodded, then scurried for the tree line. He didn't stop when he passed the first trunk. He didn't even stop when he passed the anise bush. He ran and ran, tears streaming down his face.

Until he heard the *BANG*.

THE PETALS ON AN ANISE BUSH NEAR THE BURNT
CIRCLE STRUGGLED TO HOLD ON. IT WASN'T THEIR TIME TO GO,
BUT THEIR CONNECTION WAS WEAK. ONE BREATH OF WIND,
AND THE PETALS WERE BLOWN AWAY.

The noise made Arrow freeze and tore the birds from their trees.

It was a noise Arrow wouldn't know, but I remembered it well. It had echoed around the forest many, many rings ago, when the Imposters lived under our leaves. Before I hid us away. I hated to hear it again.

The bang was followed by shouts from the machiners. Then a shout from a voice Arrow recognized.

"Let go of me. Let GO!"

Arrow ran in the direction of the voice, his feet light

and silent. When he was close, he slid behind a tree, heart thumping, and peered around.

His toes dug into the dirt. Three of the machiners towered over a smaller, skinny boy. Val. He was struggling as one of the grown humans gripped his left wrist.

I had been so concerned with the camp and the human machines, I had not noticed the boy had ventured south. I reached out now, felt for other small footsteps, but the boy seemed to be alone.

"Found this coming toward the camp," a wide man said as he dragged Val into the Burnt Circle. "Looks like that other kid wasn't telling the truth about being alone."

Wiser strode to them, eyes on Val.

Crankas hurried to the tree line, peering into the shadow. "Did you see where Arrow went?"

Val glanced at Crankas when he heard Arrow's name. His eyes darkened, then he quickly drew his gaze to the ground.

Arrow shrunk behind the tree, but no eyes were on the forest. All the machiners had halted their tasks and now glanced between Crankas and Val. The ones who had brought Val to the Circle shook their heads in answer to the question.

A hardness edged into Crankas's eyes. He turned on Val. "And where did you come from?" A sickly smile oozed onto his face.

Val's eyes narrowed, but he didn't reply.

Arrow took advantage of the machiners' focusing on Val. He crept out from behind his trunk and stalked around the edge of the Burnt Circle. I hoped he would not be discovered.

He was heading toward the tree where he and Petari had been hiding, but before he got there, he spotted her beneath a fern.

Her eyes were on her brother too, so she must not have heard Arrow when he sidled up next to her. He touched her shoulder and she jumped, letting out a scream. But it was quickly silenced by Arrow's hand over her mouth.

"What is he doing here?" Arrow whispered.

He pulled back his hand, and Petari shook her head, tears welling in her eyes.

"Val must've followed me. He can never trust that I'm okay. He always has to come after me. He makes me so mad."

"Why did you let him come?"

Petari shrugged. "I didn't know he was even here until I heard that gunshot."

"Was that the bang?"

Petari nodded. She pointed at the machiners. "Those things are guns. They can kill people. I guess I should be grateful they only shot in the air to scare him and didn't just shoot him on sight."

She swallowed. "What are they going to do to him? You're friends with them. You have to tell them to leave him alone."

Arrow glanced at Val through the trees. Crankas was still talking, and Val was still silent.

"They're not my friends. They murdered a tree like it meant nothing, because it was in their way." Arrow's gaze dropped. "You were right. They said they were going to save the forest, but they're not. They want to tear apart the Shimmer Cave, and clear trails, and build things called 'resorts' so people can come and stay."

Petari shook her head. "See? I told you they—"

"I know. I know. I have to stop them."

"And we have to get my brother away from them."

Arrow nodded. "That too."

"I know you don't like him, but he's my broth—"

"*He* doesn't like *me*." Arrow's voice lifted, and Petari brought her finger to her lips to shush him. Arrow glanced at the machiners, then started again, quieter. "He doesn't like me, but I'll still help him."

"Good. So tell them to let him go."

"That won't work."

"Why not?"

"If I go back there, they'll do the same thing to me that they're doing to him. They'll think I lied about being alone in the forest, and they'll want me to tell them where Val came from."

"So lie. Tell them you've never seen him before, and you don't know anything about him."

Arrow gawked at her. "Why would *that* make them let him go? They're still going to want to know where he came from and if there are others."

Petari gritted her teeth for a few breaths, then plopped her head into her hands. "What are we going to do?"

Arrow took another look at the camp. Most of the machiners had gone back to work, and only Wiser and Crankas were with Val now. They were talking to each other instead of the boy, locked in a heated discussion. I picked up their words from a lizard scurrying by.

"It's the best option," Wiser said. "I'm telling you; he's got friends in there somewhere." She peered into the forest. "If we go tramping around, they'll hear us, and we won't be able to defend ourselves. But keeping him here will bring them to us. We'll wait them out. I'm in no hurry, and we've got plenty of work to keep us busy."

"It makes me nerv . . . ," Crankas said, before the lizard was out of earshot.

Arrow spied the two talking and whispered, "We'll have to sneak him out when they're not around."

Petari groaned. "There are so many of them. They're always around."

"Then we'll keep watching until we find a way." He ended his sentence with a small smile, and she returned it.

"Arrow?" she whispered.

The boy looked at her.

"I really am sorry about the village. It was wrong, what they did. They were scared about the food supply getting cut off. Not that that's an excuse, but they're not bad people. We'll be better."

Arrow waved away her words, then turned back to Val, confusion swarming around him.

Wiser instructed Mora to tie Val to a chair too far into the Burnt Circle for Arrow and Petari to get him without being seen. Wiser went back to supervising the other work, unpacking more metal parts, clicking them into another six-legged beetle machine. Crankas paced along the tree line, peering out between the trunks. Occasionally he'd take a quick trip inside the shadow of the forest, just a few steps, neck craning presumably to look for Arrow. Then he'd retreat to his safety net within the Burnt Circle.

Staying out of sight, Arrow studied the metal beetle that had killed the palm and disintegrated it so quickly. Oxsen wasn't inside it now, and the machine sat alone. Its legs had curled up, making it looked like a dead insect on its back, but I knew it could quickly be brought back to life whenever the humans wanted.

It shook me to my roots to think how much more of the forest it would destroy.

As the sun continued its path and no opportunity to rescue Val had become clear, Arrow motioned for Petari to follow him to a hidden area farther away.

"We're going to have to wait until it's dark," he told her. "We can sneak him out tonight."

Petari shook her head. "We can't leave him there. What if they kill him?"

"They won't do that."

"How do you know?"

Anxiety escaped from Arrow, but he pushed it down. "I haven't been around as many humans as you have, but from what I've seen so far, they get fearful and suspicious and want lots of information. The machiners want that from Val."

"We should get the others. With more of us, we'll be able to get him out." So much worry drenched the soil around the girl. My leaves twitched for her.

Arrow leaned closer. "No!" His voice was fierce. "Even if all of your group were here, we'd still be outnumbered. They found Val, and they'll easily hear the rest of your group tramping through the forest."

Petari opened her mouth to speak, but Arrow continued talking.

"And if the machiners don't attack your herd on their way here, they'll track them after they've got Val. Just like Claw would. All the way back to the village. Back to Ruthie."

Petari chewed her lip.

"Harpy eagles don't get their prey in packs," Arrow said. "They hunt alone and capture monkeys when they're not looking. We have to be like the harpy."

Petari frowned at the boy, but her worry seemed to subside a little. She knew he was right. "Okay, so what do we do?"

"When it's dark, we'll sneak him out and cover our tracks back north."

"That will only work if they stop watching him long enough," Petari said.

"We need something that will pull their attention." Arrow narrowed his eyes, thinking.

"A loud noise is always good."

Arrow gazed at her. "When Crankas was first here, I made bird sounds to get him to look in the direction of the food I'd brought. We could do that again."

"There are so many bird noises here, I bet the Stilters have become pretty used to them. Plus we need something that will keep them busy for a while."

Arrow pursed his lips, then his eyes lit up. "Wait, I've got an idea. And I know how we can stop them from destroying the forest too."

"Perfect!"

I couldn't imagine what Arrow was planning, but if it would stop the machiners, he had to try. Still, I feared for his safety.

I steadied my roots for more.

SEEDS IN A BRAZILIAN MAHOGANY TREE WAITED FOR A WIND
TO PICK THEM UP AND SPIN THEM DOWN FROM THE CANOPY
TO GROW NEW TREES. BUT BEFORE A WIND PASSED, THEY
BECAME DRY AND BRITTLE AND FELL AWAY.

Arrow led Petari west, past the Burnt Circle and out toward the Shimmer Cave. The journey wasn't long, and before Petari could wonder where they were, Arrow pointed to a flower the color of clouds, with a long round tongue pointing at the sky.

"You're going to stop their machine with flowers?" Petari crossed her arms. "For all your forest-boy knowledge, Arrow, I don't think you understand how flowers really work."

Arrow smirked. "You'll see. We need the flowers, the stalks, and the leaves." He started pulling them off, whispering "Thank you" under his breath. "There are glands outside the flowers here, in the stalks and under the leaves, and they make nectar. See?"

He rubbed his fingers along the outside of the petal, then offered it to her to smell.

Petari leaned in and sniffed. "That's sweet."

"Yeah, and it tastes sweet too. But better yet, it's sticky. Feel."

Arrow turned over one of the leaves, motioning for her to touch it. She did, then pulled her fingertips away, rubbing the sticky substance between them.

"Eww. That's gross."

"It's not gross. It's useful. Harvest as much as you can. I'll be back in a few breaths." Arrow pushed one of the stalks into his waistband. "And keep your ears open. If you hear the slightest noise that's not made by you, get in that bush and stay still."

Petari nodded. "Don't worry. Those people are louder than my brother's farts. I'll hear them coming a mile off."

Arrow cocked his head like he didn't understand. Petari smiled. "A long way away."

"Good. And if it's a jaguar or something else?"

"I run and shout for you." She rolled her eyes. "You're just like Val, acting like I can't do anything."

"If we were in your Barbs or Stilts, I'd listen to you."

Petari opened her mouth, then shut it again. Finally she said, "I've got it."

Arrow shook his head, then began his journey again.

His footsteps scurried north and west, not traveling far, but covering a lot of ground. At times, he stopped, picked up a stick, but put it down again and kept walking. Finally he crouched next to a stick lying over a raised root. He picked it up, leveraged it against the ground to test its strength, then dragged the pointed edge across his shin to test its sharpness. Satisfied, he searched for another, until he finally found exactly what he needed.

Using the ends of the sticks, he foraged the forest floor by lifting the leaves. This way and that he roamed, occasionally crouching low, inspecting, marking with a raised twig, then moving on. After a while, markers stuck up across the ground like hairs on a porcupine. Then he hurried back to Petari.

She had piles of the philodendron flowers, leaves, and stalks around her when Arrow arrived, each pierced to release the sticky nectar.

"This better work," she said. "I've never been this sticky in my life. Are you ready?"

Arrow nodded. "Ready for the first part. Here's your stick. Let's get these over to the ant colonies."

Bending down, he reached around a pile of leaves and crushed them into his chest. Petari followed, and they took their stash to Arrow's porcupined area.

Dumping the leaves on the ground, he pointed at the

markers. "Be careful when you touch those. Each of these colonies is filled with ants and they're fast."

"We have ants in the outside world too," Petari said.

"Probably not like these." Arrow waved her to another colony. "If these big ones bite you, the pain will be so bad, you'll probably want to die. And it'll hurt like that for half of the sun's path across the sky."

Petari's eyes widened. "You can deal with those ones."

Arrow turned away, hiding a small smirk. "Okay," he said, "we make trails with the sticks and rub the nectar into the soil to attract the ants."

"You mean little ditches like this?" Petari dug the point of her stick along the ground.

"Yes. And keep the trails apart until we get close."

"Gotcha."

They got to work, rubbing nectar onto the ends of their sticks and dragging them across the ground, leading away from the marked ant colonies. At random intervals, they left a piece of a crushed philodendron leaf or stalk in the path. They worked hard, not noticing the sun ambling along its path, but soon they had trails carving their way to the Burnt Circle.

Once again close to the machiners, Arrow pulled Petari behind a bush. "Now let's get ready for the second part."

She nodded, then followed Arrow piling the rest of the leaves and stalks under the bush. They pushed their sticks into the brush so they looked as though they belonged as well.

Next, Arrow showed Petari how to weave a carrying hammock like the one he had given to the machiners. She couldn't quite get it to work, but Arrow's was large enough for their plan.

Hammock in hand, they took to the trees, moving from trunk to trunk by balancing carefully on the close branches. Arrow showed Petari how to be silent, looking for the strongest tree limbs that wouldn't creak. A few more branches, and they were high up in the tree line of the Burnt Circle. They kept their eyes on the humans below, while also searching for their prize.

It didn't take Arrow long to find frogs. He had always loved to study the frogs and lizards in the forest, predict which way they would jump and be there to catch them.

Petari scrunched up her face as her hands clasped around one, opening her mouth to release a silent *EWWWW*. Before long, though, she was picking them up as quickly as Arrow, watching for his nod or shake sign to let her know if the frog was poisonous and should be avoided.

Before the sun was too low, they had a collection of frogs croaking in their carrying hammock.

Then they waited.

Petari's heart beat faster and faster with every breath. She could see her brother from where she was perched, watched as he studied the mud at his feet. I knew she couldn't see the despair radiating around him—humans didn't pay attention to that—but perhaps she could read it in his slump.

Finally the sun waved goodbye, but the machiners didn't. They settled around a circle that had the look of fire, but none of the warmth. If I didn't know better, I'd have thought it was magic, but no doubt it was one of their outside-world "tech." They talked, laughed, ate, and drank. Beyond them, the sun-powered domes lit up paths, making Arrow shiver. He and Petari watched and watched, waited and waited, annoyance creeping into the branches around them.

Then Wiser approached the machiners' fire and clapped her hands.

"All right," she said loudly, furrowed brows pointing at each of the humans in turn. "I want everyone asleep in ten. We have a lot of catching up to do tomorrow. Oxsen, you're on duty tonight."

The female who had powered the metal beetle stood. "What about the kid?" She nodded toward Val, who was sleeping with his head hung over his chest.

Petari stiffened, but Arrow put his hand protectively on hers.

Below them, Crankas walked toward the sleeping boy. The man smiled, eyes squinting at Val, then turned his eyes out to the shadowed forest. He no doubt looked for the humans they had expected would come for the boy. Perhaps he was disappointed, but no emotion rolled off him.

"The boy needs his sleep. Let's get him untied and into a tent. We'll get some answers tomorrow."

Mora fiddled with the ropes keeping Val in the chair and released them. No longer under the pressure, Val awoke and flailed his arms.

Petari shivered, but Arrow held on to her arm to keep her close and hidden.

"Whoa," Crankas said to Val. "We're just untying you. No reason to be afraid."

Val's eyes darted around the camp.

"Are you letting me go?" His voice was shaky.

Crankas frowned. "I'd be some kind of monster to send you out there in the dark." He waved toward the forest. "Do you know what's out there? I heard all about it from your friend Arrow. Jaguars, he said. Giant snakes that would crush you alive. Gators with teeth so sharp, they'll tear into your skull. You don't want to be eaten alive, do you?"

Val shook his head slowly.

"Me neither. I like you." The man flashed the boy that sickly sweet smile that had pulled in Arrow. "Tomorrow we're going to sit down and become friends. But tonight, a growing boy like you needs sleep. That's my tent." He pointed to one of the fabric huts, tents, in the middle of the row. "You'll be safe in there. I promise."

Val's eyes grew wide. "No! I don't want to go in there with you."

"I'm not going to hurt you. I just want you to get some sleep and sitting here isn't comfortable. But do what you want." Crankas waved a dismissive hand at the boy. "You can even leave. I don't care. Just watch out for the jaguars and gators and anacondas. Oh, and the poisonous frogs. I hear this forest has a lot of those, too."

The machiners had been trickling into their own fabric huts, but the ones who were still outside chuckled.

Val glanced at the trees, his eyes wide. He was drowning in thick fear, but he didn't give in. "I'll sleep here," he said.

"Suit yourself," Crankas said. "Oxsen will be on watch." He turned to the female. "Keep him safe, okay?"

She nodded, giving Val a grin. "We'll have a party. Right, kid?"

Val didn't return her smile, just crossed his arms on the tabletop and dropped his head on them.

Crankas shared one last glance with the humans, his brow furrowed, then slid into his tent.

After the last machiner had left the fire and disappeared into their own small tent around the Burnt Circle, Oxsen took a chair near Val, one of the long, shiny guns close to her hand.

"It's time," Arrow whispered.

Petari's eyes were wide with fear, but she nodded.

"You know what to do at the machine?"

Petari glanced at her brother. So alone, so defeated. "I think I should get Val."

Arrow shook his head. "There's too much to do and you could easily be caught."

"You could too."

Arrow glared at her. "Petari, you're quiet and quick, but I've been hiding from predators in this forest for twelve rings. When things start happening, what are the humans going to look at first, the machines or Val?"

Petari dropped her chin. "Val."

"I promise I'll get your brother out."

The girl pursed her lips but finally nodded. "Okay."

She headed back across the branches until she was in a tree whose trunk was shaded from the machiners' sun-powered domes. Then she quickly climbed to the ground and slunk off to the bush where they'd hidden the piles of philodendron leaves.

Once she was clear of sight, Arrow took a deep breath. He had been truthful to Petari. He had evaded predators for many rings, but these humans were different. Arrow had never had to hide from so many, and even though only the female called Oxsen was outside now, one shout from her would bring the others. Arrow had to be silent. He had to be quick. He had to be invisible.

His eyes roamed the branches he'd mapped out as his best route down, the path behind bushes that would keep him hidden longest, and the open area before he'd reach Val.

Fear pulsed out of him.

He swallowed, then pushed forward.

In a flurry, he pulled the palm thread he'd left loose on the hammock of frogs so it opened up on the branches ahead of him. Then he pushed the tree limbs up and down to make the frogs leap off.

One by one, frogs rained down from the tree, plopping into the Burnt Circle. They leaped around the unnatural fire, leaped onto chairs, leaped onto Oxsen, who stood quickly and backed away.

"Watch out!" she shouted to Val, pushing him back as more and more frogs landed on the table. "Are they poisonous? Get back."

In his hurry, Val fell to the ground and scrambled back toward the tree line.

Oxsen pointed her gun at the frogs. *BANG! BANG!* But they were too quick and there were too many. She didn't know how to stop them.

"WISER!" She kicked at the frogs that came close. A few frogs leaped up, and landed on her chest and arms. Oxsen screamed, pushing them off.

The shouts had drawn the other machiners now. Heads appeared out of the openings of the tents, sides flapped open, and bodies stumbled out with weapons drawn. Crankas leaned out, but when a frog pounced onto his head, he gave a small scream and pulled himself back inside.

"What the . . . ?" Wiser's eyes darted around their camp, which had now been taken over by the plague of frogs. "What's going on? Where did these come from?"

"The trees," Oxsen shouted, pushing frogs off her legs. "Are they poisonous?"

Wiser looked around. "I have no idea. Get some lights burning! Get rid of them all."

The machiners jumped at her command. The frogs weren't the only ones moving quickly now. The humans ran around, setting up more lights, moving beams toward the frogs, pushing frogs off supplies . . .

And while they were busy, Arrow maneuvered quickly along his chosen path. By the time he got to the opening, the humans had focused the lights on the frogs, leaving his spot in some shadow.

"Psst." He aimed the noise at Val, as loudly as he could. "Psst."

But Val was frozen, eyes on the frogs jumping and leaping all over the Burnt Circle.

Arrow gritted his teeth, surveyed the machiners to make

sure none were looking his way, then dashed to Val's side and grabbed the boy's arm.

Val gave a small scream, but Arrow spun him around, pushing his pointed arm against Val's mouth.

Val's eyes widened in recognition and he gave a slight nod.

Arrow twisted his head toward the bush, and the two ran for cover. Arrow led Val quickly into the trees, paused, and whispered, "Follow my steps exactly."

"What are you doing here?" Val asked.

"No time. Follow exactly so they can't track us. Do you understand?"

Val's eyes flicked between Arrow's bare feet and the humans running like disturbed ants in the Burnt Circle. Then the older boy slipped off his shoes, stuffed them into the waistband of his pants, and followed Arrow.

The boys took a wide route, crisscrossing between trunks, over rocks and raised roots. Arrow jumped onto a low branch and Val followed. They scurried across to another tree, dropped down, and continued west. Finally they were on the other side of the Burnt Circle, the shouts still loud but farther away.

"Wait here," Arrow whispered to Val, then turned to head back toward the machiners' camp.

Val grabbed Arrow's shoulder. "Where are you going?"

"Just stay out of sight and wait here." Arrow shook himself free, then scurried toward the voices. He hiked himself up to where he and Petari had seen the metal birds descending on the clearing, where he could easily see the movement below while staying hidden.

The machiners were still rushing around, trying to get their invasion of frogs under control. Arrow smiled, then turned his attention to the metal beetle.

Just like he had hoped, all the crevices and holes were going dark with the abundance of ants covering the monster's surface. While Arrow had been rescuing her brother, Petari had stuffed the beetle machine full of the philodendron leaves and stalks. The ants from all the colonies Arrow had found had marched up the trails and descended on the metal beetle for the nectar feast of a lifetime.

With the ants covering the machine, the humans wouldn't be able to use it to destroy another tree. Delight flew from Arrow, and he hurried back to where he'd left Val.

"All good," he said, smiling. "This way."

They found Petari waiting at the philodendron bushes. She had been there for a while, and her fear was drowning the leaves. But when she saw her brother, she gave a small cry, then stifled it with her hands. She ran to him, threw herself into his arms, and breathed deep.

Happiness radiated around them, but Arrow's thick anxiety pierced it.

"It looks like you got everything done," he said.

Petari nodded, pulling away from her brother.

"What are you talking about? What's going on?" Val asked, but Arrow shook his head.

"We'll tell you later. Their voices are spreading out from the Circle. They're looking for you. We've got to disappear."

He ran off to the west, Petari and Val following in his footsteps, as quickly as they could.

AS THE SUN DISAPPEARED, THE MOTHS CAME OUT TO
DRINK THE NECTAR OF THE NIGHT BLOOMERS, AND THE BATS
CAME LOOKING FOR THE MOTHS. BUT THE ROOTS OF THE
MOONFLOWER HAD CURLED AND CRUMPLED AGAINST
THE BITTERNESS OF THE SOIL. THE PETALS DIDN'T OPEN, THE
MOTHS WENT ELSEWHERE, THE BATS WENT HUNGRY.

The moon peered down on the children from high above when they began to slow. The shouts of the machiners were long behind the herd now. Arrow knew the grown-up humans wouldn't venture out beyond where their lights shone, for fear of the same creatures with which Crankas had threatened Val. Still, Arrow had shown Val and Petari how to walk so their trail was less noticeable.

He had led them to the place he went when he needed comfort, the place where the moon broke into a thousand colors, and I asked a bat to send me their images, so I could make sure they stayed safe.

"This is Shimmer Cave," Arrow said as they walked through the entrance.

"I don't like this," Val said, the darkness swallowing any light from outside.

"Just a little farther," Arrow told him. "Here, hold on to my arm." Petari and Val felt around in the dense blackness, found Arrow's outstretched arm, and the three walked on. When they got to the opening at the back of the cave, Petari and Val gasped.

"Wow," Petari said.

"Amazing," Val added. "What makes it do that?"

"What do you mean?" Arrow asked.

Val grazed his fingertips over the rough, shimmering walls of the cave. "What kind of rock is it?"

Arrow shrugged. "It's just Shimmer."

"No." Val peered at the hole that let in the moonlight. "All of these colors are different types of rocks and minerals that are embedded in the walls of the cave. In the Stilts, people wear them in their ears or around their necks and wrists. They're really valuable."

"Crankas wants to dig them up." Arrow's words were heavy. "He's going to tear down this whole cave to get something called 'money.'"

Petari gasped. "He can't do that."

"He would've if you hadn't stopped him." Arrow smiled slightly, but Val frowned at his sister.

"What did you do?" His voice was harsh. Fear and anger built up around him.

"While Arrow was setting off the frogs and rescuing you, I sabotaged the machine." Excitement spiraled into the air from her words.

"Do you have a bird brain?" The rock beneath Val soaked with anxiety.

Arrow glanced at Petari. "Why would you have a bird brain?"

Petari rolled her eyes. "He means I acted like a bird, with no brain."

Arrow frowned. "Birds are very intelligent."

"See, Val? They're very intelligent. Like me."

"You could've been hurt. Or worse, killed!" Val turned on Arrow. "How could you make her do that?"

"He didn't make me do anything. You always treat me like I'm a baby, but I can take care of myself." Petari's voice lifted, and Arrow tried to quiet her. She glanced toward Arrow's "Sshh," then refocused on her brother. "*I* found this forest. *I* went through the hole. *I* got the leaves to help Ruthie. Even in the Barbs, *I* stood up to the bullies. Stop acting like I'm helpless."

"You're just a kid," Val said, his voice getting louder than hers.

"You're just a kid too," Petari shouted. "You're only a few years older than me!"

"STOP!" Arrow rushed between them with his arms up. "You need to keep quiet or we'll all be found. Crankas wasn't joking about the dangerous animals here. I told him. And believe me, there are plenty that could kill us. We don't want to draw their attention."

Val stepped back, crossing him arms over his chest. Petari did the same. They glared at each other.

Arrow sighed. "We should sleep. In the morning, I'll take you back to the village then you can all leave the forest."

"Why do we have to leave?" Val spit out the words as though they tasted bitter.

"Why would you want to stay?" Arrow's frustration soaked into the floor of the cave. "The forest is dying. You didn't help. I thought those machine humans were going to help, but they just want to tear it apart. Maybe the only way to save it is for *all* the humans to leave."

"No." Petari's eyes widened. "I don't want to leave. We're not hurting the forest. Not anymore. I promise. I want to stay."

Arrow didn't answer, just focused on the shimmering walls. They weren't giving him comfort tonight.

"We'll help to fix it. Right, Val? We want to stay." Petari's eyes pleaded with her brother, but his energy was a weight dragging him down.

"Arrow's right," he said. "Let's get some sleep."

"No!" Petari stomped her foot. "I—"

"This is Arrow's home, not ours." Val's voice was more calming now. "Go to sleep."

Petari's mouth gaped open, but any words were dissolved before they found air. Instead the girl glanced between her brother, settling on the ground, and Arrow, gazing through the hole at the moon. Sadness leaked into the ground at her feet, but she didn't say any more. She found a spot of her own, curled up, and closed her eyes.

Anguish drained from Arrow too, and it wrenched at my roots. My boy had tried so hard to mend the Anima, but nothing had worked. He had seen hope in the humans, more of his own kind, but they had betrayed him. Perhaps he felt abandoned all over again.

I wished he'd come home. Wished he'd sleep in his nest. Wished we didn't have to worry about the magic and the forest and our lives. Life is a circle in an ecosystem, but for each thing, life is a line, with a beginning and an end. If the forest were to die—if I were to die—we'd be replaced by something else, perhaps the stone of the outside world. I didn't want that, but I couldn't control it. I was at the mercy of the humans.

At least I could say that my life had been happy, especially with Arrow by my side.

He watched the path of the moon until it crept past the hole in the Shimmer Cave, then finally lay down. I listened to his heartbeat pat, pat, patting on the ground until the sun rose.

When his eyes opened the next morning, Petari was sitting in front of him. She grinned.

"Finally! Do you know you twitch in your sleep?"

Arrow frowned. "I what?"

"Never mind. It's kinda cute. Anyway, listen, you're not kicking us out that easily."

Arrow pushed himself up. "Petari—"

"No. I said I was going to help you fix the magic, and I don't go back on my promises. We're going to go to the Stilts."

"What?" Val's voice rose up from where he had been sleeping. "We're not going there. Luco said it's locked down."

Petari turned to him. "We have to find a way, Val. There's stuff you don't know about this forest. It has magic in the ground. And the magic is almost gone. That's why it's dying."

Val walked over to his sister and Arrow. "Did he tell you that? What other lies have you been telling my sister?"

"They're not lies," Petari said, standing up to face him. "I saw it myself. Arrow wasn't lying when he told the group about the Guardian. And yes, she's a tree."

"Don't tell him anything. He won't understand." Arrow narrowed his eyes at Val.

"Val's good at figuring out stuff. He can help."

"Petari, you can't believe everything this—" Val began.

"I've met her," Petari said. "She's beautiful. And she showed me the magic. I saw the forest light up, flowers bloomed in seconds, roots lifted out of the soil and twirled in the air. Tell him, Arrow."

Val crossed his arms and glared at Arrow.

My boy dropped his head, sadness piling up beneath his body. He pushed himself up to stand, then turned to Petari. "He won't believe me."

Val dropped his arms to his side. That wasn't what he had expected Arrow to say.

"It doesn't matter anyway," Arrow continued. "There isn't magic in the Stilts. Crankas showed me. Their lights are controlled by the sun. The magic is gone. I have to get to the Guardian and warn her. I don't think there's anything that can save the forest now."

My boy had lost his hope.

Arrow walked out of the cave. Petari glared at her brother, then followed. But Val stayed behind. His fingertips again touched the surface of the Shimmer, his nail tracing the multicolored gems within the rock. They weren't shining as brightly now as they did in the moonlight, but the shimmer was still there. A flash of regret twisted from his fingers; then it was gone, and he followed the others outside.

"Hey—" Val started, but quickly stopped.

*Thrum.*

*Thrum.*

*Thrum.*

"Copters!" Petari said. "They must've called them back from the Stilts."

Arrow's eyes widened like a dawning sun as he searched the sky for the metal bullfrogs. "They're coming to destroy Shimmer Cave!" Panic clawed across every word.

"It's there." Petari pointed. To the east, a metal bullfrog was hovering over the tree canopy. It moved farther east, swung back, then flew to the north.

"No, they're not coming here. They're looking for us." Val turned to Petari, eyes full of fear. "They're looking for our group."

"How do you know?" Petari asked.

"I heard them talking about how they were using me for bait. They don't want any other people in the forest. They want to get us all out."

Just like the Imposters pushing out the Forest Dwellers. Do these humans never change?

"What will the Stilters do if they find the village? Faive is so small. And Ruthie." Tears pricked Petari's eyes. She looked from her brother to Arrow.

Arrow's shoulders fell. "We'll have to bring your herd into the forest. They'll be better hidden there."

"You said the forest was dangerous." Val narrowed his eyes at Arrow.

"It is, but not as dangerous as them." Arrow pointed at the metal bullfrog.

He was right, and Val and Petari knew it.

Val shook his head. "We'll never get there in time."

"You've missed so much in the forest, Val. We'll show you how to get around fast." Petari grinned.

"Let's go." Arrow took off toward the village, the others close behind.

THE PASSION FRUIT VINE TO MY SOUTH DISPLAYED ITS BRIGHT
PURPLE AND YELLOW FLOWERS PROUDLY, BUT BEFORE THE WIND
COULD CARESS THEM, THEY SHRIVELED UP AND DIED,
FOLLOWED BY THEIR VINE.

Keeping an eye on the sky, Arrow led Val and Petari to
the closest liana-laden kapok tree. They climbed up,
perched on a thick branch, and Arrow showed Val
how to use strong vines to hold himself up.

"Are you kidding me?" Val said. "I'm not doing that. I'll
get killed."

Petari laughed. "Don't be a dust munch. You'll love this.
Come on." She twisted her vine harness around the liana,
pushed off, and flew past trunks and branches.

Val grimaced. "She makes it look so easy."

"It is easy," Arrow said. "Just look out for branches that are in your way. They sting if they hit you in the face. Now go but keep quiet." He pushed Val off the branch.

The boy flailed, angry eyes darting at Arrow, but then his hemp rope sped off down the vine.

Arrow followed closely to make sure Val stopped at the next tree with no problems. Eyes wide as the tree loomed ahead, Val swung his legs out and caught a branch just in time.

"That's . . . that's . . . ," he told Petari, who laughed.

"He likes it," Petari said to Arrow as he stopped too. "Which liana now?"

Arrow took them on four more vines, then they plopped down at Crooked Rock and headed for the root bridge.

"We thought you were dead!" Delora ran to Val and Petari as they broke through the tree line south of the village.

Arrow stayed back, anxiously glancing between the sky and the forest. I could feel the wind of the metal bullfrogs to the south. They were getting closer.

"What happened to you?" Luco ran up with the rest of the herd.

"And what's he doing back here?" Safa asked, pointing at Arrow.

"Arrow saved my life." Val's gaze turned down. "I followed Petari into the forest on the other side of the river, but I got lost and was picked up by some Stilters. They've got a camp, and they're looking for all of you now with copters."

"But Arrow's going to take you into the forest." Petari lifted Ruthie from Rosaman's arms and gave her a squeeze. "He'll hide you."

"How do we know he's not with them?" Safa frowned at Arrow.

"I thought he was at first, but he got me out," Val said. "These Stilters don't want other people here. They wanted me to tell them where you were."

"Did you?" Storma asked.

"Of course not," Val said.

Luco shook his head. "I think we should stay here. No one will find us."

Arrow stepped forward. "They can see this village from the sky. But they can't see through the forest canopy. If you're under the trees, they won't know where to look for you."

"Arrow's right," Petari said, giving Ruthie back to Rosaman. "You know what the Stilters are like in the Barbs. They've got machines and guns here, too. I've seen them."

"We need to have a talk about you going on missions on your own." Luco stepped closer to Petari. "You're supposed to be on babysitting and cleanup like Delora."

"I know, but—"

*Thrum.*

*Thrum.*

*Thrum.*

The wind of the metal bullfrog was getting closer. Like

Arrow had predicted, they must've seen the village from the air and were headed straight there.

"Hurry!" Arrow told the herd. "You'll be safe in the forest."

"Hold it." Storma lifted her hand. "Why do the Stilters want this place so badly? They don't need food like we do."

"It is beautiful." Luco motioned to the trees.

"They want to build hotels," Val said. "They've got carriers and other machines to tear down the trees."

"Sheesh. They're making it into another Stilts, just for the rich," Mercou said. "Only prettier."

"They'll get people to pay a lot, I'm sure," Delora said. "My mom said the Stilts used to be like that, until people started living there and they closed it off completely."

"Don't they have enough stuff?" Storma's words had a bitter edge. "All they do is take."

Arrow nodded, for once agreeing with Storma. "They're going to destroy it all, the forest, the river, everything. Petari and I tried to stop them, but I don't know how long it will work."

"What did you do?" Worry sank out of Val as he glared at his sister.

"We put biting ants all over their machine." Petari grinned proudly. "They won't be using it for a while."

"Ants?" Storma gave a short laugh. "That won't stop them for long."

"It's something." I liked Petari's optimism. "It'll give us some time to come up with something better."

Arrow nodded. "I don't know what I'll do yet, but I'll try again once you're all safe. I can't let them tear down Shimmer Cave."

Storma glanced at him, about to say something, but was interrupted by Safa.

"What's Shimmer Cave?"

"That's where we stayed the night. It's brill," said Petari.

Arrow frowned at the sky, but the metal bullfrog wasn't overhead yet. "It's my favorite place in the forest. It has walls that shimmer with different colors."

"They're gems," Val said. "Loads of them."

"Gems? Like diamonds and rubies and stuff?" Rosaman stepped closer, Ruthie sucking the tip of his finger.

"What are diamonds and rubies?" Arrow asked.

"There are gems in the forest?" Storma's energy had changed, no longer angry but excited.

Petari glanced at the sky. "Guys."

"I don't know which gems, but the whole cave sparkles," Val said. "It'll be worth a lot of money. That's why the Stilters want to tear it down."

"The copters!" shouted Petari.

"The Stilters have lots of money," Luco said, ignoring her.

"They have all the money," Safa said, her attention on Val.

"They don't need the gems," Storma said, her eyes narrowing.

*Thrum.*

*Thrum.*

*Thrum.*

The metal bullfrog was almost at the village.

"We have to get into the forest," Arrow said. "Now!"

"How do we know we can trust him?" Delora pointed her chin toward Arrow.

He didn't recoil at the bitter energy this time. He straightened his shoulders. "I don't want to take you with me. All you've done since you came to the forest is hurt things. But those machiners are worse, and as much as I need to get back to them to make sure they don't destroy my home, I don't want to see you get hurt. I'm trusting that if I take you into the forest, you won't damage it."

"They won't," Petari said quickly.

The younger children looked at Luco and Storma.

*THRUM.*

*THRUM.*

*THRUM.*

"They're coming!" Petari pointed in the direction of the noise.

Storma kept her eyes on Luco. "I've got an idea. Arrow doesn't want those Stilters to have this place, and neither do

I. Why doesn't he protect our group, and we'll take care of his little problem?"

"You can get rid of the machiners?" Arrow looked from one to the other in disbelief. I wondered if they could really do that too.

"It'll be fun." Storma smirked at Arrow. "We've taken care of goon groups. We can take on this camp too. It's the least we can do, right, Luco?"

She glanced at the skinny-as-a-spider boy.

He watched her as though reading words in her eyes. I couldn't see what they would be, but whatever message he found, he agreed. "Yep. The least we can do."

Storma turned to Val. "What kind of setup do they have?"

"There're about ten adults. Maybe a few more. The camp's just a bunch of tents and equipment. Nothing too substantial. Their machines are general farming and utility units. But as Petari said, they do have guns."

"Easy peasy. We've taken on bigger goon groups." Storma grabbed her sky-colored backpack off the ground. "I've got some tricks I'm looking forward to showing them."

Luco grinned at the group. "It's a plan. The younger ones will go with Arrow. A small group will come with Storma and me. We'll meet back up when everything's safe."

"I'm going with you guys," Safa said.

"Me too," said Delora.

Rosaman opened his mouth, but Luco said, "It's okay, Ros. You stay with Ruthie."

Rosaman nodded, holding the baby close.

Luco turned to Mercou. "You with us?"

Mercou glanced at the metal bullfrogs, getting closer. He nodded. "I'm ready for some fun."

"I'll go with you too," Val said. "I can help you find their camp."

Petari stepped forward. "I'll go with Arrow. I promised to help him with the Guardian, and he needs to warn her."

"You need to stay with me, Petari." Val glared at his sister.

"You go with them, if you want. I'm going to help the Guardian."

"No. You have to stay close so I can protect you."

"No, I don't!" Petari cried back.

"Yes, you do," Val shouted. "I promised Dad."

Petari gulped. "What? When?"

Val's face softened. "Before he left, Dad made me promise I'd always keep you safe. Then he never came home. I have to protect you. For him."

"But, Val—"

The metal bullfrogs were nearer. The wind was getting harder, noise louder. Luco had to shout. "Argue later!" He turned to Val. "You should go with Arrow's group. Make sure they're safe. We'll find the Stilter camp."

Storma grinned. "We'll just follow them." She pointed at

the bullfrog, coming into view. "If we can track their noise in the Barbs, we can track them in this forest."

"How do we stay safe from the creatures in the forest?" Luco asked Arrow.

"They hunt mostly at night and won't attack a bigger group. They'll also stay away from loud noises." Arrow narrowed his eyes. "But if you make too much noise, the machiners will hear you coming."

"Not over the noise of their copter and machines, they won't," Storma said.

*THRUM.*

*THRUM.*

*THRUM.*

The metal bullfrog was almost on top of the village now. The wind from its spinning arms rustled the leaves of the tree line.

"Go!" Luco motioned the others toward Arrow.

The herd dispersed, running to the large hut. Val, Petari, and Rosaman emerged with their backpacks.

"Follow me," Arrow shouted over the noise. He ran through the branches, the others close behind. Rosaman stumbled with Ruthie in his arms. Arrow ran to him, grabbed the child, and pulled Rosaman under the safety of the trees. Luco and Storma motioned for their group to follow as well.

Above them, the metal bullfrog took over the sky. It

circled around the village, the machiners inside no doubt looking for Val, Arrow, and the herd below.

The children were huddled beneath the trees, out of sight for now, but they still had to cross the bridge.

The wind strengthened as the metal bullfrog began to descend on the village. The machiners were going to look for the herd on foot. Trees bowed out of their way from the force of the wind. Animals scurried off, and birds stayed back.

Once the metal bullfrog was down far enough that its view was blocked by trees, Arrow called, "This way."

He led the herd south, weaving through the copse of trees that held our biggest secret, and out the other side to reveal the root bridge.

My roots curled, hoping this wasn't a mistake. Arrow's big heart had failed us before. But perhaps I was starting to see that following one's heart wasn't bad if it did good.

Faive was nervous about crossing the root bridge, but Arrow, Petari, and Val helped her to hurry.

There were shouts in the village now. The machiners were searching the savanna, lifting cans from the ground and knowing the contents were fresh. Eyes peered around the tree line; feet ran to the border at the north, then the south; hands pushed back branches.

Arrow kept the herd moving farther into the forest. He told them to stay quiet, but their eyes were too busy taking in these new wonders for their mouths to make much noise.

Arrow brought them to the Crooked Rock, where he had first met Petari, then stopped.

"The canopy is thick here. The humans won't be able to see us from above."

"So this is where you were hiding, eh? Pretty nice," Storma said, glancing around.

Luco gripped Arrow's shoulder. "You sure you can keep them safe?"

Arrow nodded. "You sure you can get rid of the machiners?"

Storma laughed. "Does a dog pee on trees?"

Arrow frowned. "What's a dog?"

Luco smiled at Arrow, patting his back. "You're okay, kid. Don't worry. We've got this."

The *thrum, thrum, thrum* started to pick up again.

Arrow pointed south. "Their camp is by the river to the south, that way."

Luco gave Arrow and his group a grin, then they started south.

Arrow watched them for a few breaths until Petari grasped his arm. "They'll be okay."

"This way," he said, then led the others in my direction.

THE BRIGHT RED FRUIT OF AN ACHIOTE
TREE IN THE EAST BULGED WITH SEEDS, UNTIL THEY
SUDDENLY PUCKERED AND FELL FLAT.

Arrow led his small group through the forest as quickly as he could. From the anxiety swirling around him, I knew he was torn. He wanted to help the youngsters, he wanted to warn me, but he was also worried about Crankas and the machiners' plan and whether Luco and Storma could really stop them. I was too.

Just as Petari had been slow at first, so were the others. Rosaman secured Ruthie inside his open backpack to help him keep up, but Faive's short legs kept falling behind.

"Hold it. We need to stay together," Arrow called to Val

and Rosaman when Faive fell back for the fourth time. "Can I carry you?" he asked the girl, who looked close to tears.

"I'll take her." Val knelt down so Faive could climb onto his shoulders. It looked like they'd done this before. As he hoisted her up, Val swung the girl's legs, making her giggle.

"Thank you," Arrow said, then got the group walking again.

Petari kept them entertained, pointing out all the things Arrow had taught her when he'd first brought her this way.

"A plant can stop you from farting?" Rosaman asked, and Petari replied, "Maybe not *your* farts," making the younger ones laugh.

Arrow stayed at the front, keeping his eyes on the forest and the children moving quickly.

After a while, Val got into step with him. "I didn't thank you for saving me yesterday."

Arrow glanced at the boy. He must not have expected that. I hadn't.

"Not a lot of people help others in the Barbs," Val continued. "In our group, we look out for each other, but with outsiders, it's pretty much everybody on their own."

Arrow shrugged. "The Guardian brought me up to help others in the forest." My leaves shook with pride. "You can thank her."

"You mean the tree?" Val narrowed his eyes.

"Yes, the Guardian Tree." Arrow glared at the older boy, daring him to not believe.

Val looked away. "Anyway, I know you're probably worried about the forest, what with the Stilters and everything, and the last thing you want to be doing is helping us. So, I just wanted to say thank you."

Arrow slowed a little, his energy softening. Val was right, and even though Arrow was still guarded, I could tell he liked being seen.

"Do you really think the others will stop Crankas?" Arrow asked.

Val opened his mouth to answer, but Petari shouted, "Arrow, look!"

He followed her gaze to the river's finger. It looked very different from when they'd last come through. Many of the water lilies had large rips and browned holes.

"They look terrible," Petari said. "What happened?"

Arrow shook his head. "The Anima is depleting faster. Use the solid ones. We have to hurry."

Petari frowned but didn't say anything more. Instead she helped Arrow show the others how to slide onto the lilies safely to get across.

It wasn't long before they were running to my trunk, and joy lifted my leaves. I had worried I'd never talk to Arrow again, never feel his weight on my soil. I had worried the machiners would destroy him, just like they wanted to destroy the forest. I had worried, but I hadn't needed to. He had come back to me.

"Guardian!" Arrow shouted as I came into sight. He flung his arms around my trunk. Happiness warmed my bark and soaked into my cells.

Curly greeted Arrow with a screech. Still slow on her healing paw, she swung down and hugged his arm.

"I missed you, Curly." Arrow kissed the top of her head.

"I'm glad you're back, Arrow," I said.

"Hi, Guardian!" Petari jumped up and down, waving to me.

"Hello, Petari." I liked this girl's enthusiasm.

Arrow repeated my words to Petari, then turned back to me. "You were right about the machiners. I'm sorry I trusted them."

"Don't be," I said. "I heard what you told Val on your way here. And you're right. In this forest, we do try to help each other. It's not your fault that they betrayed your trust. I am very proud of you."

"This is the Guardian?" Val gazed up at my branches. "Looks like any normal tree. Doesn't even look too healthy."

"What do you mean?" Arrow asked.

Val pointed to my leaves. "Got some yellow and brown spots. Could be a disease or something."

"How do you know that?" Worry drilled into the ground as Arrow saw my yellowed leaves.

"Our dad taught Val about plants and stuff," Petari said proudly.

"Yeah. He was a gardener and worked in the Stilts sometimes, looking after the few trees they had. He used to teach me stuff about soil and trees. That was before he disappeared." Val kicked his toe against the hard ground.

Arrow glanced up at me. "Guardian, are you okay?"

"I've had to give nutrients to help others. If I sacrifice a few leaves for that, it's all right."

"Does he really hear the tree talking?" Rosaman whispered to Petari.

"Uh-huh." She smiled up at me. "I wish I could, but I did see her use the magic. It was amazing."

"Don't listen to her, Ros," Val said. "I love trees, but they're not magic. There's no such thing as magic."

"That's not true!" Petari turned to Arrow. "Could the Guardian show them like she showed me?"

Arrow shook his head. "We need to preserve the Anima."

Arrow was right, but perhaps shielding the forest from the herd hadn't been my best idea. Arrow was reminding me of the lessons I had taught him, about how the forest had worked together with humans in the time of the Forest Dwellers. I hadn't trusted the herd from the north, but Petari was proving me wrong. She wanted to help. When the Imposters had pushed out the Forest Dwellers, I had hidden away our home. I had turned my back on the humans. But had the Forest Dwellers always lived in harmony with us? Had there been a time when they had needed lessons too? Had I given up on humans too quickly?

"Arrow," I said, "stand so you can't see Val, so he's behind you, close your eyes then tell him to point to something around him."

Arrow frowned. "Okay." He relayed my message, even though doubt squeezed from his toes.

"Why?" Val asked.

"Because the Guardian asked you to," Arrow said. "Because I'm asking you to and I helped you before."

Val sighed. "Fine."

Arrow closed his eyes and turned his back to the boy.

"Tell him he's pointing at me," I told Arrow, relaying what the ants had seen.

"You're pointing at the Guardian?" Arrow said, as though he weren't sure. He should trust me more.

Val's eyes widened, but his heart was still hard. "You could've guessed that. Do it again."

"He turned around and is now pointing at the rock that was behind him," I told Arrow.

Arrow repeated my words, and Val's mouth dropped open. "How did you know that?"

"I told you," Petari said, grinning.

"That's . . . That's . . ." Val peered at me, as though I suddenly looked different, like I was impossible.

"Umm wow?" Rosaman stepped back, gazing into my branches.

"That's the Guardian Tree." Arrow opened his eyes and smiled at them.

"Let me try," Faive said, jumping up and down.

But her request was interrupted by Ruthie starting to cry. "She's hungry," Rosaman said, swinging the backpack off his shoulders and pulling out the baby.

"Bananas are over there." Arrow pointed to the tree to the east.

Rosaman glanced around. "Will we be safe?"

Arrow smiled and patted my trunk. "Don't worry. The Guardian won't let anything touch you here."

Rosaman smiled at me and nodded. "I can believe that. Come on, Faive. Help me."

As they went to the tree, Arrow hung his head. "I have to get back to the machiners' camp. I don't know how I'm going to stop them from destroying the forest, but I can't leave it to the others. I have to try."

"Arrow, Storma was right," Val said. "They've taken out groups bigger than this. Not ones with so many guns, but . . ."

"I've been thinking about that." Petari crossed her arms. "You said the Guardian could keep the forest safe if you had more of the magic, right?"

Arrow sighed. "Yes, but I've tried to grow the Anima, and nothing has worked."

"We haven't gone to the Stilts yet," Petari said.

"The Stilts doesn't have magic." Val scrunched up his face

as though he was wondering how she could think otherwise.

"How do you know?"

Arrow shook his head. "He's right. Crankas showed me how they made the light. It was another lie."

"But if this Anima is in the earth in the forest, doesn't it make sense that it'll be in the earth everywhere?" Petari looked from one to the other, making sure she had their attention. She did, and mine as well. "Arrow, you told me it's not that trees can't talk, but that we're not listening. Well, now we know that trees can talk to the people who listen. Right, Val?"

Val nodded, glancing at me. "I don't know how, but yeah. . . ."

"So just because we've never seen real magic outside of this forest, doesn't mean it's not there," Petari continued. "Dad always said that bush near our house lasted much longer than it should've, didn't he?"

Val nodded.

"Maybe that bush had some magic and we didn't know," Petari said. "There used to be trees and bushes and flowers growing all over the Barbs and the Stilts. You told me that, Val."

"That was before you were born. Before I was born even," he said.

"So? If they were growing there, maybe there was magic. Maybe there's still some magic, but no one knows about it.

If we can find some and get it to the Guardian, she can protect the forest from the Stilters for good." Petari looked from Arrow to her brother to me and back again. "It's something, isn't it? We could at least look."

I liked her thinking. Arrow did too.

"But how long will it take to go there?" he asked. "We need to mend the Anima fast."

"It will take you too long to walk there," I said. "But I can show you. Birds have been saying they want to help the forest. They can fly over and look for healthy trees."

"Do you have enough Anima?" Arrow put his palm against my trunk.

"I will have to disconnect from the root network for a while." I didn't like to do that, but we were in desperate need. "As your friend said, it is something. If we can find magic there, it will be worth it."

Arrow glanced at Petari, warming at my calling her his friend.

The girl responded with, "What's she saying?"

"She can help us," he said, "but I'm worried about time. Guardian, before you disconnect, can you see what Crankas is doing at the Burnt Circle?"

"I will look."

Val frowned. "She can—"

"She's connected to everything in the forest," Arrow explained.

"Yeah, Val." Petari slapped his arm lightly.

"The root network has been breaking since the magic has been dying, though," Arrow continued. "Can you see them?"

The frogs showed me the scene, angry machiners, a chaotic mess. "It looks like your ants have done their job for now. The humans are still cleaning up."

"Good." Arrow told Petari and Val the news. "The Guardian's going to show me the Stilts."

"She can—" Val began, and Petari slapped his arm again.

"Will you stop asking that? Anytime you wonder if the Guardian can do something, just say to yourself, 'She's magic. She can do anything.' Got it?"

"I was just asking." Val glared at his sister.

"It could be useful to have them as a guide," I told Arrow. "Show your friends how to hold on to my root."

I released my connection to the root network, suddenly feeling cold without the forest's constant touch. It was the first time I had not been in full contact with the fungi since I'd sprouted. I didn't like it.

But if I couldn't mend the Anima, there would be no forest to connect to.

I wriggled away some soil, while Arrow explained the daydreaming to Petari and Val and showed them how to get ready. When they were all settled, each with a hand around my root and their eyes closed tight, I reached far, far, far out to the birds.

"Wow," Petari said, as the daydream began.

"What the . . . ? How . . . ? What . . . ?" Val stuttered.

"Watch," Arrow said.

The bird had left the forest and flown high above. Arrow let out a breath as he saw the green of the canopy, and the patches of yellow where the Anima was depleted. The bird's view swooped north, past the curtain and into the arid space beyond.

Nothing was green and alive. The few trees that still stood were brown and dead. The soil was light and dusty. Farther away, structures sprouted from the ground, straight and tall, gray and black. Vehicles like the ones I had seen the Imposters maneuver through the forest so many rings ago crouched in corners. A few humans trudged along a road, heavy on their feet. Dogs, small cats, and rodents scoured for food. But there were no trees, no bushes, no flowers. The only color came from the blue sky above, completely clear with no sign of a nourishing, water-filled cloud.

"That's the Barbs," Petari cried.

"There's our old building," Val said.

"Where?" Arrow asked, but the daydream had moved on with the bird.

We followed a road with houses on both sides, squares of barren dirt laid out before them where once grass had grown. Houses with chipped walls, broken windows. Parks of concrete littered with trash. Rows and rows and rows of empty roads, lined with brown, cracked twigs of bushes. And not one tree in sight.

I felt a tug on my roots, something calling for my attention. But I had too little Anima to reconnect to the root network and stay with the bird.

The bird flew on, past gray tongues of concrete that crisscrossed over more roads and stout buildings, onto a grove of sparkling towers that rose high enough to block out the sky.

Arrow's right hand shook against my root.

"There it is," Val said. "That's the Stilts."

The bird swooped around the towers, eyeing itself in their sides, which reflected like water.

The Stilts was vastly different from the Barbs, full of color and life. Specks of people roamed the streets, and Arrow gasped at the sight of so many humans, more than he'd ever seen in one place. They strolled and hurried and laughed and talked. Their hum could be heard high in the sky.

They shaded from the strong sun under green trees that stood tall along the roads. Perfectly sculptured bushes sat on street corners, and parades of flowers bloomed in tidy beds and boxes. Yet there was something wrong about them, something too even and perfect.

The bird got closer, and I asked her to land on a branch. I could immediately see the problem.

"These look like trees but they're not," I said.

"How can they have trees that aren't trees?" Arrow asked.

"They used to have more real ones, but now it looks like they're almost all fake." Sadness dripped from Val's voice.

"But why have these when they can have actual trees?" Arrow asked.

"Real trees won't grow," Val said. "There's barely enough water for people, so they won't waste it on trees. Plus the soil's so bad, trees would get diseases and die. They used these chemical fertilizers, but it didn't help for long." Val swallowed, unease seeping from his hand into my root.

"So where should we look for the magic?" Petari asked.

"We'll have to find some real trees," Val said. "I think I know where."

"Any trees here will be in desperate need of that life magic," I said. "I can't ask for it for ourselves."

Arrow repeated my words to Petari and Val, then said, "Maybe if we can combine their magic with our magic, it'll grow faster and help both the forest and the trees in the Stilts."

"Yeah, like mold on cheese," Petari said. "The more mold that's on the cheese, the faster it'll spew out spores and grow more mold."

Now it was Val's turn to reach out and slap Petari on her arm.

"What?" she said, protesting.

"Mold? Seriously?"

His reaction was amusing, but the girl's analogy wasn't

bad. "It's worth a try," I said. "But how can we connect the two?"

"The river!" Val started to stand in his excitement, but when the dream images began to slip from his mind, he sat and clasped my root again.

"What river?" Petari said. "There hasn't been a river in the Stilts since long before you were born."

"It's dried up now, but it might be just dried up on the surface. There could be a river underground, and it could be joined with the river here. Could the Guardian connect to magic in the Stilts through the river?"

"The river is part of the Anima," I told Arrow. "We can try."

Arrow repeated my words, hope building beneath him.

"Okay," said Val, "can I tell you where to go? We can see how close the river gets to the trees in the Stilts. Maybe the Guardian can connect to them."

"Go ahead. I'll ask the bird," I said, and Arrow repeated me.

Val gave a series of directions, and I passed them on to our hosting bird. She followed, swooping between buildings and around corners. We flew down a road that headed away from the shiny towers. Shorter buildings with dull, dust-colored walls sat along the sides.

The road weaved farther and farther out from the Stilts until we were moving back toward the Barbs. Then the road ended at a group of connected buildings and towers. Smoke rose from pipes on the roofs. And on the walls was a symbol I remembered well—the emblem like the stinkbird's fan.

"Fenix," Arrow whispered.

"Yeah," Val said. "This is the plant that gives all the power to the Stilts. It also recirculates the water. It was built next to the river, way back before the river dried up, but it still gets water somehow." He paused, then his eyebrows rose. "Maybe the plant pulls water from underground."

The bird flew around the buildings. Humans hurried along paths below, opened doors, slammed others. Carriers, like the ones at the Burnt Circle, transported items from one area to another. And the smoke billowed and billowed, making clouds above. But not the nourishing clouds that fed the earth. These left a bitter taste on the wind, like the taste in the soil that had been dying.

At the back of the concrete village was a building that blew more smoke than any other. Pipes protruded from behind it, pointing to the earth. And at the ends of the pipes were piles of some gray substance. A human operating a large vehicle with a clawed bucket on its front scooped up the material, carried it away from the building, and dumped it into a large hole, then pushed mud on top.

The bird swooped around the hole but immediately pulled back. There was something she didn't like, something that hurt. Next to the hole was a long dent carved into the earth, like a deep scar that ran from far in the north and headed south toward us, toward the forest.

"What's that?" Arrow asked.

"That's where the river was. We can follow it to—" But Val's words stopped. His hand started to shake. "Oh no! That's it."

"What is?" Petari asked.

Val didn't answer immediately. Anger was swelling on his fingertips.

"Fenix is dumping their chemicals into that hole," the boy said. "I think they're killing the earth."

THE ROOTS OF A TANGARANA TREE IN THE NORTH SHRUNK
AND CURLED UP TIGHT, UNTIL THEY COULD NO LONGER SUPPORT THE
TRUNK. AFTER A BATTLE TRYING TO STAY UPRIGHT, THE TREE FELL
WITH A *CRASH*. THE ANTS THAT HAD LIVED PEACEFULLY WITHIN
THE HOLLOW TRUNK FLED TO FIND ANOTHER HOME.

Fenix powers things, Val said.

Fenix makes things, Val said.

Fenix controls things, Val said.

After he let go of my root and I gave the bird my thanks, Val sat with his head in his hands. Anxiety grew under Petari as she watched her brother, not fully understanding his worry. Arrow peered at them from under furrowed brows.

"Dad used to talk about Fenix a lot, about how terrible they were," Val said, eyes on the ground. "I thought he hated them because they made the power and only gave it to the

Stilts. I always liked them because at least they made power and water, and I hoped we'd get in there one day and have it for ourselves."

He shared a glance with Petari, who thinned her lips.

"But this is what he was talking about," Val continued. "I get it now."

"I don't understand. What are they putting in the ground?" Arrow asked.

"Dad said there are bad chemicals that pollute the sky and the water and the earth. They kill soil," Val said. "He told me soil was one of our most valuable resources because it takes thirty years to make the kind of soil that helps trees and plants grow the best way."

I agreed about the value. The soil in our forest was our greatest treasure. It fed us, nurtured us, kept us connected.

"This forest makes its own soil." Val sifted the decomposing leaves around him through his fingers. "But out there, in the Barbs and the Stilts, the soil is dead, which is why nothing grows well. People have to have chemical fertilizers to make anything grow, but it doesn't last long."

"Crankas talked about fertilizers." Arrow frowned. "He said he was going to fix the forest with fertilizers in the soil."

"He also said he was going to tear down the Shimmer Cave." Petari rolled her eyes. "Like we should trust what he says."

"True," Arrow said. "But why would Fenix kill the soil, then fix it?"

"Well, for one, Fenix had lots of side businesses, and one is making fertilizers," Val said. "So they get money when people buy their fertilizer. But mostly, I think they just don't care."

Arrow jumped up. "How can humans not care?"

"People out there don't know trees the way you do, Arrow." Petari rose too. "I didn't care about them in the Barbs. Not like Dad did."

"We didn't have many trees in the Barbs," Val said. "And besides, we were too busy finding stuff to eat."

Petari pursed her lips.

"So why do you think Fenix is killing the earth?" Arrow asked.

Val swallowed. "You saw that smoke. You saw that stuff they were dumping into the riverbed. That's not natural. Dad said the waste from those plants was poisonous. If it's poisonous to us, it's probably poisonous to the earth, too."

"And if they're dumping it on top," Petari said, "the poison could be bleeding into the earth and getting into the underground river." Pieces were starting to fit into place.

"Then the poison is floating down here," Arrow continued. "Into the river, into the soil, into the Anima."

"It's killing everything it touches." Val's words dropped from his mouth like a bird falling out of the sky.

"Dad always said pollution was like lies." Petari cast her eyes down. "He hated it when I lied. He said that untruthful words pollute our souls just like the chemicals were polluting our land. I always thought he was trying to get me to own up to stuff. But maybe he was right."

"That's why the Anima is dying," Arrow whispered.

"That's why we're dying," I said. These chemicals, this poison, was making the bitter taste in the soil, the bitterness that had begun when the Anima had started to wither.

I felt a tug from the root network, but I was too engrossed. We were close to understanding our problem. To finding a solution.

"What can we do to stop it?" Arrow began to pace in front of the small group.

"I don't know." Val paced behind Arrow. "It was when Dad was trying to get a job at Fenix that he disappeared. He thought that if he could work there, he'd change our lives and could help the plants, too."

"You think they killed him?" Petari ran to keep pace with her brother. Fear vibrated in the air around her. "Do you think that's what happened?"

Val shook his head. "They didn't have any reason to. He could've been robbed. He could've been hurt. Or he could've just left." He looked at his sister. "He was never the same after Mom died."

Sadness spread out from them both.

Arrow stopped walking, crossing his arms over his chest. "So what does this mean? How do we fix the magic?"

The other two halted as well. They looked at Arrow. Arrow looked at them. They all looked at me.

"I don't have an answer," I said, wishing more than anything that I did.

All were silent, deep in thought. Searching for options. It was as though none of this small pack of humans wanted to say a word unless it professed a fix.

And when none came, the silence drew out further.

"Hey." Rosaman walked back up with Ruthie and Faive, arms laden with bananas. "Anyone want a—"

Curly shrieked from the nest above them.

She jumped onto Arrow's head, pulled at his ears. Her high-pitched scream echoed in the branches above. She was scared.

And she wasn't the only one. Her brothers and sisters ran to us, skittered up my branches, and curled into a tight ball together.

Faive tucked herself behind Rosaman, dropping the bananas.

Val jumped back. "What are they doing?"

"I don't know." Arrow brought Curly into his arms, trying to soothe her.

I felt that tugging in my roots again. I hadn't reconnected to the root network after our trip with the bird. I opened my roots to them again and . . .

Ripping.

Tearing.

Crunching.

Lives had already been lost. Birds and animals had screamed their distress. Fear was so thick, it was a fog that crawled up the tree trunks.

"Arrow! ARROW!"

He whipped toward me, his eyes scared. "What is it?"

Petari and Val looked between Arrow and me, questions filling their faces.

"It's the Burnt Circle."

"The Burnt Circle?" Arrow pushed Curly onto the branch with her family.

"The Fenix camp?" Petari asked. "What's going on there?"

"Have they left?" Hope buoyed Arrow's words. "Maybe they left because we killed their machine."

The pain was excruciating. So much disaster coming from one section of the forest.

But I couldn't understand why. And I couldn't find an insect, bird, or other animal to show me what was happening there. It was as though all life had left.

"No," I told Arrow. "They haven't left the forest. They've done something. Something . . . I . . ."

He ran, ran, ran to the kapok tree.

"Be careful!" I told him, but I wasn't sure he heard.

"Where are you going?" Petari shouted after him.

"Come on." Val ran after Arrow, Petari close on his heels. "Ros, look after Faive. We'll be back."

Arrow's heart pounded as he sped along the liana. Val and Petari followed, anxiety growing thicker around each of them with every breath.

The closer they got, the more Arrow's energy darkened. Noises echoed around the trunks.

Crunches.

Rumbles.

Shouts.

And SCREAMS.

Screams from the birds. Screams from other animals. Screams throughout the whole forest.

Swinging onto the last liana, the one that would take them closest to the Burnt Circle, Arrow peered around to find the cause of the noise. But before he saw anything, he dropped.

Something was wrong.

The liana was no longer tight. It sagged. And with Arrow's weight, it sagged more.

He looked back to Val and Petari. "Don't get—"

But his words were swallowed when he heard a loud *CRACK*. He fell, tumbling through the air. He hit branches, but they were weak and broke at the slightest touch.

Arrow shrieked, then crashed onto the ground with a *Thud*.

He lay there, pain streaking through his body and out into the soil. My boy!

"AAAAAHHHH."

Arrow lifted his eyes in time to see two more bodies tumbling after him. Val and Petari had gotten his warning too late.

The liana had broken close to Arrow, so he had been able to ride it down to the ground. But Val and Petari had only swung a short distance before the liana had snapped. They had farther to fall.

*THUD.*

*THUD.*

Val groaned. Petari screamed.

Arrow picked himself up and rushed to her. "Are you okay? What's hurt?"

Val hurried over. "Petari!"

Tears glistened in her eyes. "My hand." She lifted her arm. Her palm had a deep gash running from under her thumb to the base of her smallest finger. Blood fled from the wound and soaked into the ground below. "It hurts." Her voice was weak.

Arrow took her hand in his. "We need to wrap it with blood leaves. There's some where the Fenix people had placed their lights. Wait here."

He rushed off, running through the trunks, gazing up to see why the liana had fallen, taken them all down.

Then he saw and froze.

The path he had shown Crankas, the path the Kiskadee Man had lit with glowing light, the path that was home to the blood leaves, anise, and so much more, was gone.

In its place was a strip of land bare of any green, bare of any trees.

Bare of any life.

Bare.

THE DRY TOPSOIL CRACKED
AND DUSTED, SO LIGHT WITHOUT NUTRIENTS
THAT IT BLEW AWAY WITH THE SLIGHTEST BREEZE.

My roots shook.

A cockroach too weak to leave showed me what Arrow saw. It looked like a giant eagle had raked a sharp talon through the forest and dug up everything it touched.

The bushes were gone. Leaves were gone. All that was left of the trees—trees so tall they had touched the sky—were golden circles dotting the dirt. As far as Arrow could see, there was a line of earth, yellowed with the dust of chopped wood, pointing toward the Burnt Circle.

At its nearest end were six metal monsters like the one Arrow had tried to destroy. One had stains on the side—what was left of the ants. Somehow the humans had removed the ants, then built more of the machines. And the humans had constructed two more types: One had a large dome on its front with claws to scrape across land. The other had a barrel on its body, with a lid of teeth.

Blades whirled out of the arms of the tall machines. They sliced through the bottoms of the trees, while the clawed arms picked up the trunks and dumped them to be ground up by the teeth of the barrel.

*RUMBLE.*

*SLICE.*

*CRACK.*

*CRUNCH.*

With each noise, Arrow flinched.

With each cut, the forest bled.

Arrow stared at the devastation before him.

Until he heard the cry. Petari was hurting.

He searched for the blood leaf tree, but it was gone. Destroyed. Crushed into dust in the machiners' barrel monster.

Gritting his teeth, Arrow backed away from the raked land, then ran to his friends.

"They took . . . They took . . ."

"What's wrong?" Val asked.

Arrow fell to his knees, put his forehead to the earth. He tried to breathe, but air had left him. "It's gone. So quickly. Just gone."

"What do you mean?" Val held Petari's hand up and nudged Arrow with his elbow to make the boy answer.

But Arrow couldn't speak. No words would squeeze through his throat, thick with hurt. Tears rimmed his eyes, then streamed down his cheeks. "I'm sorry," he whispered. "I'm sorry."

He grieved for the loss of the forest, a loss I knew he felt in his blood as much as I felt in my cells. These trees were his home, his life, his family. And now they were gone.

"Help Petari." Val placed Petari's hand in Arrow's, then ran off in the direction of the destruction to see for himself what had upset Arrow so much.

Tracks of tears shined on Petari's face. "What happened, Arrow? What did you see?"

He shook his head, unable to put it into words.

Val came crashing back then. "They're tearing up the forest." He turned to Petari. "We've got to go. Now!"

"They've done what? How?"

"That's why the liana came down." Val's eyes followed the vine. "The tree it was connected to is no longer there. It's their fault we fell."

Petari stood up, but the pain in her hand made her cry out. Arrow swallowed hard. "I can wrap your hand with a palm frond until I can get some blood leaves. It'll at least keep the pressure on. Wait here."

He hurried to the nearest palm, pulled off some fronds with his right hand, and whispered, "Thank you." When he returned, Arrow cradled Petari's injured hand on his arrow arm, tucking one end of a frond beneath it. Then with his right hand, he wrapped the palm tight against her wound.

"How could they do that?" Petari asked. "How could they?"

Arrow shook his head. Grief still tore at his heart, at his gut, pouring into the air around him, thick and harsh. It ripped through me as well. All those voices snuffed out too early.

"What are we going to do now?" Val glanced around, fear spiking the earth beneath him.

"There are more blood leaves near the Guardian," Arrow said, making sure the palm fronds were secure.

"I'll be fine," Petari said, worry weighing her words. "We have to stop them!"

"Luco! And the others!" Val's eyes were wild. "Do you think they're okay?"

"I don't know." Arrow sucked in a breath. "Wait." He tilted his head and sniffed.

"What is it?" Val searched their surroundings more urgently now.

Arrow turned to Petari. "Can you walk a short way?"

She nodded.

Arrow hurried away. "Follow me."

He took them around the path of machines, which were still destroying trees. Staying behind the trunks that hadn't yet been touched, Arrow kept Val and Petari far enough out that they wouldn't be seen by the machiners. Then the children skirted around closer to the Burnt Circle and crawled behind a rock that already hid some human heartbeats.

"Lu—" Val started to shout, seeing the skinny boy, but Luco clapped his hand over the boy's mouth. Val nodded, then Luco released him.

"How did you find us?" Luco pulled Val into his chest for a hug.

Delora and Safa were huddled with him and patted Petari on the back.

"Arrow found you." Val pointed at the boy, who was peering around the rock for the machiners.

"Good job, Arrow." Luco pulled on my boy's arm, inviting him into their circle. Through his grief, this gave him some warmth.

"Where's Storma and Mercou?" Val asked.

"In the Fenix camp," Delora said.

"No!" Val whispered, clapping his own mouth shut so the word came out muffled.

Delora grinned. "Our plan worked beautifully."

"What do you mean?" Petari sat on the ground, resting her hurt palm on her knee.

"Storma and Mercou let themselves be captured by the copters," Luco said.

"Then the rest of us followed them down here," Safa continued.

"It took us a lot longer," Delora said.

"And my feet are killing me now," Safa mumbled, slipping her feet out of her shoes and rubbing them.

"We even saw some of your dangerous creatures." Delora pointed at Arrow. "You were right, they're mega scary. Lucky for us they were running away from the Stilters' machines. But I don't know how you haven't been eaten in here."

Despite his grief, Arrow gave her a light smile. The herd were seeing him differently now, and at least that was better.

The grinding and crunching stopped. Then there were shouts, and the machines began to make their way back to the camp.

"Why'd they let themselves get caught?" Arrow asked.

"It's all part of the plan," Safa said.

Arrow peered around the rock at the Burnt Circle. It looked different now. The new raked path, golden with the remains of the torn trees, was a sharp contrast to the dark scorched earth of the camp. The people and machines were the same, though. And still frightening.

Petari pushed against Arrow's shoulder, trying to get a look of her own while staying hidden.

"I can't believe they tore down all those trees, Arrow. I'm so sorry."

Arrow shook his head. Tears still glistened in his eyes. I felt his pain deep in my roots.

"You guys couldn't have stopped the machines from doing this?" Petari turned on the rest of the others.

"Keep your hair on. We only just got here a few minutes ago," Safa said.

"How are you going to get Storma and Mercou out?" Fear spiked the earth beneath Val as he no doubt remembered when he'd been tied up alone in that camp. At least this time, Storma and Mercou knew their friends were close. I just hoped their plan worked.

"You'll see." Safa grinned. "We'll be killing two birds with one stone, so to speak."

"We've been trying to see what kind of tech they have, so we know how well they can follow us," Luco said.

"They've got trikes." Val peered around the rock and pointed at a collection of the machines Arrow had ridden with Crankas. "I saw them when I was at the camp."

"Those things are quick," Safa said. "I got to ride one once. The rich people have all the fun toys."

Petari peered out farther. "I want to ride—" Her brother pulled her back quickly.

"You won't ride anything if they see you," Val whispered.

Petari slunk back, holding her injured hand to her heart.

"I don't see the two leaders," Arrow said. "There's a woman called Wiser and a man called Crankas. They must be with the machines heading to Shimmer Cave. We need to get there and stop them."

"Don't worry." Safa stretched her clasped hands in front of her, releasing a *pop, pop, pop* of her knuckles. "They'll be on their way here soon. When we get the signal, everyone needs to run out to the part that they've cleared shouting that you're being chased by some kind of animal."

"Safa and me will hang back and see if we can get the trikes so they can't follow," Luco said.

Everyone nodded.

"Are you sure they'll leave the forest?" Arrow asked.

"If they don't leave after this," Delora said, giggling, "I don't think they ever will."

"Really?" Arrow smiled, but confusion bore into the ground beneath him. I didn't understand either.

"What are you going to do?" Val asked.

"Mercou's the science wiz," Luco said. "He's figuring out—"

"AAH HA HA HA HA!"

The hum of noise coming from the Burnt Circle was suddenly broken with a loud, harsh laugh.

"AH HA HA HA HA!"

Delora's eyes widened. "It's Storma. That's the signal!"

"Okay, everyone, get out there and make some noise." Safa leaped from behind the rock, screaming, "Jaguars! Jaguars biting me!"

The others followed, Delora shouting, "Snakes! Gators!"

Val, Petari, and Arrow trailed after. They all screamed and shouted, jumped and hollered.

It had the desired effect. The machiners turned their way, many running out with their guns pointing at the imaginary animals. But also at the children.

Fear raked up my roots, but there was nothing I could do.

"Where are they?" Arrow whispered to Val. "What do we do now?"

Val shrugged. "They've got it figured out. Just keep them chasing us." He kept the group moving forward away from the camp, pursued by the angry machiners.

Until they heard a shout.

"Fire!"

The cry had come from Mora, the machiner who had first arrived in the forest with Wiser and Crankas. Arrow started running back toward the camp, followed by the other children.

When Arrow got close enough to see, he gasped. Mora was right. Flames twisted into the sky from one of the tents.

The machiners stopped chasing the children. Instead all eyes were on the fire as confusion filled the air.

Val pointed to Mora, who stood a little away from the camp and was talking into something he held up to his ear.

"He's probably calling the others back. What do we do now?"

Arrow was mesmerized by the fire. It no doubt reminded him of the day Crankas had crashed.

It pushed dread into my roots. There had been much destruction of the forest that day too, but I feared this would be worse.

A peal of laughter and slapping hands drew Arrow's attention. Storma, Mercou, Luco, and Safa were running up to the group of herders.

"That was awesome," Storma said. "Easy peasy to get that fire going."

Arrow spun around. "You set that?"

"No, it sprung up by magic." She smirked. "That'll keep the Stilters busy for a while."

"Don't you think that's extreme?" Val said. "This isn't the Barbs."

Storma turned on him. "They're Stilters. We need extreme!"

"It's okay." Mercou smirked. "It'll burn itself out even if they're such dust munchers, they can't figure out how to stop it themselves."

"But—" Arrow glanced back as a shout pierced his words.

"There!" Most of the machiners had retreated to the camp to help with the fire, but Fratos shouted to a group with guns ready. "Get those kids!" He pointed a stubby finger at Arrow and the other children.

"Run!" Luco shouted, and the children obeyed, falling and stumbling into the forest.

Machiners pounced after them, guns aiming.

Arrow's heart thumped harder, louder, faster with every footfall. He had been chased before, by animals quicker than these humans, but never with weapons that could stab him from afar.

He had to do what I'd taught him: trick, evade, outsmart. But how?

Delora screamed as a machiner grabbed the back of her shirt while she hid behind a tree trunk.

"Let her go!" screamed Mercou. Luco tripped the machiner, pulling Delora away.

"There's too many of them, and they can run faster than us," Val shouted at Arrow. "We need to climb up the trees or something."

Arrow's eyes had been scanning the forest. He glanced over to Val, shaking his head. "No, this way. Follow me!"

"This way!" shouted Val at the others, and the rest of the herd turned east after Arrow.

The change in direction didn't slow the machiners. One grabbed at Arrow and narrowly missed clamping onto the end of his left arm, but Arrow's feet pulled forward faster. Caught off guard, the machiner's foot slipped in some sloth dung, and the woman fell to the ground. She quickly pushed herself back up and resumed the chase with the other machiners.

But they were gaining fast.

A few more steps, and the children saw sunlight and a clearing up ahead. They'd come to the southeast finger of the river, which twisted down from the north. This patch was wide but covered in water lilies.

"Yes!" shouted Petari behind Arrow.

But the other children screamed.

"I hope that's shallow, because none of us can swim," Luco shouted.

"You don't have to," Petari said.

"Get onto the lilies," called Arrow.

"What? Are you kidding?" Storma slowed her running, glancing around. "We need a place to hide!"

"Trust me." Arrow pushed Safa onto the nearest one. The lily swayed but stayed afloat with the surprised girl lying on top.

"Get back here!" "Stop!" called the machiners, but the remaining children pushed ahead toward the swampy finger.

"Move forward," Arrow said to Safa. "Get on," he said to Mercou.

The boy hesitated, fear in his eyes. Petari stormed past him and jumped onto a lily of her own, keeping her injured hand high in the air.

"Come on," she shouted. "It's easy. Just watch out for gators and snakes."

"What?!" Safa searched the water around her in alarm.

"Just stay above the surface." Petari moved across the lily to the next, then the next, beckoning the others on.

The machiners were almost to the finger now, and Arrow was helping Val and Delora get onto the lilies.

"How is this going to stop them?" Luco pointed at the machiners.

"Go. You'll see," Arrow said, helping Val.

Luco reached out to the closest lily tentatively. "Are you sure this will hold Storma and me? We're bigger than you."

"It'll hold, but spread out your weight," Arrow said.

Luco shook his head but followed Arrow's instructions. Slowly he moved from lily to lily, almost tipping into the murky water when his knee pushed too hard on the edge of one of the lilies, but Val caught him. Storma went next.

Arrow was the last to get onto the lilies, and almost all of the children had crawled safely to the other side with the help of Val.

"A little water won't stop us," Fratos said.

"Don't go in there," Arrow shouted from his lily near the other side of the river. "Caimans and anacondas are under the surface. They'll kill you."

The machiners glanced at one another. Then the woman who had powered the beetle machine, Oxsen, said, "Just do what they're doing."

She began to crawl onto the nearest lily. Arrow stayed, watching.

"Don't!" he shouted as one of the men reached out for another lily. "That's a very bad idea."

"You know what's a very bad idea?" Oxsen said, shifting her weight onto the lily. "Messing with our equipment and—AAAHHH!"

The lily beneath her buckled, sending her tumbling under the water.

"Oxsen!" Fratos shouted. He turned to help her, but his momentum was already moving toward a lily, and he fell right through.

On the far side of the finger, the children laughed. Arrow didn't. He kept moving over the lilies until he got to the other side. When he looked back, the rest of the machiners were trying to pull Oxsen and Fratos out of the water.

*SPLASH.*

A black caiman as long as Fratos was tall sped toward them. Its maw was open. Sharp teeth glinted in the sunlight.

"Go!" Arrow motioned for the children to head west, away from the water.

Behind them, shouts and screams and *BANG*s rang out, but the children didn't look back. They followed Arrow past the water, leaving excitement and dread along their path.

"That was great," Petari said, running up to Arrow. She kept her injured hand tight against her belly.

"What were those things?" Luco glanced back, but trees covered his view.

"Giant water lilies," Arrow said. "They're strong enough to hold us, but they can't hold a caiman. I figured they probably couldn't hold a grown-up human either."

"Glad you were right," murmured Storma.

"This way." Arrow pointed to a wide tree that bent over a narrow part of the water. He trod over the trunk, then jumped off on the other side. The others followed him quickly. "We can get back to the camp from here."

"Why do you want to go back there?" Safa scrunched up her nose.

"To make sure they leave, of course," Petari said.

Arrow nodded, trying to hurry the others. "We can stay hidden this way, but—"

"We're not going back to the camp." Storma pulled Arrow to a stop. "You need to take us to that cave. Our little distraction will have pulled all the Stilters to the camp now. We need to get to the cave so we can get the gems for ourselves."

"What?" Arrow's eyes widened. "You didn't say anything about taking the Shimmer."

After everything, the herd had lived up to my expectations for them. I had so hoped they wouldn't.

Storma laughed. "You think we're fighting your battles for charity?"

"Or care what happens to a bunch of boring trees?" It was Safa's turn to chuckle.

My roots curled in anger.

"You want the gems?" Val's voice held disbelief.

At least some of the herders had changed.

"They're not boring trees." Arrow's words filled with rage. "You haven't listened to what we've told you."

Petari stepped between them. "They listened all right. They just didn't believe us. But you believed the part about the treasure, right?" She spat out the word "treasure" as she glared at Storma with narrowed eyes.

"If there's something here that's good enough for Fenix, it's good enough for us," Luco said. "Jom will get us a brill price for this stuff. With any luck, we'll get enough to pay for a place in the Stilts. A place all our own."

"We can live like the rich people for once." Storma smirked. "But don't worry, I'll take you and Val with me."

"I don't want to live in the Stilts." Petari's teeth were gritted. "I want to live here."

"Fine. Don't come," Safa said. "Just show us the cave."

"Arrow, look!" Val pointed to the sky. Gray clouds of smoke billowed over the canopy, but they weren't at the Fenix camp anymore.

"The fire." Delora's eyes grew wide. "It's spreading."

Mercou shook his head, but fear sparked from him. "It can't be. I made sure."

Arrow ran as fast as he could back to the Burnt Circle, the other children close behind. They didn't worry about hiding now. No one was looking for them anymore.

All eyes were on the flames.

The fire had spread to the other tents and attacked the boxes and equipment the machiners had brought. Mora had a tube that sprayed foam on the flames, but it was barely taming them. Other machiners filled buckets from the river, but the fire was too big.

"Why is it spreading so fast?" Petari said.

"It shouldn't be," Mercou said. "It was supposed to put itself out. Damage all their stuff so they'd leave, then put itself out."

"It's dry," Val said. "And windy. If they don't get it under control soon, they're going to be in trouble."

"The rainbow liquid was all around there." Arrow's words were quiet. "This whole place burned when Crankas crashed. He almost died. His leg caught fire. He left, but the rainbow liquid stayed."

"Rainbow liquid?" Delora asked.

"Oil. He's talking about oil." Mercou's voice shook. "Where was the oil, Arrow? Where?"

"Everywhere," Arrow said. "They dug it out, but . . ."

"What if they missed some?" Petari asked.

No one answered her. They watched the burning camp, fear soaking the ground they stood on. It filled my roots, too. The root network was alive with warnings, but what could we do?

"You think—" Val didn't have time to get the words out before the fire jumped to the table where he'd been tied up.

"They're not putting it out." Panic pricked Arrow's voice.

"This is ridiculous," Storma said. "They'll put the fire out. But we've got to get to the cave." She turned to Luco and Safa, her eyes screaming, *Come on.*

"That's right," Luco said. "Tell us where the cave is. We'll do all the hard work to get the gems out."

"No more fighting for food," said Safa. "No more sleeping on the floor. No more—"

Her dream was interrupted with a loud *BOOM.*

Flames rocketed into the sky from the far end of the camp.

Arrow and the herd ducked behind the trees. The machiners flattened on the ground.

*BOOM.*

A ball of fire surrounded the beetle monster.

*BOOM.*

A barrel at the front of the camp went up in flames.

"Gas cans," Val said, his hand in front of his mouth. "The fire caught the gas cans."

Storma backed up a few steps. "I didn't know they had gas cans."

"Of course they'd have gas there," Val said. "How do you think they're running the copter and machines?"

"I just . . ." Storma's mouth stayed open, but no more words were released.

"It was supposed to go out," Mercou repeated. "It was supposed to go out."

The machiners ran around, more frantic than ants without a trail, but their efforts to put out the flames weren't working. The fire roared larger. The wind pushed it farther.

"YOU!" Crankas pounded over to the group, face red with anger. "What did you do? Why did you do this?"

He turned to Arrow, shaking his head. "We were going to build something amazing here. We were going to save this forest."

"You weren't going to save it," Arrow shouted. "You were going to tear it apart to make money. You are the reason it was dying in the first place. You! Fenix! The chemicals you leach into the soil. You're killing this forest. You!"

Rage emanated from the boy, more than I'd ever seen.

"Crankas!" Wiser's voice called from the camp. "We're not going to get this under control. We've got to bail."

"We can't leave." Crankas watched the flames as he hurried across the path. "I've invested so much. All the plans. We don't have the gems."

Wiser shook her head. "We're not going to have our lives unless we go now. We can come back when the fire's down." She turned to the other machiners. "Get in the helicopter fast! Before the fire gets too close."

Crankas surveyed his camp. Metal monsters red with flame. Fabric huts devoured to dust. Glowing lights melted into dull discs.

"Now, Crankas, or I swear I'll leave you," Wiser shouted.

The two ran to the metal bullfrog. Other machiners were already inside. The arms on top began to spin as the last of the machiners ran out of the forest.

"Let's get out of here." Wiser pushed Crankas into the bullfrog. With all the machiners inside, the blades turned faster and faster.

Wind tousled the flames devouring the camp. Some were snuffed out. But others fought back. The fire rose up, caught the wind, and jumped again, this time to the trees.

Then again, to the bushes across the raked path.

Then again, to the trees farther in.

The metal bullfrog rose out of reach of the flames.

The children watched as it lifted higher and higher into the sky, then sped off toward the Stilts.

The machiners were safe, but the fire kept growing. The wind from the arms of the bullfrog had given the flames energy. They wanted more.

Sparks flew across the path to where the children stood.

Burst into flames that caught the dry leaves.

Spread into fires that devoured bushes and trees.

Petari screamed. Arrow pulled her clear of the heat.

"This way," Arrow shouted. The children ran, ran, ran

toward the river. They were farther from the flames, but the fire was growing.

I felt the losses.

The lack of rain had left the forest dry.

The downed leaves provided kindling.

The hungry flames devoured it all.

In the soil, bushes and trees took to their roots to say their goodbyes, passing on their knowledge to others through the network of fungi. Above, animals fled north. Birds winged high in the sky. All the residents of the forest tried to get away from the bite of the flames.

But the trees were stuck.

"It's burning the forest," Arrow cried. He turned on Storma, Luco, and Mercou. "Look what you've done. Look at it!"

Tears filled Mercou's eyes. "I set it to go out quickly. I didn't know it was going to spread."

Luco's shoulders dropped. "It was supposed to draw them back from the cave. That's all. Just clear the way for us."

"It's Fenix's fault." Storma glared at the burning camp. "They couldn't even put out a stupid fire. Then they left like cowards. It's their fault it got this big. Not mine. It's their—"

"No!" Arrow collapsed on the ground. "It's my fault. I should've never trusted you or the machiners. I should've listened to the Guardian. I should've fixed the magic myself. I should've found a way to protect the forest. I should've—"

"Arrow!" Petari and Val had run off to the north, tracking the flames' hungry path. Now they dashed back to the others. "ARROW!"

Arrow turned. "What?"

Petari pointed. "The fire is spreading toward the Guardian!"

THE ROOT NETWORK LIT UP WITH DYING TREES AND
BUSHES PASSING ON THEIR NUTRIENTS AND KNOWLEDGE,
BUT THE FUNGI THAT CONNECTED US WAS PATCHY.

Arrow sprang up, turning toward the kapok trees.

"We can't use the vines," Val said. "They might be burning farther down."

"The trikes!" Petari cradled her hand and ran through the charred bushes toward the razed path. Val, Arrow, and the others followed quickly.

Petari was right. The trikes were sitting patiently by the camp. And the fire hadn't surrounded them yet.

"I don't know how to make it go," Arrow said.

"I can figure it out. Come on." Val jumped into the

driver's seat, while Petari and Arrow took the other seats.

"You're not leaving us here." Storma jumped onto one of the other trikes. "Everyone, get on." She motioned for the others to load up the machines.

Luco climbed into the driver's seat of one, and Safa in another. The rest of the children pushed and pulled to find their own spots.

"Push the button," Val shouted to the others, then took off with Petari and Arrow. He maneuvered the trike around the flames, and Arrow shouted directions over the roar of the machine.

The other trikes followed, heading my way.

I had felt the fire's path cleaving toward me. I had begun to prepare. My knowledge, my history, the story of this forest was being shared.

I was glad Arrow was coming back to me, happy I'd feel his feet on my roots again. But I worried for his safety.

As soon as his trike barreled to a stop, Arrow climbed off and darted toward my trunk. "Guardian! Guardian!" He threw his arms around me.

The other trikes pulled up, and the children climbed off. They looked at Arrow embracing a tree. They looked at me. They whispered to one another.

But Arrow didn't care. Tears streamed from his face filled with sadness and worry.

"You're here!" Rosaman joined them with Ruthie in his

backpack, followed by Faive. "What's going on? All the monkeys suddenly left like their house was on fire."

Storma's eyes hit the ground.

"There *is* a fire," Petari said. "It's taking over the whole forest, thanks to them." She pointed at Storma and Mercou.

Mercou's eyes were still wide with fear and regret. "I didn't know. I didn't know," he mumbled.

"What are we going to do?" Rosaman hiked his backpack farther up his shoulders, Ruthie murmuring inside. "Are we leaving?"

No one answered him, just peered at Arrow, who was searching my branches. "Where's Curly?"

"I sent her north with her family. They're safe."

"Good. That's good." Arrow wiped the tears from his face. "What are we going to do, Guardian? How are we going to save the forest now?"

"With the little Anima that's left, I'm not sure what we can do," I said.

Arrow turned to the herd. "You should leave. Run as fast as you can north. Stay together as a group. Find the hole and go back to your Barbs."

"What are you going to do?" Petari asked.

"I'm staying here, in my home." Arrow collapsed on the ground at the base of my trunk.

The children glanced at one another, but no one moved.

"Arrow," I said, "you must go too. Go with the herd. Go north with Curly."

Arrow shook his head, silent tears running down his cheeks. "I failed, Guardian. I failed. I couldn't save the forest. I couldn't be like the Forest Dwellers."

"No!" I wished I could wrap my branches around my boy, wipe his tears with my leaves. "I asked too much of such a small boy."

Arrow gazed up at me. "You believed in me, but I couldn't fix the magic." He looked at his arms, one with a hand, one with a pointed end. "I was abandoned because I'm broken."

"You might've been abandoned once," I told him, "but to me, you were found."

He hugged me again, but his head still hung low.

"What are you talking about?" Petari tugged on Arrow's arm until he looked at her. "Look, I don't know why someone left you by that wall when you were a baby. But it wasn't because of you. It's because of them. Seriously, if you're broken, I must be completely useless."

Arrow wiped his tears. "That's not true."

"Dude, you grew up the only human here and figured out how to do all these brill things!" She gestured at the forest around them.

Seeing the blood-soaked palm leaves on her hand,

Arrow stood quickly, ran to the bush near my trunk, then returned with the leaves to help heal Petari's cut.

"See what I mean?" Petari said, as Arrow clasped her hand in the crook of his left elbow and began to unwrap the old palms. "You're amazing at tracking things. You know how to move through the forest without being seen or heard. And you can heal people with a bunch of leaves. That's more useful than all of us combined."

She nodded to the other children, who stood looking at Arrow as though seeing him in a new light.

"I did have help," Arrow said, rubbing the blood leaves carefully into the gash on Petari's hand. "And besides, I don't know all that stuff about making good soil like Val does."

Val smiled. "That's why we're a good team."

"What's a team?" Arrow asked, wrapping Petari's hand with new palm leaves.

"It's when people work together." Petari paused. "And, I'll admit, I'm not great at that. I wanted you to teach me about the leaves so I wouldn't need your help. I don't like needing anyone's help. I'm always afraid they'll leave, and I'll be on my own. But you can do so many things way better than I can. Like this." She lifted her injured hand.

"It feels better already." Petari focused on Arrow's eyes. "I need you. And right now, this forest needs you. You know it better than anyone, except maybe the Guardian." She smiled. "I'm not leaving here. There must be something we can do as a team."

"I'm not leaving either." Storma stepped closer. "Tell me what you need."

"Me neither," said Mercou, standing next to Storma.

"Nor me." Luco got in line. One by one all the herders moved closer, eyes on Arrow, waiting to know what they could do.

Flames licked the edges of a large capirona tree south of us. The ground was being scorched.

"I don't know. I don't know," Arrow said. "If only it would rain. I wish we could call the clouds and make it dump a heap of rain on us."

"That's the kind of request the Anima would help with," I told him. "You're thinking like a Forest Dweller now." Pride rippled through my leaves for this boy, my boy.

Arrow's eyes widened. "I am?"

Petari gazed up at me. "What did she say?"

Arrow told her, then said, "Maybe that's what I've been missing. Maybe I've been asking the Anima for the wrong things. Or asking in the wrong way."

"Go on," Petari said. "Try it again."

"I . . . I don't know if I can," Arrow said, not moving.

Petari flung her arms into the air in exasperation. "Mercou, tell him about that science guy who tried a lot."

"Thomas Edison?" Mercou said. "Oh yeah, he got his light bulb wrong thousands of times before he did it right."

"Exactly!" Petari said, turning to Arrow. "Have you tried this thousands of different ways yet?"

Arrow shook his head.

"Then what are you waiting for? Stop the fire!" Petari stepped back, as though she were giving Arrow space to act.

The other children stepped back too, perhaps suspicious of the idea of magic and what it would mean.

"Thousands," Arrow whispered to himself. "Thousands of tries. Ask for the rain. Dig deep."

A tree branch CRACKED a short distance away, then CRASHED to the ground.

"No pressure or anything," Storma said, her voice shaky, "but the fire is getting closer."

Arrow was trembling, but he got down on his knees and scrabbled in the dirt. Suddenly he stopped and lifted his palm, examining the dry soil in his hand.

"Maybe I don't do it like you, Guardian. You dig deep with your roots, but there's no way humans can dig like that. Maybe we access the magic by digging deep with our hearts."

Petari started nodding rapidly. "Yes, that sounds good. Try that."

"Perhaps that's what the Forest Dwellers meant. We'll

do it together," I told him. "Me with my roots and you with your heart."

Val smiled. And Luco. And Storma. And all the other children.

Arrow's lips thinned.

Kneeling, he placed his palm and the end of his arrow arm on the ground, took a deep breath, and closed his eyes.

His emotions rained through his arms and knees deep into the soil. Fear, mixed with love, mixed with courage.

He thought about the forest, his home, about the animals who lived here, about these children who had accepted him—who believed in him. He thought about the fire, the loss, the grief. He thought about the rain.

"Please, clouds, come and rain over us. Take out this fire. Save our forest."

He held his emotions in his heart, put them all into his request.

Waited.

Pleaded.

Breathed.

But nothing happened.

"The rain has been too dried up," I told him. "We haven't had clouds for moons. There isn't enough Anima to create them."

Arrow slumped.

The CRACKLE of fire was louder now. A palm close to us burned up in a poof of flames, then clattered onto its side.

Petari gasped, her hand over her mouth. She started to step toward Arrow, but Val held her back. "He'll think of something. You'll think of something, Arrow."

Arrow looked at his new friends. Sorrow poured from him. Despair curled around his toes. He pushed it away and sat up again.

He thought of all the parts of the forest. He imagined Shimmer Cave, and the giant water lilies, and the river with its powerful waterfall . . .

Arrow sat up straighter. "The river! The waterfall! That's already here. That's what we need."

"Do it! Do it!" Petari jumped up and down.

"Yes, Arrow," I said. "Ask."

He looked down at the ground, readying himself, then glanced back at me, worry clouding his eyes.

"But what about all the animals?"

"I'll warn them," I said. "But if you don't do this fast, they'll be dead anyway."

Arrow nodded, nervousness swirling around him.

As I sent word to all the residents of the forest to get high, to get safe, Arrow placed his palm and the end of his arrow arm on the ground again, breathed deeply, and closed his eyes.

"River, we need your water. We need you to save this forest, to banish this fire. Please, River, help us. Send your water over the edges of your beds. Send it to the trees and bushes. Make it douse this . . ."

A crackle tugged at my attention. The fire had reached my branches. Flames burning into the leaves and bark. I pushed the pain away. I had to concentrate on the magic. I had to help Arrow bring it up.

Then, suddenly, my roots tingled. Deep down. The Anima was pulsing in the soil. Pulsing in my roots. I hoped Arrow could feel it too, but in case he couldn't, I said, "It's working, Arrow. It's working!"

The river had heard. Water sloshed against its banks. I pulled up the magic and sent it that way. *Listen to the boy*, I told the river. *Listen and help. Save the forest.*

"Keep asking, Arrow," I told him. "Keep asking."

And he did. Filling his request with all the love he had for the forest and the creatures living under its canopy. He thought of Curly, playing with her brothers and sisters in the nest. He thought of the sloths, and how the monkeys teased the babies for being slow. He thought of the jaguars and black caimans and anacondas, who were dangerous, but also part of forest life.

He thought of the trees and flowers and fruit. The acai berries that had made him feel happy whenever he was sad. The malva leaves that had healed rashes. The blood leaves that healed his cuts. The anise that made his stomach better after he'd eaten too many acai berries.

The river roiled and splashed. The waterfall bucked and swelled.

"Help us!" Arrow screamed.

And the water from every finger and leg of the river pulled together. Lifted. Rose into a giant wave. The tip was taller than the towering kapok trees.

It held there for a breath, two, three.

Then the wave crashed down and tumbled through the forest.

The *ROAR* was louder than any animal. Louder than the metal birds.

It raced past bushes. Carved around trunks.

It picked up burnt logs and leaves and twigs. Carried them with its tide.

"It's coming!" I shouted to Arrow. "Get everyone up high!"

Arrow opened his eyes, and there, not too far away, he could see the giant wave of water heading toward them.

"Climb!" he shouted. He pointed to the lianas leading up to my highest branches. "Go! Quickly!"

The children screamed and hurried toward my trunk.

Petari was the first one up. Then she pulled up Rosaman with Ruthie in the pack on his back. Then Faive, Val, Safa, and more. They were like ants, linking and helping one another to the next branch and the next.

"Get as high as you can," Arrow shouted up, as he waved over the last of the herd.

"I can't climb," Storma said. Thick fear held close to her body. "I don't like heights."

"You can do it," Arrow said. "You have to. Take this." He gave her the vine that he used to hoist food into his nest. "Hold on to the vine and the tree, and look out, not down."

Storma nodded quickly, her breath ragged. Then she held on to the vine and pulled herself up.

The giant roll of water was closer now.

Flames had been snuffed out.

Sparks had been crushed.

But the water could still do a lot of damage of its own.

In just a few breaths it would be on top of me. On top of these children.

"Get up, Arrow," I said. "Now!"

He was helping Storma onto the branches. They climbed higher as Arrow pulled himself up. His hand on one branch, his elbow crooked around another. But he was still too low.

"Go, Arrow! GO!" I shouted.

He glanced back. Panicked. His toe slipped.

The wave hit me.

The wall of water slammed into my trunk, ripping leaves and twigs as it doused the last of the fire.

In my branches, the children held on, Rosaman cradling Ruthie in the pack against his chest. As water raced upward, they all screamed.

All except Arrow, who sucked his breath tight into his lungs.

Leaves and mulch and twigs swarmed around Arrow as he clung to my branch underwater. He held his breath for one, two, three, four . . .

Finally the wave passed.

The fire was out.

The children peered down.

"Arrow!" Storma rushed to Arrow's body, slumped against my branch. She pushed him, hit his back. Arrow coughed, water rushing out from his mouth, and Storma smiled.

The water began to recede, back to its home in the river.

The forest was saved.

THE DEATHS LOOMED LARGE IN THE FOREST. THE
POLLUTION HAD DONE ITS DAMAGE. THE MACHINERS HAD TORN
US DOWN. THE FIRE HAD SWEPT US CLEAN. ONE MORE DEATH
WAS TO COME. ONE TO HOPEFULLY SAVE MANY.

The children quickly descended my branches, but not
before they marveled at Arrow's nest.

"You really sleep here?"

"How did you build it?"

"Can we build nests too?"

Arrow was pleased. He liked the attention—the appreciation. His energy was no longer stuffed full of doubt and
fear but swirled around him, light and warm.

"That was amazing," Petari said when they were all safely
back on the forest floor. Ruthie cooed as Rosaman brought

her out of the backpack, making the children laugh as their anxiety shredded away.

Petari put her arms around Arrow, squeezing him into a tight hug. "You did it. You saved us and the whole forest. You saved our home."

Arrow's eyes bulged with surprise, but his face lit up. He had only been hugged by Curly and her family. This was better.

Word of the fire's demise spread quickly throughout the forest, and the residents that had fled north began to return. Curly was among the most excited to be back. Nervous to go, she had stayed as close as possible. Now she barreled through the trees and launched herself onto Arrow's head.

He staggered back from the force, laughing all the way.

"Curly! I missed you."

The monkey jumped onto Arrow's arm, hung off his fingers, twisted around his back, then climbed up to nuzzle his neck.

"That's a pretty mega monkey, Arrow," Luco said, stepping forward. "You're pretty mega yourself."

Arrow frowned. "I'm big?"

Luco laughed. "No, you're mega. Like, great. You're one of us . . ." He glanced at the other children for help, but Arrow laughed.

"I understand. You're pretty giant yourself." He smirked,

but now it was Luco's turn to swim in doubt. He wasn't sure if Arrow was telling a joke.

Storma slunk up to Arrow then, her head hung low. "I'm really sorry about the fire. I didn't think any of this would happen. I didn't . . ."

Arrow nodded. "I know."

"I don't want to take those gems, either," she added. "They should stay where they are. Everything in the forest should stay exactly as it is."

"I'll show you Shimmer Cave one day," Arrow said. "You won't want to give it away once you see it." He smiled, then turned back to me.

"Guardian, is the magic back now? Did I help it?"

I was slow to answer. What I had to tell the boy next he wouldn't like, and possibly wouldn't understand, but it was the only way.

I had underestimated the boy. I had always known he was smart, but his doubts about himself had prevented him from seeing how much he could do.

That had all changed today, though. He had called up the Anima. He had put out the fire. He had saved the forest. And now he saw through my stalling.

"Guardian!" His voice held an edge of despair. "Your leaves."

He pointed to my leaves, which had turned yellow, then brown, and begun to rain around the herd.

"What's wrong, Guardian?" He hugged my trunk. "What's happening?"

I didn't want to tell him the truth, even though he would discover it soon enough. But Petari's father had been right—untruths pollute us, and this forest had enough pollution from the outside world.

Petari and Val hurried to my side as well.

"What is it?" Petari asked.

"I am too weak, Arrow," I said. "I have been giving my nutrients to help the younger trees. Ones that were burned. Ones that were suffocated. Ones whose soil is more scorched than mine."

"But I'll help them," Arrow said. "We'll help the other trees, right?" He turned to Petari, Val, and the rest of the children. They nodded, murmured, "Yes" and "Of course."

But that would not be enough.

"They need help that only I can give," I said. "And if I don't help them, they will die."

"But you're too weak." The pitch of Arrow's voice was getting higher and higher, filled with panic. "If you help all the trees in the forest, you won't have any nutrients for yourself. You'll die. You can't die, Guardian. Please, don't die."

Petari gasped. Tears sprung to her eyes.

Tears were in Arrow's throat and voice, and now flowed down his cheeks.

"It's all right, Arrow." I tried to make my voice as gentle

as possible. "I have lived for many, many, many rings. More than you will ever see. And I will never fully be gone. Many of the trees in this forest grew from my seeds. I will be in them and in every animal that has lived in my shade and every insect that has feasted on my leaves."

"But—"

"Listen to me, Arrow. I was wrong about the humans."

"What do you mean?"

"Not all humans are like the Imposters. And even when humans make mistakes, they can change," I said. "You trusted that they could be good. You believed in them, Arrow. When you believe in someone, you open a door and hope they'll step inside. I had forgotten that, and how much the forest needs humans to be a part of our lives, just like humans need the forest. When we live together, we are better than when we live separately. I hope that one day, the curtain will no longer be needed."

Arrow smiled, a tear-filled smile, and hugged me tighter.

I pulled on some Anima, wriggled a few of my roots, and lifted them from the soil. Wrapping them around my boy, I hugged him close.

"You are the very best thing that has happened to this forest for many rings," I told him. "You, Arrow, are our magic."

Tears streamed from the children's eyes. Curly leaped into my branches and wrapped her arms around me. Petari flung her arms around my trunk. Then Val. Then Safa. Then

Storma, and Luco, and . . . all the herd piled up to hug me.

"I love you, Arrow," I said. "You are strong. You are good. You will protect this forest."

"No!" Arrow screamed. "Don't die."

But my end had come. The last of my nutrients and knowledge passed through my roots to the other trees and flora in the forest.

My rest . . .

came . . .

now . . .

"Arrow . . .

"Arrow, can you hear me?

"Arrow, are you there?

"Arrow! We have work to do."

Arrow doesn't look up. He's still sobbing by my mother's side, arms wrapped around her trunk.

But there is movement among the children. The girl, Petari, pokes her head above the others and says, "Did you guys hear that?"

"Petari," I say. "You can hear me?"

She pulls herself out of the huddle of children and glances around. "Whoa! Who said that?"

"It is me, the Guardian."

Her brother looks up at her then, eyes wide, heart thumping. "Tell me you just said you're the Guardian."

"You heard it too?" A slow grin breaks out on Petari's face. "Does that mean . . . ?"

"It's nice to meet you, Petari. And you, Val. Could you tap Arrow on the shoulder for me?"

Petari, eyes still bigger than the sun, does as she's told. "Arrow! Did you hear that? The Guardian's not dead. The Guardian—"

Arrow lifts his head and blinks in the sunlight.

"Hello, Arrow."

"Guardian?" he says. "But you're not—"

"No, I'm not the Guardian you know. Not the Guardian who brought you here. I am the new Guardian of the forest."

Petari gasps, but Arrow frowns. "New Guardian? We don't need a new Guardian. We need . . ." He breaks into sobs again.

"I understand how you're feeling, Arrow. I'm also grieving. The Guardian, your mother, who brought you into the forest, she was my mother too. She had been the Guardian of the forest for more rings than I know. And I'd hoped she'd be the Guardian for many, many more."

Arrow nods slowly.

"But she knew this time would come," I continue. "And she knew that a life lived in the service of others is the best life of all."

Arrow presses his lips together. "So you're . . ."

I give him a breath. Sometimes we need a moment to let a new reality sink in. "I am the new Guardian," I tell him again.

"Yeah." He sniffs. "But you're the Guardian's daughter?"

This seems to make him the most happy.

I laugh. "Yes, I am. I am her oldest. I grew from one of the first seeds she dropped as a new tree. She has been teaching me to be the Guardian ever since I sprouted, long before you arrived."

"This is incredible." Petari gives a little jump.

Arrow turns to her, understanding dawning on his face. "You can hear!"

Petari nods rapidly.

Val says, "Me too!"

Arrow smiles, then turns to the others. "What about you? Can you hear her?"

Luco frowns. "What are you guys talking about?"

"The new Guardian," Petari says. "She's talking to us now."

Storma shakes her head, and I can feel sadness below her feet. "I can't hear anything."

"Maybe it's because we were connected to the Guardian before, when we saw the Stilts," Val says.

"I want to hear," says Faive.

"Yeah," says Rosaman, Ruthie cooing in his arms as though she agrees.

The others join in, and finally I say, "Children. Children!" Petari quiets them.

"Right before she died, the Guardian told me everything that has happened in the forest, from the crash of the metal bird until now. You have all been wonderful, but we don't have much time. The forest is not out of danger yet."

"What do you mean?" Petari asks, after repeating my words for the others. "The fire is gone."

"And the Guardian's nutrients helped the damaged trees," Arrow says.

"Yes, but the forest was dying long before the fire. If we're going to survive, we have to fix the Anima."

Val, who has been pacing around my mother's trunk, stops and says, "It's the pollution, remember? From Fenix."

Luco steps forward. "Fenix is polluting this place? Why am I not surprised?"

"Those mutants don't care about polluting," says Storma. "But they put their factories out in the Barbs, not in the Stilts. Then the rich people don't have to breathe in their disgusting fumes."

"Everyone breathes it in," says Val. "It doesn't matter where you are. Pollution travels in the air. The people in the Stilts are breathing it in, even if they don't know it."

"They did create the problem," says Luco.

"And they should suffer for it," Safa says.

"Hold on!" Storma lifts her hands. "We can't put all the blame on them. We've done bad stuff too. We threw out all that trash in the village. I know it hurt Curly, and I'm sorry." She gives the monkey a weak smile. Curly sticks out her tongue, which makes Storma smile bigger.

Then Storma shakes her head. "No more 'them versus us.' I mean, look at this. This whole forest was almost destroyed because we were fighting them. And we were doing that to get what they had. What I'm saying is, it's our fault too. I don't know how we fix it, but I'll do whatever you need."

"Thank you." Arrow collapses onto his butt on the ground. "How do you stop something that's so far away? And how do you fix something that's been dying for so long?"

The children fall silent, then Storma speaks up again. "You restore it."

All eyes turn to her. Hope spins across the ground, and I feel it grow inside me as well.

"Before she died, my mom used to go to the dump and find old things people had thrown away and restore them, like tables, and cabinets, and benches. She used to say we didn't need to build new things if we could restore and reuse our old ones. People thought she was weird." Storma shrugs. "But what if we can restore the forest somehow?"

"Yes!" Val raises his finger in agreement. "The pollution

has been killing the soil, so we have to restore it. That's it!"

"Can we do that?" Arrow asks.

"You showed us that the forest has everything it needs," Petari says. "Like all those leaves and things that can heal us. Can't they heal the forest too?"

Luco nods, picking up on the thread Petari has begun. "Yeah, I see what you mean. We have to figure out how to restore the soil the way the forest would."

Petari smiles. "Exactly."

I like how these children think.

Val shakes his head. "Good soil takes a really long time to make, like years. Rocks have to break down; then worms eat pieces and poop them out in another way so plants can use them.... It's a whole thing. That's why Fenix makes their chemical fertilizers, to speed it up."

The group's hope begins to fade, but Arrow slowly stands, excitement growing around him. "But what if the forest can speed it up?"

"I will do whatever I can," I tell them.

Val turns to Arrow. "What do you mean?"

Arrow grins, like he knows a secret. "I just asked the river to flood the entire forest to put out a fire, and it did. Maybe we can ask for what we need to make the good soil faster."

Val's eyes light up. "Yes! That'll do it."

"Was what you said about the rocks and worms and stuff all we'd need?" Arrow asks.

"Ummm." Val studies the ground. "I'm not sure. I can't remember everything Dad told me. But microbes, grubs, and worms decompose leaves and dead stuff, and that gives nutrients. Some plants have roots that go deeper than others, and they can bring up nutrients from below. Oh, also, when rodents bury themselves and dig, they turn the soil over, which helps too."

Delora scrunches up her nose and picks up her feet, eyes watching carefully for any moving bumps across the ground.

"I'll bet those snakes slithering around help to spread the leaves too," Petari says.

Delora's eyes roam for the creatures.

"Anything that will help," Storma says. "What do you think, Arrow? Will this do it?"

Arrow shrugs. "The Guardian didn't teach me about this stuff, but maybe it'll be enough to push away the pollution. We can try."

He gets onto his knees and places his arrow arm and his palm on the soil again, just like when he worked with my mother to call the river. Closing his eyes, he sucks in a deep breath. Then I feel his pull on the Anima. He puts what Val has told him into his head and makes the requests, infused with his love for the forest.

His requests dig down deep into the ground. Worms wriggle faster. Leaves shrivel up and release their nutrients.

Trees and other plants spread their roots. Rats race through the soil to turn it over.

And buds and leaves begin to peek out from dying branches.

"It's working," Petari shouts. She points at the coconut tree near her whose leaves had drooped. Now the leaves have pulled up, up, up until they're rising proudly above their trunk. Buds start to sprout on a heliconia bush. And the camu camu shrub begins to brim with baby berries.

The children gaze around them, watching the transformation, eyes wide and hearts blooming.

"Keep going," Val shouts, eyeing the dried orchids on branches. "It needs more."

I can feel that he's right. The Anima has only reached the smallest part of the forest around my mother's trunk.

Arrow begins to shake, gritting his teeth.

"Come on, Arrow!" Petari says.

But sweat pours off his brow and down his back. It is taking too much out of him.

"Stop," I tell him. "It's too hard, Arrow. Stop."

"AAAAHHHH!" The scream races through him, filled with frustration, disappointment, anger with himself. "I can't do it."

"You tried, Arrow," I tell him. "You were great. You helped a lot."

He curls forward, his arms hugging his belly. "The forest is too big. I'll never be able to fix it all."

"We'll do little parts," I tell him. "We'll keep it up."

Arrow shakes his head. "The pollution will keep coming in. What if I can't clear the forest fast enough?"

Sadness rolls around each of the children as they watch Arrow. Then Petari looks up.

"Why don't we try it?"

"What do you mean?" Val asks.

"We can hear the Guardian now," Petari says, looking at her brother. "Maybe if we can do the same thing Arrow's doing, we can cover more ground."

Arrow's eyes light up. "Yes, let's try it." He looks at the other children too. "Let's all try it."

Storma points at her chest. "Us too? We can't hear the tree."

Arrow shrugs. "So what? Do you believe that the Guardian and the magic are there?"

Luco laughs. "After seeing what happened with the river and the roots hugging you? Dude, I'd believe it if you said fairies lived in the forest."

The children chuckle. And I can feel warmth filling the air, the ground, the soil.

I like it.

Arrow picks up his feet, like he can feel the warmth too,

then he gazes at the group again. Children who were lost or abandoned like him. Children who have made a family together.

"Why didn't I think of this before?" he murmurs to himself, then says louder, "That's it!"

Petari frowns. "What?"

"Us. The forest. Us and the forest." Arrow waves his arms to show them the trees and grubs and monkeys. "The Guardian always said that everything has its place in the forest, everything has a job to do. Whether it seems like it or not, each living thing helps the forest as a whole. That's like you and your group. You each have jobs that help everyone."

The children smile at one another, happiness forming waves around them.

"Until Crankas crashed and I met you, I'd been the only human here for my whole life," says Arrow. "But the Anima was so broken, I couldn't fix it all by myself. Just like the old Forest Dwellers who lived here, we all have to work together to save the forest."

Storma steps forward. "I'm ready. Tell me what to do."

Luco does the same, then Safa, Petari, and Val. One by one, each of the children steps forward to join in. Even Ruthie gargles as Rosaman nods in agreement. Some are filled with trepidation, nervous pulses thumping against the ground, but excitement sparks in the air around them too.

Arrow grins, and his nervousness thins out and dissipates. He has found his place, bringing people together.

"Let's hold hands," he says. "So we're connected to one another. And sit on the ground so we're connected to the forest."

The children quickly move into a circle, Rosaman tucking Ruthie into his lap. Petari gives Arrow a warm smile as she wraps her fingers around the end of his arrow arm. He smiles back.

"Val, you say what we need out loud," Arrow continues. "Then we'll all ask for it from the forest, in our hearts. But..." He pauses, looking each of them in the eye. "Let the forest know how much you care."

The children nod. Storma lets out a loud, "Whoop!"

"I like this plan, Arrow," I tell him. Then I prepare to do my part too.

Val clears his throat. He's nervous—it drips into the ground below him—but he peers at the circle of children, all ready to follow him, and his heart lifts.

Together, the children call on the worms and the grubs. They ask the monkeys and sloths to throw ripe fruit onto the ground. They ask the snakes to push through the leaves, the fish to stir up the water, the birds to scratch at the soil. They ask the plants to reach in, to dig deep, to pull up nutrients.

The children put all their care of the forest into their

thoughts, and soon, love builds and spirals within their circle. With each request, it grows stronger and faster, building and building until there's a whirlwind of love sparkling with magic rising from within them.

All around, dying trees and bushes spring to life. Leaves bud then grow bigger, some going their full cycle, then dropping to the ground to be digested quickly and turned into more nutrients. Roots twist and lengthen, pulling up the nutrients from below to the roots that need them.

I can feel the Anima building and building; then suddenly the earth below the forest ripples around me. Waves of magic push outward, turning the soil and feeding the plants all the way to the edges of the forest.

The leftover stumps from the trunks the machiners tore down find new life growing within them. The burnt tents and machines are turned over and kneaded into the ground. Grass and bushes twirl up in their place, strong and bright.

All around the circle of children breathing their love and life into the forest, flowers bud, then grow, then bloom.

As far as the humans can see, every tree and branch has a brilliant orchid smiling at them. And they all glow as brightly as the sun.

IN THE NORTH, PALM SEEDS SPROUT. IN THE EAST, BUDS POP ONTO A MALVA BUSH. IN THE WEST, A NEW BROMELIAD UNCURLS. IN THE SOUTH, A WIMBA TREE STRETCHES OUT A NEW BRANCH. BEES RETURN TO POLLEN. ANTS RETURN TO NECTAR. ANIMALS VENTURE FROM THEIR HIDING PLACES. ALL OVER THE FOREST, NEW LIFE BEGINS AGAIN.

"You did it," I tell the children. "The forest is brighter and healthier than I have seen it for many rings. Even the curtain is complete again."

Arrow beams.

Storma says, "Who's saying that?"

"Yeah, who's talking about rings and curtains?" Luco glances around.

"I heard it too," says Safa.

"Me too," says Delora.

"Yeah, me too," says Mercou.

One by one, they all say they heard me, and when Arrow tells them, "That's the new Guardian," his smile gets even bigger.

My leaves dance in the wind. The chlidren are one with the forest now, and we are one with them.

Mother always used to say she missed the Forest Dwellers. But now we have new humans to live among us.

The herd throw questions at Arrow about the forest, the Anima, and me, until he raises his hands and says, "I don't know everything. We'll have to figure it out together."

Then Faive asks one more. "Will we always hear the Guardian? Will she always hear us?" The others gather in closer for his answer, but he shrugs.

"I've heard the Guardian for as long as I've been in the forest," he says. "I imagine that as long as we live with the land and as long as we open ourselves to listen, we'll always be connected to the forest."

He goes quiet for a breath, a small frown forming on his forehead, then says, "Guardian, where are you?"

Oh! In all the excitement, I hadn't shown the children where I am.

"You know the Crooked Rock?"

Arrow nods.

"East of that, look for the largest tree, with branches that make the shape of a circle."

"Come on," Arrow says, and the children come pounding

toward me. When they near the spot, Arrow slows, and the others follow. All eyes are on the branches, looking for the circle. Looking for me.

"You are close," I tell them.

Then Petari points. "There!"

I see myself through Curly's eyes, from Arrow's shoulder. Tall, strong, golden leaves shining in the evening sun.

"Hi, Guardian." Arrow smiles at me.

"Hi, Arrow."

Over the next few days, the children decide where they're going to make their homes, at the village or in the forest, closer to me. I like that they move close to me. Storma and Luco are still looked at as the leaders, and they hand out tasks that are completed with a smile. Arrow is consulted on everything for the forest and in charge of training the others in medicines and food. He enjoys this job. Soon, work is underway on new homes for them all, with the design of Arrow's nest the most appealing. But Mercou finds ways to improve it.

Even Curly is happy with her new home, and her brothers and sisters have adopted the herd as their family too.

Everyone seems happy, rested, at peace . . .

Except Arrow.

As the herd work and play, Arrow wanders off. But he doesn't do the things he used to enjoy: fly along lianas, hang with the sloths, swim in the river.

He takes long walks around the forest, searching . . .

· He peers at leaves.

He touches buds.

He sifts through soil.

Curly tries to drag him into playtime with her brothers and sisters, but Arrow smiles with a sadness in his eyes, then climbs to my highest branch and gazes out.

I feel the worry in every one of his actions, the anticipation before each of his breaths.

So I'm not surprised when, over a meal of nuts, breadfruit, and, of course, acai berries beneath my branches, Arrow goes quiet as he holds Ruthie. He feeds her a piece of mango, steels himself, then says, "I have to go."

Petari frowns as she wipes mango juice from her chin. "What do you mean? Go where?"

"To the Stilts."

Curly screams from his shoulder, slapping his head. Petari sits straighter, quickly followed by the others.

"Why do you want to go there?" Petari says, wrinkling her nose.

"After everything we did, you want to leave?" Luco frowns.

Arrow hands Ruthie to Rosaman, then waves his arms. He swallows. "Wait." I can feel the nervousness twist around his feet. "It's not that I want to go. The pollution is going to come back. The magic won't last forever. Not unless the people in the Stilts live with the forest like we do."

"So what are you saying?" Petari asks.

Arrow hugs Curly close and swallows. "I need to go there and stop them from polluting the earth. I have to make them see that they must live *with* the earth like the Forest Dwellers did with the forest."

Silence trembles over the children.

I feel it too. I don't want Arrow to leave. And yet . . .

"You're right," Petari says. "I don't like that Fenix is polluting everything and the Stilts people are letting it happen, but maybe they don't know."

"They know," Luco says. "At least some of them do. And the others don't care."

Murmurs of agreement come from the other children, but Arrow stands up.

"It doesn't matter what they did in the past. What matters is what they do now and going forward." He glances at me and the other trees nearby. "I can't let this forest die. I won't. It has to stay alive for a long time, for us, for Ruthie, for every creature here. But even if we stay hidden away, we'll still be affected by the cities outside. I have to make the humans in the Stilts understand."

"But you can't leave," Delora says. "We need you here. Those people don't need you."

Arrow talks a deep breath, his shoulders sagging. "I don't want to go, but I also don't want the Anima to be in danger anymore. Pollution is already coming back in."

He smiles a sad smile. "You can take care of the Guardian and the forest. I trust you. But out there . . ." His eyes gaze toward the north. "We'll never be completely safe until that pollution is gone. And besides, the Guardian hoped that one day the forest wouldn't have to be hidden behind a curtain. Won't that be a good day?"

There's a silence in the forest, all the children and animals soaking this in, until I say, "Yes, Arrow. That will be a good day."

Curly whimpers, curling around his neck.

The children look at one another, uncertainty thick between them.

Petari stands. "I'll go with you."

"No," Val says. "You should stay. I should go. I'm the one Dad taught about the trees and stuff."

"He taught me, too." Petari crosses her arms. "And besides, these guys need you here to help, right?"

Luco shrugs. "We can always use your help, Val. But I think Arrow's mission needs you more." He turns to Petari when she opens her mouth to protest. "It needs both of you. But you three can't go alone. It's too dangerous."

Petari rolls her eyes. "I can take care of myself. And them."

"Remember what you said about being part of a team?" Arrow chuckles.

"Okay." Petari sighs, but she's smiling.

Storma stands. "I'm going with you. Not that you need a bodyguard, tough one." She winks at Petari. "But I've got friends there who can help."

Petari grins. "Brill."

"Thank you," Arrow says, but a sadness still seeps from him. "What if we can't get them to listen?"

Storma stalks over to Arrow. "Kid, you convinced me. And if you can convince me, you can change the whole world."

The next morning, as the sun rises, Storma, Petari, Val, and Arrow say their goodbyes. Curly clings to Arrow's ankle, but he tells her she has to take care of the herd until he comes back. The monkey looks around at the children, nods, then jumps into Delora's open arms.

"Be quick and be safe," Luco says.

"We will." Storma smiles, then the group leaves their camp.

Before they head toward the north curtain, Arrow takes them west, to the place he loves, to his home.

"I won't be long," he says, then scurries up my mother's branches.

"Hi, Mother," he whispers, a small smile crossing his face as he runs his fingertips over his nest. He reaches down and pulls out the knife he had kept in its folds, the knife the monkeys had collected after the Forest Dwellers left, the knife my mother had told him to use to carve his arrow in her bark. Then he turns, finds the lines of the arrow, and whittles the section away. Holding the piece of bark in his palm, he says, "I will always remember who you taught me to be, Mother. And you'll always be with me."

He begins to put the knife back into the folds of his nest, but reconsiders and stuffs it into the pocket in his shorts instead. Then he leans to my mother's trunk, kisses her, and climbs down.

"Okay," he tells the others. "I'm ready."

"About time," Storma says. "At this rate, the Stilters will pollute the whole world before we get there."

"Really?" Arrow asks, anxiety pulsing from him.

Storma laughs. "I've got to teach you about sarcasm."

Petari and Val laugh too. Arrow smirks and says, "That could be difficult."

And he chuckles with them.

When they get to the north curtain, I check the soil outside, but there are no footsteps. I open a small hole for them to go through.

"I will miss you," I tell them. "But the curtain will always be open to you."

"I'll miss you too, Guardian," Arrow says, before they walk through. "Take care of the forest."

"I will."

I feel for their footsteps for as long as I can, until finally, they are too far away in the dusty earth.

Arrow, the boy who was named for being straight and true, is right: We won't be safe until the whole world lives with us. As hard as it is to let him go, this boy, this human who doubted himself then saved us all, I know that I must. This is his destiny.

My mother, the Guardian of the forest, would be proud.

# Author's Note

This story came out of a few pieces of inspiration that all happened around the same time. A boy with one hand who lived in a tree popped into my head, but I had no idea what this boy's story was. Then I saw a TED Talk by Suzanne Simard, a professor of forest ecology at the University of British Columbia, on how trees in a forest talk to one another (TED.com/talks/suzanne_simard_how_trees_talk_to_each_other), and I knew I wanted to share this with the world. Around that time, construction crews around my neighborhood were tearing down trees to make way for more apartment buildings, a hideous noise I couldn't keep out of my ears.

These three things gave life to this story, but really its birth began when I was ten and first went into the Amazon. My family is from Guyana, where I was born, and my parents grew up with the rainforest, rivers, and creeks of South America in their backyard. Unfortunately, my family's safety was threatened due to political problems in the country, and we were forced to leave when I was very young. The last time

I was there, I was ten, but the trip impacted me for the rest of my life, especially when we went into the "interior," as the rainforest is locally known. Sitting on the edge of the boat as we floated down the river weaving into the Amazon, I was in awe of the enormous trees, the songs of the brightly colored birds, and the smell of the soil, flowers, and animals. I also loved when we stopped to give supplies to the AmerIndian tribes living inside the forest. They had big smiles and even bigger hearts. Even though I've lived most of my life away from Guyana, the country and its rainforests are a large part of my early years and will always have a place in my heart.

Most of the rainforests in Africa and Asia have been destroyed, and while much of the rainforest in South America is still intact, a lot has been taken for cattle ranching, logging, agriculture, oil, mining, and more. After much destruction, Guyana put environmental laws in place in 1995 that have helped—some of my cousins work with rainforest conservation organizations there—but in Brazil's portion of the shared Amazon, less than 20 percent of the rainforest is officially protected. And with every election, the Amazon's future could change for the good or the bad. Indeed, while I was working on this story, Brazil, which houses the majority of the Amazon, had more fires causing deforestation than at any other time in history.

The technological advances humans have made in the first world have given us many benefits, but we have forgotten that it's the indigenous tribes around the globe who truly understand the beauty, importance, and potential of nature. That became abundantly clear while I was revising this book under lockdown because of COVID-19. A study from Harvard, supported by other studies from elsewhere, found that an increase of only one percent of air pollution led to an increase of fifteen percent in COVID-19 deaths. And while the majority of air pollution is in cities and industrialized areas, studies have shown that air pollution doesn't stick to boundaries but instead travels across the world, potentially damaging the immune systems of every person on our planet. Plus to survive COVID-19, people needed medicines, a lot of which are found only in the rainforests. Saving our rainforests is not just about helping the environment, although that should be reason enough. It's about helping humans thrive.

Thankfully, I see a lot of reason to hope for improvements in our future, thanks to such child activists as Isra Hirsi, Xiuhtezcatl Roske-Martinez, Ayakha Melithafa, Jamie Margolin, Autumn Peltier, Helena Gualinga, and Greta Thunberg, among so many others around the world. Children like these have been leading the charge to protect the environment and stop further damage to our planet. Xiuhtezcatl in particular talks about how the connection he has with the natural world, born from his indigenous Aztec culture, influences his work and ideas, and how important it is for people to return to living with the earth. These people have been working hard for years to change minds and policies to save our earth—and they are still young. They inspire me and make me feel encouraged that we can have a better connection with our beautiful world in the future.

For now, this novel is my love letter to trees, the rainforest, and the people we should be learning from every day to help our world flourish—a hope that as we humans grow, we do so in partnership with nature's ecosystem and not against it.

# RESOURCES

While *Arrow* is a work of fantasy, many aspects of the story are based on fact. Pollutants around the world are damaging our most precious resources, and the effects aren't felt just locally. Evidence shows that pollutants travel through the air, down streams, and across oceans, carrying dangerous chemicals far away to other parts of Earth. When you think about it on these levels, you can see that Earth, our home, is really quite small.

We are all part of an ecosystem in which we depend on one another to survive and thrive. We need good air to breathe, and trees help to clean the air. We need good soil, so trees and plants can grow to give us food, medicines, and that clean air. We can still have cities and cars and industry, but if we live smarter, we can also save our planet.

We must all do our part to protect Earth, for ourselves, for our neighbors across the sea, and for those who come after us. Luckily, there are lots of places where you can learn about rainforests and lots of things you can do, big and small, to help preserve our environment. A partial list is on the next page, including resources about limb differences like the main character's in this book. For a longer list and other downloadables, go to SamanthaMClark.com/Arrow.

The Nature Conservancy's Nature Works Everywhere program (Nature.org/en-us/about-us/who-we-are/how-we-work/youth-engagement/nature-lab/elementary-lesson-plans) has lessons, including videos and downloadables for multiple grade levels.

Fridays For Future (FridaysForFuture.org), started by teen activist Greta Thunberg, helps to organize Friday strikes to raise awareness for environmental protection issues.

Soils4Teachers (Soils4Teachers.org), from the Soil Science Society of America, teaches about the importance of soil and how to protect it.

The Rainforest Alliance (Rainforest-Alliance.org) supports the protection of rainforests around the world and has school curricula, games, and activities.

The Mongabay environmental science and conservation news platform (Education.Mongabay.com) has a resource center for children.

Earth Day Network (EarthDay.org) brings people together to take action to protect their world, including Earth Day on April 22 every year.

The National Audubon Society (Audubon.org/get-outside/
    activities/audubon-for-kids) works to protect natural eco-
    systems and has resources for kids.

National Geographic Society (NationalGeographic.org/
    education/classroom-resources) uses science, education,
    and storytelling to promote and protect the wonders of our
    world, and it offers classroom resources and publishes the
    *Explorer* magazine, aimed at children.

Don't Hide It, Flaunt It (DontHideItFlauntIt.com) encourages
    acceptance and understanding by celebrating the differences
    in people of all ages.

Shriners Hospitals for Children—Northern California
    (ShrinersChildrens.org/handdifferences) has a list of
    resources about congenital hand differences that was created
    by Sarah Tuberty.

# ACKNOWLEDGMENTS

Just like a rainforest is an ecosystem, where everything inside needs the others to survive, this story received a lot of help on its way to becoming a book.

I couldn't be more grateful to the team at Simon & Schuster for their support and love of *Arrow*. Thank you to my incredible editor, Sarah Jane Abbott, and publisher Paula Wiseman at Paula Wiseman Books for seeing the potential in this story early on. Together with art director Laurent Linn, managing editor Morgan York, and production manager Chava Wolin, they helped *Arrow* become a book I could only have dreamed of. Thank you also to all the sales, marketing, and exhibits staff at Simon & Schuster, not to mention all the administration staff who take care of Simon & Schuster's authors. I feel incredibly lucky to be part of your family.

A big thank-you to illustrator Justin Hernandez, for wrapping Arrow's story inside such wonderful art.

I had four amazing expert readers for *Arrow*, all of whom helped make this book better. Thank you to:

Nicole Kelly and Sarah Tuberty of the great *Disarming Disability* podcast for making sure Arrow's limb difference is represented accurately.

Kayla de Freitas and Candace Phillips for helping me with the representation of the rainforest and the culture of the indigenous people. I had to take a few literary licenses, but I wanted to make sure that all the fantastical elements still held the spirit of reality.

All of these women are dedicated and inspiring, and I can't thank them enough for their input on this book.

I also want to thank Bob Allen of The Nature Conservancy for helping me better understand soil, Suzanne Simard for her wonderful TED Talk about her research into how trees communicate, and Peter Wohlleben for his fascinating book *The Hidden Life of Trees: What They Feel, How They Communicate—Discoveries from a Secret World*.

Before *Arrow* got to Simon & Schuster, it was nurtured with support from my personal and professional ecosystems, which I can't live or work without.

My fantastic agent, Rachel Orr, loved this boy and his rainforest from the first words I sent her. Thank you, Rachel, for always being my champion.

My wonderful husband, Jamie, believed in this story and my ability to tell it even when I didn't. I couldn't be an author without him. Thank you for being my partner in life.

Thank you to my fellow children's book authors and illustrators who inspire me, especially my friends at SCBWI, the Electric Eighteens, and my fabulous Lodge of Death family, who have rooted for this story since I wrote the first words while gazing out the lodge windows.

Thank you to my parents and all my de Freitas and Gomes family, who took a chance on a new life in Guyana so many years ago. Without them, I might never have gone into the Amazon and fallen in love with rainforests.

I also want to extend a huge thank-you to the Amerindians who protect the Amazon, to all the indigenous people around the world who have always and continue to live with nature, and to the amazing people, especially the children, who are spearheading environmental efforts globally in spite of corporate and political pushback. Your courage, passion, and dedication inspire me. I hope others will follow your lead.

To God, thank you for allowing me to tell this story about this glorious world we are so lucky to call home. We haven't always treated it as well as we should, but I pray that will continue to change.

And finally a thank-you to all the librarians, teachers, and parents who are handing this book to children, and who are growing a love of reading in kids. And a big thank-you to all my readers. Without you, this story would be just words, but through you, these characters and this forest live on.